6 - 10 - 06

For Peggy

Second Thursday Circle

by
Charlotte Schreck Burns

Charlotte Schreck Burns

Published by Dream Street Prose
in cooperation with Fusion Press
A publishing service of Authorlink
(http://www.authorlink.com)
3720 Millswood Dr.
Irving, Texas 75062, USA

First published by Dream Street Prose
in cooperation with Fusion Press
A publishing service of Authorlink
First Printing, December 2001

Printed in the United States of America

ISBN 1928704905

Dedication

For Jim

Though they bear no responsibility for any imperfection,
some whose advice and critique have encouraged
and helped me in writing this book are:
Rebecca Balcarcel, Margot Blewett, Elaine Bucheri,
Jerry and Barbara Burns, David Dennis, Meg Files,
Patricia Hilborn, Wanda Horton, Kaye Hushour (deceased),
Carolee Jacobson, Betty Kurecka, Doris Lakey,
Elaine Lanmon, Karley Martin, Dulce Moore, Dorothy Pray,
LaNelle Pierce, Shirley Shepherd (deceased),
Margaret Shultz, Jackie Weathers,
Don Whittington, Carolyn Williamson, Sharon Woods.

Author's Notes

This is a work of fiction. All the names, characters, organizations, and events portrayed in this book are either the product of the author's imagination or are used fictitiously for verisimilitude. Any other resemblance to any organization, event, or actual person, living or dead, is unintended and entirely coincidental.

One

The Reverend Pierce has announced he will explain the difference between fornication and adultery. I imagine people wonder which sin applies to Dexter Gilpin and which to me. Redbud nibbles on gossip about my behavior, but our small town has a feast over what they think they've learned about Dexter.

I don't fault the town for not knowing quite what to make of me. I'm Maggie Gilpin, slimmer at fifty-five than I was at forty, better dressed, and no longer controlled by secrets. Sweet memories play in my head while I'm sitting in the choir loft, my concentration far from Brother Pierce's admonition about the wages of sin.

Elsie Wickfielder, loud and just a beat ahead of the congregational responses, smiles across the choir at me from her place in the soprano section. She is flanked by the uprightness of Flory Santos and the moral certitude of Amelia Crabtree. Elsie has worked hard to restore Dexter's and my reputations. The more she defends us, the more people are convinced we've lain in more beds than Don Juan. But I love her for trying.

Everything in church comforts me today, seems so vibrant, rich—the stained glass window of The Good Shepherd glowing in the morning sunlight, Albert Santos and the other basses blending in the "Three-fold Amen," callow teenagers passing notes along the pew where my own Lori and Gil used to sit with their friends. I let the memories and the beauty wash over the sadness, allow myself to feel at peace.

I catch Richard Mitchell staring at me as he passes the collection plate. He looks quickly away, his thick neck swiveling as he tracks the plate along the row of worshipers. I wonder which stories he's heard. Against the weight of questioning glances, I try to manage an enigmatic smile. Perhaps I should emulate Victorian ladies and hide behind a flowery paper fan.

We're all sinners, I want to tell them. I've repented, confessed all the earthy details to those best able to dispense spiritual advice.

Only last year Redbud thought me a cold, new widow because I did most of my crying in private and because I accepted a date with a man who later would be carried naked from my home. I didn't wear ashes and sack cloth or share with them the fact that, for weeks, the mention of Dexter's name was more than I could bear.

They didn't know I couldn't walk into a bakery where the yeasty aroma of sourdough bread would remind me of Dexter standing by the maple butcher block in my kitchen. Bread baking made me think of flour clouds dusting the work island, my husband masculine and out of place in one of my aprons, his trimmed mustache in sharp contrast, his powerful hands kneading dough. The recollection used to make me hurry home to shut myself in our bedroom, to bawl like a baby. But those are private memories I won't share, not even with my grown children.

Dexter's treachery deserved the avalanche of anger that settled into my soul, but my own pride and sexual lust hurt most to recount. It has been over a year and finally it is less painful now to examine the last days of my marriage and the trauma that followed.

At Dexter's request Elsie Wickfielder had given us the sourdough starter along with solemn instructions, "You've got to feed it every few days with potato flakes, sugar, and a cup of warm water or it will die."

Dexter thought I'd be the one to feed starter and bake sourdough. "I can manage the rest of my life with store-bought white bread," I told him.

So he scattered measuring cups and spoons, shiny pans,

containers of oil, sugar, salt and lard on my neat counter top. Then he lugged fifty pounds of bread flour into my well-ordered kitchen. The recipe made three batches and a sink full of dishes. Dexter stacked plastic bags of brown loaves in our spare refrigerator in the pantry.

After a month of baking, he hardly needed to measure. His plaid western shirt pushed to his elbows, he'd dump flour and starter into an old porcelain wash pan. When he saw me he'd say, "If I'd known how much fun this is, I'd have retired twenty years ago, Maggie." He baked with a frenzy, as though the pounding and kneading released pent up demons, as though the energy he'd used to make us a fine living and a comfortable retirement now poured from his hands into the loaves.

The starter grew, took on a life of its own. Before long the teaspoonfuls Elsie had given us filled a quart jug. "Pour some of it down the drain," I said, wiping sticky liquid he'd spilled on the tile counter and shoving a can of shortening and the box of salt into the cupboard.

On mornings I woke to the sweet-sour smell of baking bread, I'd slouch into the kitchen and plop down on one of our country oak chairs. "Hello, bright eyes," he'd say and plant a kiss on my forehead. Butter melted on thick slices so sweet no jelly was needed, only hot coffee in my favorite mug and a quick smile from Dexter as he settled behind the newspaper.

"Don't you hate having him underfoot all the time?" asked Elsie. She'd phoned to read me the twelve-month schedule for our Second Thursday Circle meetings and to remind me I would be the January hostess. But every call from Elsie included enough news about our town to fill the pages of *The Daily Oklahoman*. Dexter always said his cousin was the only person he knew who could make a camping trip to Lake Eufaula sound like Hannibal crossing the Alps.

I wasn't about to admit that too much "togetherness" could be irritating, that I resented the times I had to fix lunch or hurry from an afternoon bridge game because Dexter was home waiting. I didn't want to hint at dissatisfaction beginning to color our lives. My words would have circled back to me before noon the next day.

"I probably saw more of him when he was working," I lied.

"He still drives to Tulsa twice a week to see his buddies. And he usually works outdoors when he's home. Last week he lined my rose garden with railroad ties and painted the back deck."

Maybe Elsie's curiosity was sparked by my visit to Dr. Combs. I wasn't sure Redbud knew the rule about doctors respecting patient confidentiality, but it hardly mattered; Elsie Wickfielder's snooping abilities out-distanced the C.I.A.

She couldn't have guessed the problem because, on the surface, Dexter's and my relationship was as loving as ever. Neither of us would have talked about how his performance in bed, which had always been enthusiastic, now seemed to be more a matter of duty than ardor. He was just attentive enough to let me know I wasn't forgotten. It wasn't the infrequency I minded, but the vague notion Dexter labored to fulfill a husbandly obligation—that he'd tired of me. I scolded myself for giving in to my too finely tuned sensitivity, for expecting more from a man who said he loved me, who had always sheltered me in privilege and safety as his wife.

Still, there was a wariness on my part. There might have been no substance to my concern, but I thought I sensed a distancing.

And then, a new thing—the nights when he cried out in his sleep.

Over morning coffee Dexter suggested it was my remembered nightmares, not his. I nagged for an answer. "After thirty-three years of marriage, Maggie darling, maybe your cooking has finally turned on me." He smiled then, but there was no laughter in his eyes. When he glanced quickly away, I was certain he hid a problem.

One morning he threw a flour-laden dish rag through the kitchen toward the laundry room. His aim was off and the rag took something to the floor with it. The pretty elephant teapot he'd bought when he was stationed in Korea shattered on the floor into blue and white pottery shards. I moved to help him clean up. "Wild pitch. Guess I've lost my curve ball," he said. But then he wept. And that was not like my husband—to shed tears over a broken teapot.

Dexter's nightmares intensified. His long legs pumped beneath the covers as if he were pedaling his mountain bike through rice paddies. Only after weeks of thrashed bedclothes and denials did he admit, "A locomotive chases me. Over and over. It lays its own tracks as it goes and I can't escape... can't get away."

This from a man whose restful sleep I'd always envied.

"It's too silly to get all worked up about, Maggie."

I wanted to ask if such "silliness" could make him emotionally frail, could tire him so much he couldn't love me as often as he used to, but I couldn't think how to phrase those questions without making them sound like accusations, without wounding. He'd pulled away from me somehow, and I was afraid bluntness would make things worse. So I only suggested, "See Dr. Combs and ask him for something to help you relax."

He didn't answer.

"Maybe I should move to the back bedroom," I said, keeping my voice light.

Before he looked away I saw the hurt in his eyes. When he left for lunch with our insurance agent, I dropped by to see Dr. Combs.

Sitting across from his cluttered desk, I softly recounted Dexter's symptoms. He leaned back in his chair and fingered his stethoscope.

"For a man of fifty-nine Dexter was in great shape the last time I examined him. Prostate the size of a thirty year-old's."

His office door was open, and I was painfully aware of how clearly I'd heard him diagnose Flory Santos' urinary tract infection as he'd examined her in the adjacent room.

Ignoring my embarrassment Combs fingered his stethoscope and peered through his bifocals. "Without examining Dexter I can't help you much, Maggie. You might try giving him one of those over-the-counter medications. They're mostly aspirin or acetaminophen and won't do him any harm. But it sounds to me like Dexter's uptight about something. Maybe you two haven't adjusted yet to his retirement. You'd know more about that than I would."

As if it were all my fault, I thought. As if *I* hadn't reordered my life to accommodate Dexter.

That evening I dressed for bed early, then went into the den. I stood behind my husband, not seeing his face, but sensing his concern. He sat before a computer screen. White words against a blue field proclaimed, *Estate Planner.*

He said without turning, "After I'm gone you'll find everything about our finances on these disks."

His preoccupation with wills jogged my memory. A couple of Dexter's army buddies had died recently, and he'd been very moody after their funerals. Was that the key to our problem? Experiencing the loss of friends his age probably made him worry about his own mortality. I told myself I'd found the answer to his restless nights.

Seduction could be a powerful distraction. In my arrogance I decided to employ all the sensuality I'd learned in our years together to exorcise my husband's demons. I put my hands on his shoulders, bent and nuzzled his neck. I felt a love for that man so fierce he'd have to respond.

"Maggie, honey, even if I weren't pushing sixty, it only makes sense you know about our investments."

"Dex, dammit, I'm wearing a see-through nightie and Paris perfume." His eyes were still on the screen, so I bent to nibble his ear. I whispered, "Estrogen supplement is coursing through my veins, and you'd better come to bed before I smash that electronic hussy to smithereens."

The moment he turned to look at me, I spun his chair and eased myself onto his lap. I kissed his mouth, then drew back to search his face. "Honey, you can teach me about our investments tomorrow. This time I promise I'll listen. But for now can we just go to bed?"

His hands were on my arms, and for just a moment I thought he would push me away. Then his eyes softened. "Maggie, you wanton witch." He smiled and drew me close.

"I'm going to turn off the computer, Dex." Grateful he did not argue, I pressed my breasts against him as I twisted from his embrace to disconnect the machine. Standing and taking his hands, I pulled him to his feet and drew his arms behind my back, then leaned into his chest.

He stood there, tan and muscled and husky of voice, naked under his terry robe. "You're wearing too many clothes," he said.

"I thought you'd never notice."

I took my gown off and threw it onto his chair, then pulled at his robe and led him into the bedroom.

The phone rang. "It might be one of the kids," he said.

"So? Let the answering machine get it."

I eased into bed and stretched my arms to reach for him. "There's no one in the whole world but you and me, Dex."

And then we were kissing. He caressed me as if his yearnings held as much passion as mine. Nothing existed but the pleasure surging through me as we drowned in intimacy.

When our bodies were sated I snuggled naked against his back and purred, "I like it, Dex. That was good."

"That's what all the women say."

The corny litany of our affection was comforting. I put my hand on his chest and waited to hear the soft rhythm of his snores. I wondered if tonight's sleep would be untroubled. But he shifted from my embrace, rolled toward me and propped himself on his elbow.

"There's something I need to tell you, Maggie." His brow furrowed, and his tone was serious.

Ah, I thought, *it's about time*. But I kept my voice level. "What's bothering you, sweetheart?"

"Maggie, I..." He touched my head and brushed his fingers through my hair. "You know I love you."

"Yes, and I know that's not what you're trying to tell me." Did I sound shrill? Was it his fear or mine now gripping my thoughts? "Dex, what's wrong?"

He spoke so tenderly. "If anything happens to me I want you to remember, I love you."

"Of course, darling." I reached for him, still believing I could comfort him. He came to my arms like a child needing reassurance from a parent. "Dex, please talk to me about it. Let me help you."

"I'm scared," he said, his voice breaking. "Just hold me and promise you'll never let go."

Two

Elsie Wickfielder once gave a report on Hindus. It was straight from CNN, but she gave it her own spin as she informed us that devout widows have been known to immolate themselves willingly on their husbands' funeral pyres, though some receive assistance from in-laws. She had cited the "true facts" which contrasted the value of women in Indian society with our own. The members of Second Thursday Circle had gasped at her graphic description of suttee. I pictured hot flames licking a pious woman, reducing her to a pile of cinders, and thought the act unfathomable and barbaric.

Now as I stood by the open grave, Dexter's mahogany casket sat waiting to be lowered into its concrete, waterproof vault. I recalled someone telling us, "It's guaranteed not to leak for a hundred years, but in reality the manufacturing process seals the casket so your loved one's remains won't ever deteriorate." For a split second I suspended my Christianity and contemplated the rationale of the Hindu response to widowhood.

For three decades I had defined myself as Maggie-the-wife of George Dexter Gilpin. I had no quarrel with women's liberation—I espoused equal pay for equal work and thought beauty pageants a tremendous bore. These opinions made me a flaming liberal in Redbud. But with Dexter's death my identity hovered in limbo, nebulous and fragile.

I focused my hate on the small-town quack who'd pronounced Dexter healthy. He'd never monitored Dexter on a treadmill, never run more than a cursory EKG. His stethoscope probably couldn't have detected a heart attack in full sway, let alone the aortic embolism that took my husband's life. He was lucky I didn't spot him among the other townsfolk who'd been at the church.

The promise of snow scented the air, and I shivered under my wool tweed coat. Hymns, slow and mechanical, tolled across the cemetery from the carillon but did not obscure my granddaughter's plea to Lori. "Mommy, can we go home now? I'm about to wet my pants." Her urgent little voice was more comforting to me than any dirge.

I nodded at Lori. She, Don, and Peggy left to settle the little ones into the black limousine while the funeral director, Albert Santos, and my son, Gil, stayed by my side.

The other mourners had returned to warm cars, only the Wickfielders lingered near the canopy. With her red eyes and crumpled handkerchief, Elsie Wickfielder could have been mistaken for the grieving widow. I nodded to her.

Apparently mistaking my acknowledgement for an invitation, she walked over, grabbed me around my neck, and wailed close to my ear, "Poor Dexter. He looked real natural. Praise the Lord, he didn't suffer long. If you need anything, Maggie, all you have to do is call Orin and myself."

At that moment I thought no more of my surroundings than I imagine an embryo thinks about the darkness of the womb. My actions were automatic. There was nothingness, and I felt no need to probe the possibilities. Dumbly, I nodded at Elsie.

Orin, his jug-ears red, hands clenched in leather gloves, came to stand beside Elsie. He nodded in agreement, hugged me stiffly, and patted Gil's shoulder.

"I appreciate your serving as pallbearer," I told him.

His eyes misted. "I cain't believe he's gone, Maggie. Seems like he ought to be ready to go hunting with me and the boys next week."

Orin's grief, visible as a festering sore, brought my own into sharper focus. "I know," I said, trying to maintain control. I turned and touched the polished wood of the casket.

Albert spoke softly. "It's time to go, Maggie."

Sobs choked my voice to a whisper. "Until we meet again, sweetheart."

Gil took my arm and led me to the limousine. Elsie followed at our heels.

"Oprah Winfrey had a panel of experts," said Elsie, "who said the worst mistake a widow can make is to leave her home and her old friends. You're not thinking of leaving, are you, Maggie?"

Without turning to face her I dismissed her question with a wave. How could I answer what I had not begun to settle for myself? My senses were too dulled to feel irritation. Which is always the best way to accept Elsie's advice and friendship. Besides, I knew she loved Dexter, that she'd admired him as the shining star of her family though they'd shared only a great -great grandfather.

Even in my numbed state I sought to sidetrack her, to keep her sorrow from touching my own. When we reached the car I wiped my face with a tissue and asked, "Elsie, did you see that short, dark-haired man who came to the funeral?" The stranger's noisy sobs had penetrated my cocoon of grief as I sat with my children in the church. If anyone could identify him it would be the Wickfielders who had walked behind him as he made his way in the line of mourners.

"Do you mean the stranger with the ponytail who acted so tore up? He drove a silver Accord with Okmulgee County plates and a bumper sticker that said, 'I'm proud to teach at Pepperwood Elementary.'"

"Elsie, you saw all that?" asked Lori as she shielded her children from the cold air.

Albert and Gil helped me into the limousine, then Elsie leaned through the door and across me to continue her report to Lori and the others. "I was almost to the parking lot when he raced ahead of me. I tried to catch up to him before he got into his car, so I could introduce myself, but he was hurrying to beat the band. I called to him, but he didn't seem to hear. And it wouldn't have been proper to yell right outside a church after a funeral. He wore little bitty black loafers, but I couldn't see enough of his face even to tell how old he was. He was still crying into his handkerchief."

"Is he some of yours or Dexter's kin?" asked Orin, coming to stand outside the car window. Behind his question I detected sympathy for the relatives of any young male who wore his hair in a ponytail.

Albert started the engine and tapped his knuckles on the steering column. My youngest grandson cried.

"I don't remember ever meeting him, Orin, but I suppose he will be at my house with the others," I said as he gently pulled Elsie from the limousine. With a show of finality, Albert pushed the button to roll up the window.

On the way home Sara Jane and Chet argued over who would be first to hold their baby cousin, and no one had the energy to reprimand them.

It seemed everyone but the stranger came to our home to offer condolences. People brought food in aluminum pans, in microwaveable throw-aways, and in vessels with their names written on tape. A crowd of out-of-towners stayed to eat from paper plates. There was almost a festive air. Occasionally a mourner would laugh, then check his mirth so as not to offend Dexter's loved ones. As if it were possible to heap more offense on my little family than that we were already suffering.

More than once I heard faint conversations regarding the tiny man who seemed so upset at Dexter's death, but people were too polite to risk offending me with their questions.

They brought me drinks and plates of food. "You should eat to keep up your strength," they said.

People I barely knew embraced me, their hugs tentative, as if they sensed my fragility. Just in time I stopped myself from saying, "Excuse me while I go look for Dexter. I know he'll want to see you before you leave." And, hearing Gil tell his cousin Brent of his new dental practice, I thought, *I must remember to get Dex to talk to Gil about helping him with a loan for the new office equipment.*

Each moment of reality brought a fresh sense of loss. Why did life have to be so unfair? Dexter must have had some warning, some hint of pain. Why hadn't he gone to a heart specialist? Why had he left me?

Someone stood close and spoke softly in my ear. "Maggie, I'm going to stay and clean your kitchen for you." It was Elsie. An unidentifiable strand of green stuck between her teeth.

"Thanks, Elsie. I really appreciate your offer, but Lori and I will do the dishes. There aren't all that many, and we need some time together before they drive home to Tulsa."

"They're leaving tonight?"

"They are if I have anything to say about it. Don has missed enough work, and Peggy and the baby have appointments for their six week check-ups tomorrow. After they all leave I'll need to be alone for a while."

"Well, if you're sure…."

"I'm sure."

When the last visitor left I went into my bedroom to shed my girdle and shoes. Dexter's cat, Furr Schleggener, met me and rubbed against my legs. I wondered if either of my children would be willing to take him home.

As I hung my dress I thought how empty the closet would look when Dexter's clothes were gone. I held the sleeve of his blue serge jacket to my face and drank in the smell. But it was the sight of the battered hat he wore on fishing trips which sent me sobbing.

I took a cloth from my side of the bathroom cabinet and wet my face with cold water. Then I dressed. When I returned to the family room, my grandchildren were wearing their play clothes, and my son his blue jeans and sneakers.

"Dad would have loved the music," said Gil.

"Yes, I think he would have been pleased with the whole service," I replied.

My voice sounded false and bright to me. "Lori, why don't you put in a video for the kids to watch."

Peggy held George Dexter Gilpin III, his mouth resting on the burp rag covering her shoulder. "Skip is such a good baby. I didn't hear a peep out of him at the church," I said.

"Maggie," said my daughter-in-law, "it would be real easy to move the computer into our dining room. You know, we've got that new sofa bed, and Gil and I want you to stay with us. For as long as you like."

Lori looked up from the VCR. "Mom, my kids would love having you with us year round. They hate the daycare center."

I was sure she hadn't conferred with Don, but Lori couldn't allow her sister-in-law to be more generous than she.

"You can sell this place, move to Tulsa, and we'll shop for a house large enough for all five of us. If you help with the financing we can buy something with a mother-in-law suite." She stood, crossed the room, and gave me a hug. Her words came faster as she grew more excited by the possibilities. "We could have the large house I've always wanted and you could have your own rooms in it."

I looked from my son to my daughter. Gil's hair was thinning. His eyes were as brown as Dexter's, but they were set wide apart like mine.

Lori had chewed her nails to the nub. She had inherited her fine bones and wavy auburn hair from me. It fell across her shoulders. Her eyes looked naked without mascara.

They were strong, capable adults. Dexter and I had raised them well, and I knew either of our children would find a place for me and make the best of things.

"Thank you, but I'd put my clothes in a shopping cart and take a turn at being a bag lady before I'd move in with either of you."

"Moth-er," said Lori. My bluntness had irritated her.

"Honey, it may sound like a good idea to you now, but that fine house you want would come at quite a price. Would it be your house or mine? And you sure wouldn't want me interfering with the way you raise your children. No, I'm too set in my ways to give up my own home for a mother-in-law suite."

Until that moment I hadn't realized I'd already made the decision to carve whatever life I was going to have right there in Redbud, in the house where Dexter and I had raised our children. I pictured Oprah's panel of experts applauding me.

Gil hugged me, tears in his eyes. "Just so you know, you can call on us... for anything," he said.

I smiled. "You've walked into a trap of your own making, Gil. Just now, I wish you'd all help me with these acknowledgements. The funeral home gave me a box full of cards, and I'm afraid I won't have the energy or the inclination to do them after you leave."

We sat at my dining room table to write our notes. The few names I didn't recognize were known to my children, except for one. His name was Wilmer Darling. *So*, I thought, *that was probably the name of the stranger everyone had been talking about.*

Later, as she helped me wash dishes, Lori said, "A couple of people asked me about that fellow who made such an ass of himself at the funeral. Who do you suppose he was?"

"I didn't think he made an ass of himself."

"Well, he cried harder than any of us."

"Maybe that's because we'd done most of our crying before the services."

"I still thought he acted a bit dramatic for someone outside the family. Don asked Mr. Santos, but he said all he knew was the guy wasn't from Redbud."

"I've wondered if he might be Wilmer Darling, the person in the guest book none of us recognized."

"Wilmer Darling." Lori repeated the name as if it left a bad taste in her mouth.

"He's probably someone your father met on a business trip," I said as I found containers and organized the casserole bowls for delivery to their owners. "And I think he might be Asian— there was something like a Chinese character by his name— but Darling doesn't fit, does it."

She blew a wisp of hair from her face. "I wonder why he didn't leave his address. Did you get a good look at him?"

Even in my haze of grief it had been impossible not to notice the stranger. "Just his general appearance, the way his clothes hung as if he'd recently lost a lot of weight. I suppose, if he only knew your dad professionally, he didn't feel comfortable going to the cemetery or stopping by the house." Which made his flagrant mourning seem more improbable to me.

Lori frowned. "Mother, what if he didn't know Daddy at all. What if he's just some weird character who likes funerals?"

"Likes funerals?"

"Weird Wilmer. He gets off on funerals, loves a good cry."

"Lori—"

She put her hand to her mouth and bit a nail. "Or, and this is even better, maybe Weird Wilmer went to the wrong funeral and didn't know it until he got right up to the casket. Can you imagine the poor guy's reaction when he finds out? Does he try to steal the floral spray and take it to the right funeral, or what?"

"Lori, honestly."

"And then Elsie chases him down the sidewalk. No wonder he left town in such a hurry."

We both started giggling. When Gil walked into the kitchen we tried to explain why we were holding our sides and laughing. My son looked at us and shook his head. He looked just like Dexter when he did that.

After the dishes were put away I helped Peggy find her curling iron, then we looked for Sara Jane's shoes. I held each of my loved ones close, wanting them all to stay but needing them to leave. It was late evening. My children closed themselves into two cars and left.

I had no mooring. The future was uncharted, frightening. I stepped back into the emptiness of my home. For the first time in my life, I was alone.

Three

I slid between king-sized satin sheets and cried myself to sleep. I dreamed, and when I woke I was blessed with a pleasant feeling of amnesia. I smiled. "Who am I?" It was good not to remember so much as my name. I felt weightless. Without memory, I felt no hurt.

Reality crept into my brain, much like smoke creeping beneath the bedroom door of a burning house. *Oh. I know who I am. I am the woman whose husband died.* A moment later grief swallowed me again. I cried indulgently, affirming no one could hear me.

At this point I tried to bargain with God. "Lord, I know you could do it. You could make this all into a dream and you could bring Dexter back to life." I prayed so hard, but Heaven did not repeal the sentence I'd been given. I couldn't even bargain with God. He held all the chips.

My feet were slabs of ice, so I threw off the covers and sprinted to the thermostat to turn up the heat. On my way back to bed I called, "Here, kitty, kitty." Furr Schleggener dutifully scampered from my closet. I caught him and tried to use him for a foot warmer, but I had thrown that cat off too many times for him to trust me now.

I made trips to the bathroom as necessary, fed and watered Schlegg, filled the pitcher of water on my night stand, engaged in feeding frenzies, and changed television by remote control. Time did not exist. I found a package of leftover Halloween candy, the chocolate turning white, and ate twelve small bars while watching *Mr. Smith Goes to Washington.* I finished the meat loaf brought over by one of the church ladies, but I poured her gelatin salad down the sink before returning to bed. I was eating ripe olives with tuna when *Nightline* came on. It was then I realized I had been in bed all day.

The next morning Lori called. "I can't believe Daddy's gone," she said, her voice husky with tears.

"I know, darling. It's like a nightmare, and I want to wake up."

"What are you going to do?"

I knew she meant what would my life be like without Dexter. In those moments when grief didn't consume me, I listened for him. Stretched my leg to rub against his warm, hard muscles. Rolled to snuggle against him in our bed. I couldn't give Lori answers until my heart knew I was alone.

I swallowed my tears and forced a laugh, hoping to reassure her. "I'm being a real slob, honey. I'm sure there are things I should be doing, but all I want to do is sleep. I don't seem to care if I never get up."

"You wouldn't... Mother, you wouldn't—"

Not that suicide didn't sound attractive, I thought, *recalling the practice of suttee.* But I was Christian, not Hindu. "No, I would never take my own life. I wouldn't do that to you kids."

"I shouldn't have asked."

"It's all right. But I do need time... I just can't seem to take it all in. You know?"

"Take all the time you need. We'll all be back in a few weeks to help you... that is, have you decided what you're going to do with Daddy's things?"

"I can't think about that now, Lori."

I didn't explain how seeing Dex's clothes hanging in the closet, catching sight of his toothbrush still in the holder, and leaving his favorite brown loafers by the dresser comforted me with the illusion he might reappear at any moment.

"We love you. Call us if you need anything, Mama."

When I had not emerged from my home by the third day, women from the Second Thursday Circle at church began to telephone. It was as if they had met and decided I needed "cheering up." Their pleasant voices assaulted me as they tried to restore warmth and gaiety to my life.

"I just thought I'd stop by for a while this afternoon," said

Elsie, "and bring over some of my homemade chicken-noodle casserole."

"Don't come yet, Elsie. And there's still plenty of food left from the day of the funeral."

Flory Santos invited me to ride to the country with her family. "We thought we'd hike up to the bridge on Redbud Creek. Ray wants us to dig up some trees for his and Susan's new house."

"I can't go this weekend, Flory." I searched for a valid excuse. "There's so much to be done, you know."

Amelia Crabtree wanted to bring a baby gift for Gil and Peggy's baby, "before Little Skippy outgrows it."

"I'll call you next time they're here, Amelia. That way you can give it to them yourself."

My second decision: no parade of do-gooders or friends to distract me from pain. I turned on the answering machine so I could screen my calls.

Days and nights ran together. As I lay in bed on New Year's Eve, I saw fireworks explode over the high school stadium. For exercise I bathed and changed gowns. When my teeth felt fuzzy I brushed them. When my head itched I washed it. Pressed against pillows, my uncombed hair knew no pattern or style. My pink razor went unused. I let Schlegg in and out as he demanded.

I fixed cereal with milk, but the milk tasted sour; so I poured the whole mess on top of the aging, melted gelatin. The next time the phone rang I unplugged it.

At six AM, ten days after Dexter's funeral, the doorbell chimed. "Yoo hoo. Yoo hoo, Maggie, are you there?" It was Elsie Wickfielder. "I tried to call you first, but your phone is out of order."

Though our houses are on half-acre lots, the entire neighborhood would hear her yelling at my front door. If I didn't answer, someone would call the police.

Opening the door a crack, I spoke softly. "I'm just not up to visitors today, Elsie."

Elsie pushed the door open and swept past me. The mess in my kitchen drew her like a magnet. She hung her parka on the coat rack, threw her purse on a kitchen chair, picked up dishes, scraped them, and began to load my dishwasher.

"Elsie, please don't do that."

"Do what? Oh, I don't mind. Where's your soap?"

"Elsie, I don't want you to do my dishes. I just want you to leave."

She did not slacken her pace. "You don't mean that, Maggie. If I don't help you, you'll never be ready in time."

"Ready for what?"

"Have you forgotten tomorrow is your day for Second Thursday Circle?" Her smile was smug.

I looked at her in disbelief. Elsie Wickfielder was often indelicate and insensitive, but even she couldn't have expected me to host our church women so soon after Dexter's funeral.

"Elsie, I can't host Circle."

"My mother lay a cold corpse in December of seventy-two, and I had to sing in the Christmas cantata. You don't know what grief is until you've sung 'Sweet Visitor from Heaven' while your mother is laying on a slab at the undertaker's. No one else could sing the solo, and people depended on me. Dexter has been dead thirteen days, buried ten. You need to see to your duties, Maggie. Go wash and get dressed. Then we'll see about making refreshments for the meeting tomorrow."

I retreated toward the bathroom, beyond the reach of Elsie Wickfielder. I locked the door and took a long shower, hoping to outwait her.

People like Elsie are the best reasons for living in a small town. They are also the worst. Concern and friendship motivated her to see about me. And after she left she would be able to tell everyone in Redbud how she'd rescued me from self-pity. It would be beyond her imagining that I would want to continue the grieving process in solitude.

When I finished blow-drying my hair, I heard the vacuum cleaner. By the time I dressed she was caroming around my living room with a bottle of O'Cedar furniture polish and a rag.

She stopped to look at me. "That's a sight better, Maggie. You look almost human again. Dexter wouldn't want you going to the dogs."

"Elsie, I will not allow Circle here tomorrow."

"I know. The girls and I talked about it the day of Dexter's funeral, and we decided to reschedule Circle. Amelia traded with you, so your turn will be next October. I was just trying to get you off your backside."

I thought about hitting her, but days of wallowing in bed had robbed me of energy. And the truth of the matter, I grudgingly admitted, was Elsie's ruse concerning Second Thursday Circle had set me on my feet.

"As soon as I finish dusting the dining room, we'll drive to Thompson's," she said. "You're nearly out of Cokes, coffee, toilet paper, and cat food."

"And bread and milk."

"No. You're *plumb* out of bread and milk."

I gathered the florists' cards and the guest book from the dining table and put them in a box.

"Elsie, do you know someone named Wilmer Darling?"

"Mm." She sucked her lower lip and wrinkled her forehead. "Is he related to the Darlings who used to run the dairy?"

"I don't remember the people who ran the dairy. It closed before I moved here."

"Come to think of it, their name was Carling. Are you sure you don't mean Carling? They moved to Stillwater after the flood. On the other hand...." Elsie rattled on. She required minimal responses as she discussed former and current residents of Redbud. "...and Mrs. Doctor Finney is just the bravest woman you've ever met."

"*Mrs. Doctor* Finney?"

"Used to be Louella Watson, but she married a doctor."

I could hear the awe Elsie reserved for missionaries, celebrities, and anyone who'd met Elvis.

"When I think how that dear woman has been left alone to live out her years by herself... well, you could take a leaf from her book. Not many people know how much Louella has suffered."

"She calls herself 'Mrs. Doctor Finney'?"

"The point is, you're not the first woman to lose her husband, Maggie. It's past time you started back to church and choir practice. I know you haven't worked in years, but you might even see if they'd hire you back to teach at the high school. If you don't get out of this house, you're liable to develop agoraphobia." She paused, her face a portrait of concern as she warned, "Jenny had a panel of recovering agoraphobics on her show. It's a pitiful state to be in, and you do not want to turn into one."

"You're sweet to worry about me, but I don't want to see people just yet."

As I protested Elsie carried a tray of dishes from my bedroom to the kitchen sink. After she crowded them onto the dishwasher rack so close they were nesting like canned sardines, she sprinkled washing powder over them, closed the door and turned the switch. Heat would weld every speck of leftover food onto the plates. I watched as she scalded the dish cloth and draped it over the sink divider.

"Who is Wilmer Darling, anyway?"

"Remember the small man at Dexter's funeral, the one who cried so? No one seemed to know him, and Wilmer Darling is the only stranger in the guest book."

She grimaced. "Orin wondered where Dexter ever met a fellow like that."

"Like what? Small?"

"Oh, you know what I mean," she said, smirking. "Dexter was so manly. And that little shrimp looked real effemi-nite."

"How could you tell he looked effeminate? I thought you couldn't see his face."

"Orin and I wondered if he wasn't one of those con artists from the city who prey on new widows. I just hope you'll be careful about meeting people, Maggie. And, even if this is Redbud, you might ought to start locking your doors at night."

"I've noticed locked doors don't stop some people."

"Staying locked up in this house won't bring Dexter back," she said.

"I know." I wondered how I could make her understand the effort required just to talk to her. "But I don't feel sociable. I don't have anything to say to people. And without Dexter, nothing matters anymore. What's the use of it all, Elsie?"

"The use of it all is the choir needs you. Sharla is as sweet as she can be but she goes flat if you're not there to sing alto with her." She paused to adjust her bifocals before continuing in a softer voice. "And I miss you. It's not like you to stay shut up by yourself all day." She drew herself ramrod straight again and turned toward the kitchen window. "Your children and grandchildren love you. There are probably other reasons too, but I haven't had time to think about it."

"Aren't you going to say time will heal my sorrow and that everything will work out all right?"

"I'd like to, Maggie. But right now, short of The Resurrection, I don't see how things could possibly work out all right with Dexter dead in his grave."

A dam seemed to burst, and I cried until I got the hiccoughs. I blubbered, "Elsie, I suppose I should thank you for not sugar-coating the truth."

"You're just feeling sorry for yourself again, Maggie. Dry up so we can go to the grocery store. I told Orin to stop by after he closed the shop and we'd eat tuna-noodle casserole here. I already put the ingredients on the shopping list."

Four

After the Wickfielders left I took stock. Ten days in bed hadn't changed a thing, except I had laundry spilling from clothes hampers, a sack of unopened mail, and I could hum the theme songs to four daytime dramas. If I went back to bed I'd have to exist on leftover tuna-noodle casserole. It was motive enough to take Elsie's advice about getting out of my house.

I telephoned Lester Quinn, Dexter's insurance agent in Tulsa, and he instructed me to mail him a copy of the death certificate. "Your husband left the option to you, sweetie. You can take your benefits in a lump sum, but I'm sure you'll want us to send you a monthly check instead. Most of our widows do."

Widow. I hated the word almost as much as I hated him calling me sweetie. At that moment I hated Lester Quinn. "I'll want payment in full," I told him.

Our finances were Dexter's domain. He gave me an allowance, and I seldom had to ask for more money. The thought of shouldering bills and managing a budget made my stomach queasy, but asking my children for help was unthinkable. I planned to make an appointment with our accountant for a course in investments and I put Dexter's *Money Magazine* on my reading list.

A few days later Quinn's secretary called from the insurance agency. "You can stop by for your check on Monday, dear." I could hear the two-inch fake fingernails in her voice.

"Can't you mail it to me?"

"Mr. Quinn would like to talk to you in person. Could you come by Monday around ten o'clock?"

So on Monday I drove thirty miles to Tulsa, allowing extra time to find the agency. My disposition did not improve while being kept waiting until eleven-fifteen. Following Quinn's secretary, I walked into the paneled office. Quinn continued a phone conversation while motioning me toward a chair.

I never understood why Dexter didn't buy life insurance from Moore and Pilmont in Redbud where we had our homeowner and automobile policies. "It's a business decision, Maggie," he'd said without further explanation. I had no grounds to argue my husband's business decisions, but Quinn's pompous and chauvinistic attitude toward women repulsed me. I couldn't see why Dexter counted him among his friends.

Dexter told me, "I've known Quinn since we were in Boys State together. And we shipped over to Korea at the same time. We tried to keep each other from going crazy with homesickness over there, and if I can throw some business his way now, I will."

I remembered Dexter bounding down the steps of our front porch last October, wearing his Sooner jacket and carrying his O.U. thermos. "I'm late to meet Les," he told me. I didn't want to sit in the icy stands to watch a game I could see in comfort on my TV screen, but Dexter never left for a game with Quinn that I didn't feel a twinge of jealousy.

Waiting for my check, I watched Quinn's pompadour bob in rhythm with his speech. He laughed softly into the phone, and one curl slipped low on his forehead. I imagined some girl telling him thirty years ago he looked like James Dean. I bet he thought he still did.

Phone conversation ended, he turned to me. The smile left his face, replaced by a properly sympathetic expression. "I'm sure going to miss my football buddy."

He flashed a broad, patronizing smile. "But you're a fortunate woman, Margaret. You wouldn't believe the number of men who leave their widows absolutely destitute. But, even if he didn't have all those mutual funds, this policy will keep you fixed comfortable." He scratched his chin as though in deep thought. "My, my, Dex was a good one. He left you a tidy sum all right. And I'd hate to see you get took and lose all his money in one place, so you really ought to leave your benefits with the company. It'd be the safe thing to do. I've got it written up so you'll have a supplemental check coming in every month. It'd keep my old buddy's wife pretty darn comfortable."

I considered explaining that waking in the middle of the night to fear cold as ice, fear which crept into the scared place in the hollow of my back, was not comfortable. And there was nothing fortunate about being fifty-four years old and single and knowing one survived as the remnant of a truncated marriage. I pictured myself wearing wool socks to bed as Grandma had. Why had I not understood her sooner?

"Dexter always took good care of his family," I said.

"That he did, Margaret, and I do feel a certain obligation to offer you the advantages and protection of our firm. It's the least I can do. On this policy we can guarantee you an income of—" He opened a book and drew a line across a chart, then turned it so I could read the numbers. "See, the company bases your income on three point seven per cent, and they augment that with the principal. We could guarantee you a nice annuity for the next thirty years, which is virtually the rest of your life."

It may have been the way he patted my hand, it may have been the three point seven per cent, or it may have been that anger over my husband's death bubbled beneath the surface of my grief, but I had to struggle to be civil. "That's very kind of you," I said, "but I don't believe an annuity would be as useful to me as the full payment."

He cleared his throat and pushed the intercom button. "Miss Tremont, I need you to notify the head office we'll be delivering the check on that policy for George Dexter Gilpin as soon as we get the paperwork signed."

After several minutes Miss Tremont burst through the door carrying a stack of documents. "Sorry I took so long. I hadn't re-filed Mr. Gilpin from the time his daughter was here for her annuity, so of course it was...."

She trailed off as though embarrassed, and I took some satisfaction in telling her, "Lori Margaret didn't have a policy on Dexter."

Quinn's face turned florid. "Tiffany, I don't know what the

hell you're talking about. This here is the widow of Mr. George Dexter Gilpin, and she wants her insurance check."

Miss Tremont blanched. "Oh, oh my gosh. Of course, Mr. Quinn. I always get the names mixed up—Gilpin and... Gillman. Sorry about that." She smiled at me. "At least I got the right name on the papers for you to sign."

Miss Tremont's incompetence didn't surprise me. I thought Quinn probably hired her because he enjoyed the way she swung her hips. I thought it would serve him right if she scrambled all his files. He cleared his throat and thanked her.

After Tiffany closed the door Lester began his apologies, barely meeting my gaze. "I'm sorry for the mix-up. Miss Tremont's usually so reliable."

"That's all right. If you have a client named Gillman, I can certainly understand how someone could confuse one for the other."

He picked up the papers, laid them down again, and drummed his fingers on the desk top. "I sure hate to give up on you," he said. "Why don't you have lunch with me, and we can talk some more." He rose, walked from behind his desk, and took my hands in his. At close range his mouthwash tried to overcome smoker's breath. "We could discuss the advantages of a monthly annuity, Margaret. I'm sure Dexter would have felt better knowing someone with good old-fashioned horse sense looked after you."

I withdrew my hands. "Don't worry. I hired an advisor to assist with my investments."

"Oh, really?" He looked nonplussed. "Anyone I might know?"

"Crash something or other. He's a recent graduate of Texas A & M who financed his education playing blackjack with the other Aggies. He swears he can teach me his secret system."

"You're joking," Quinn said, though his frown seemed to say his worst expectations were confirmed.

The merchants who wrote and called me were no less interested in the disposal of my insurance money than was Lester Quinn. When I returned from his office I tackled the stacks of papers on my dining room table. There were letters from a few concerned friends and relatives and a half-dozen bills, but the bulk of my mail consisted of advertisements. Some described fail-safe investment opportunities. A siding company notified me an on-site inspection of my property revealed wood rot in the eaves. A tree service warned any storm might bring limbs crashing into my house. Three residential security firms sent brochures, including the one that had installed its product two years earlier.

While I plowed through the paper blitz, the phone rang. "Con-grat-u-la-tions!" said the honey-voiced recording. "Today's your luck-ee day. Your friends have nominated you to join other attractive singles and avail yourself of our dating services. And if you call today—"

"Call back," I said before I slammed the receiver, "when you've signed Harrison Ford."

That night I wore one of Dexter's shirts to bed. I sprinkled his aftershave on my pillow.

Outside, wolves howled for Margaret Gilpin to bring her checkbook and play with them. Inside my house were shadows, a cat who walked on piano keys in the middle of the night, creaking boards, skylights popping with expansion, and an ice maker that released its offspring with a reverberating clank.

I hugged my pillow and thought of Dexter. He had eclipsed all other men I'd ever met. I knew I'd never remarry because my standards were too high, and that was unfortunate. Even if his armor were a bit tarnished, another knight by my side might have tilted the battle in my favor—might have punched Lester Quinn in his annuity.

Five

In the weeks that followed, Elsie continued to search for "something useful" for me to do. My behavior right after Dexter's funeral convinced her I'd lapse into permanent depression if I didn't keep moving. While I suspected she might be right, I couldn't utter a sigh, a single mournful word in her presence, without her scolding.

"Your trouble is, you're what the psychiatrists call too self-absorbed. That means you don't spend enough time helping others."

"Which talk show evaluated me this time?" I asked.

"Maybe you could increase your hours at the Thrift Shop from one day a month to four. And I read in the paper that they're looking for people to take in foreign exchange students."

"Would Oprah consider having a panel just for me? You could act as sort of a guide—tell them about my deficiencies. Maybe we could make the circuit. Two shows would probably cure me completely."

"You're not too old for the Peace Corps," she said. "Lillian Carter was older than you when she castrated all those men."

Only the Wickfielders could equate vasectomies with castration, I thought. "Until now, Elsie, I hadn't seen castration as a peaceful activity."

Though I didn't tell Elsie, I had strongly considered returning to the classroom. I gave it up years ago while Gil was still a baby. At one tense homecoming Lori had clung to Mother Gilpin and refused to accept my outstretched arms. At that moment I decided to devote my full energies to raising my children and to being Dexter's wife. As a widow I would not have a problem of divided loyalties. But teaching required stamina, and I finally concluded I didn't have energy or incentive at this time of my life to wrestle gerunds and participles for hormone-saturated teenagers. After some soul searching I consigned them to their *bustier* clad idols, and to all who mumbled the shocking lyrics which set their fans screaming and writhing.

"You could run a free day-care for poor children. Of course, you might have to charge some so you could hire help when you wanted to go to the bathroom, or something."

"Maybe I could turn the basement into a lab and make explosives for anarchists," I suggested. "Or stand in the town square and distribute literature for Planned Parenthood."

She shook her head in disgust. "That sort of talk turns my stomach."

Elsie was a convenient lightning rod for my anger, and I felt ashamed for using her. I grappled for alternative topics. "Elsie, when did your nails get so long? Let me see."

She held up both hands. Her skinny fingers ended in sharp talons of bright purple.

"I did it when Candace came home for Orin's birthday. She helped me glue them on. Aren't they pretty?"

"How is Candace?" I asked. "We just don't see enough of our kids these days, Elsie."

"My daughter is probably the happiest woman that ever lived now that they've moved into that gorgeous new home I told you about. Do you like my nails?"

Candace worked as a computer programmer for a large oil company. "Does she still like her job?"

"She loves it, and I guess she's just about the fastest programmer they've ever had." She paused and furrowed her brow. "I don't mean that the way it sounds."

"Candace is a principled, married woman, Elsie. I know that."

She held her hands just inches from my face. "You haven't said what you thought of my nails."

"Elsie, they're… they're certainly… riveting."

"We can do yours when we get back from Happy Heart Care Center. I got a kit in the car."

On the visit with Elsie to see Orin's mother at the nursing home, we read a notice on the bulletin board for part-time jobs.

"They need nurses in the worst way," said Elsie. "Jobs don't grow on trees in Redbud, Maggie. Too bad you only got a degree in education. Besides, you're what my mama used to call 'too long in the tooth.'"

"Long in the tooth? Hah! Elsie, this place would hire anybody who could walk and chew gum at the same time." I pointed to the job notice. "Look there. They want people they can train as orderlies. 'High school diploma required.' I do have one of those."

She smiled as though she'd put the winning quarter in a Vegas slot. "But I'm definitely not interested in working here, Elsie."

"Well, it would get you out of the house and give you something useful to do. That is, if they'd hire you."

"I told you—getting hired would not be a problem."

"You got to consider, it's back-breaking work for someone like yourself. Not like reading *Hamlet* to a bunch of tenth graders or shuffling around the house with your nose in a book."

"And you think I couldn't do it?"

"You wouldn't last a week."

Maybe it was just what I needed to occupy my mind, I thought. On an impulse I walked to the receptionist's desk. "I'd like some information about the job you listed."

Barely glancing up, the receptionist handed me an application.

"Getting your hands on an application doesn't prove a thing," said Elsie.

A few days later I sat in the director's office waiting for my first job interview in thirty years. The fact I was there at all says much about my mental state at the time. I did need something to do. And, even with Elsie and my other Circle friends, I was so lonely. I imagined it might be interesting to spend an hour or two a month visiting with people the age of my parents.

But now my palms were sweaty. Ways to murder Elsie leapt to my mind as I waited to be interviewed.

J. Ronal Patrick, Ph.D. strode in, shook my hand, and sat behind his desk. He wasn't what I expected. He frowned as he leafed through my application. "I'm afraid we don't have any openings in our business office," he apologized. His words were accented with a faint Irish brogue that matched the auburn strands left in his graying hair. "My receptionist didn't go over your qualifications very thoroughly before she called you in."

"Oh, I don't want a desk job, Dr. Patrick. I'm looking for something more physical." He raised an eyebrow, reminding me of Peter Jennings delivering a particularly distasteful news story. I hurried to explain, "I'd like to interact directly with the residents. I want to help people."

He studied me a moment, tapping a pencil on his desk. His gaze was so intent, I had to look away. "Somehow, I can't see a woman like yourself emptying bedpans, Mrs. Gilpin."

"I can empty bedpans," I said.

He looked doubtful, as though he'd found me wanting. And I imagined Elsie's smirk when I told her he hadn't hired me.

"Dr. Patrick, I've raised two children. I helped take care of my grandparents when they were terminally ill. I spent summers on their farm where we had to use an out-house and a slop jar. I know what it's like to... what I mean is I'll be happy to do whatever needs doing."

His yellow pencil turned to rubber as he shook it fast. "I'll be frank with you, Mrs. Gilpin. What I don't need is another do-gooder who sees herself as Florence Nightingale. Then, when she has to clean shit from underneath somebody's nails, or change a full diaper, leaves me stranded without anybody to cover her hours."

I must have winced. His descriptive language was at odds with his impeccable grooming, but his craggy face looked serious and uncompromising. "I'm sorry if I've offended you. But I've fired the third girl this quarter for pilfering and I don't have time for a prima donna, no matter how well-meaning she might be."

"Prima donna, Dr. Patrick?" I felt the heat crawl my neck and didn't know who most deserved my anger, Elsie or the pompous ass who couldn't see how lucky he'd be to hire me. "Florence Nightingale? I'm amazed that someone with your charming manners and glib tongue has trouble keeping employees." I rose to leave.

He didn't flinch, but a smile played on his lips. Then he burst forth in a lovely booming laugh. His teeth were even and white, and his eyes crinkled pleasantly. "You may have a point, Mrs. Gilpin. Please stay a moment and give me time to make my apology to you."

"There's no need, Dr. Patrick." I moved closer to the door.

"You see, most of the kids who sign on are high school dropouts, and I'm their last resort. They stay with me a month or two, and then, about the time we've got them so they can give a decent bed bath and know how to read a thermometer, they quit and go to work in some hospital that pays half again as much as we do."

As he talked I noticed how clean and manicured his hands were. Not smooth as if he'd never baited a fish hook or held a paint brush, but groomed and capable.

"And if one of them happens to be brighter than average," he continued, "he or she'll usually figure how to supplement their income here with petty theft. We don't exactly attract the cream of the crop." He smiled again. "I didn't mean to take all that out on you. Please stay and at least drink a cup of coffee with me." He came around his desk and held out a chair for me, and I sat down.

Relief and sanity flooded my mind. I had honorably discharged my duty, but who was I kidding? My baby grandson's diapers were unattractive, not to mention those of some poor, senile adult. I would have to endure Elsie's implied "I told you so," but that happened often enough I was used to it. I thought about telling her the position had been filled but knew she wouldn't believe me.

"I tell you what, Mrs. Gilpin. If you like, I'll put you on two days a week, starting at a dollar over minimum."

"I... I could never work for that, Dr. Patrick." A lump in my throat made my voice small. "After all, I do have a degree, and I... I'm not some unskilled kid fresh from high school." Ronal Patrick's icy blue eyes held me in their gaze. "Besides," I continued, "I can see you don't need someone like me. I don't even know that I have the time... what with volunteering once a month at the Thrift Shop and all. I—"

"There I go again, stepping on toes," he said, his voice sweet as honey. "Sorry. I'm just not used to working with people of your caliber. I didn't understand you were volunteering."

I opened my mouth and closed it. I felt like a frog who hears truck tires singing on the pavement.

"When you do leave us I'll see that you get a fine letter of recommendation—in case you ever think you want to go on to a paying job. It seems the least I can do for you."

"Yes," I nodded, "the least."

We settled on four hours twice a week. "We'll furnish your uniforms."

He put me on a rotating schedule. "So the system won't suffer as big a jolt when you go on to bigger and better things."

Widows are notoriously easy prey. My quick acquiescence seemed to define the genre. But, much as I hated to admit it, Elsie was right. I did need to get out of my house, to do something useful. It was difficult to feel sorry for myself while confronted with feet whose toes were lost to diabetes, or while comforting a wizened creature who mourned the loss of her only daughter.

On the first day I reported for work, I arrived early by half an hour. Dr. Patrick invited me into his office for coffee and doughnuts.

"I'm working on a theory, Mrs. Gilpin. Half the people here die before their eightieth birthday, the other half just seem to go on forever. And, while it's not a scientific survey, the really long-livers seem to load up on caffeine and sugar every morning."

"So do some prima donnas," I said. I ate a doughnut and drank two cups of coffee before checking in with the floor supervisor that morning.

At the next Circle meeting Flory asked me, "What kinds of things do you do there?"

"I don't give the clients medicine but I do almost anything else."

"Yuck," she grimaced, "how do you stand the smell? I hate the way nursing homes smell."

Elsie volunteered, "You get used to it. Orin's ma has been there so long, she don't notice it at all."

Happy Heart Care Center wasn't the liveliest place I'd ever been, but those residents with functioning minds appreciated the extra attention I gave them. Ron Patrick painted a darker picture of my assignments than necessary, and I delighted in reminding him I could leave those urine-scented halls any time I chose. After the briefest of training, the staff happily allowed me to carry food trays to the residents, help with baths and feeding, and to assist them with their feeble attempts at recreation. Playing checkers with Bella Shariff and untangling yarn for "Aunt Betsy" Todd did not equal finding cancer cures or joining the Peace Corps. But when Miranda Chase, tears in her eyes, thanked me for braiding her hair "the way Mama used to do it," I knew I was onto something.

And while I was there, I forgot to be lonely.

I reported early nearly everyday I worked, and Ron Patrick would wave me into his office. We'd talk about politics, religion, our respective families—he had three sons and four granddaughters—and literature. It was his passion, and though I'd taught Literature in high school, I felt outclassed.

"Dickens wrote passionately, from the heart," he said.

"But he used too many words. And his women were cardboard."

"Ah, Maggie, I'd rather have cardboard than those self-absorbed lesbos and libbers your modern novelists write about."

"No doubt you use Chaucer as a yardstick," I said.

He grinned and pulled a book from his desk drawer. "Maybe we can agree on Miller."

"Henry Miller?"

He handed me his copy of *The Crucible*, the part of John Proctor highlighted in yellow marker. "I starred in a little theater production in Boston." He pronounced it "Bahstun."

"That's in Georgia, isn't it?"

"I think you'll find the parallels to McCarthyism brilliant," he enthused, ignoring my insult. "A wonderful play."

I bit my tongue to keep from remarking on his unique insight. The way his eyes crinkled I was sure his condescension was playful teasing—a response to my sarcasm. I smiled, and was rewarded with that laugh. I loved the way it seemed to fill the room. Ron was making life fun for me again. Having conversations with a man near my age was a pleasant distraction as I warred against grief. Our conversations were innocent, the door to his office always open, the picture of his dour wife always visible on the bookcase along the wall.

From the safety of marriage I'd often flirted harmlessly with men I trusted. I'd enjoyed the controlled chemistry that benignly energized our relationships. Dexter knew my game for what it was and felt no jealousy because there was no threat.

But the rules were different for widows. I thought it required a keener discipline to keep from overstepping the bounds of taste and morality.

I found myself looking forward to the days I "worked."

Six

Those first several months were a time of transition for my family, for me.

"Where's Paw-paw?" asked Sara Jane.

"We already told you," said Chet. "He's up to the sky with Jesus."

"When he gets back he's going to take us to the zoo," she said, pushing her doll buggy into the living room.

Five year old Chet rolled his eyes, and Lori looked perplexed, as if she couldn't decide whether to offer her daughter more explanations or to shush her.

I visited in Tulsa for the first time since Dexter died. Sara Jane wasn't the only one who needed to make some adjustments. I missed the way Dexter roughhoused with the children, slinging one over his shoulder as if the child were a sack of potatoes, then acting oblivious to the up-side down tot bouncing on his back.

"Where's Sara?" he'd ask, twisting and turning, but not finding her. "I don't see that little gremlin anywhere."

Screams and giggles, followed by scolding the gremlin for attaching itself to his back. Then Grandpa's fierce punishment of growls and tickles.

Dexter had loved his grandchildren, but Lori's letting them run through our house at top speed, yelling and bumping into things, made him nervous.

"They're going to hurt themselves or break one of your heirlooms, Maggie. Shouldn't they be made to behave the same as our kids were? We wouldn't have put up with that wild screaming for a minute." Even when I child-proofed our home for their visits, he couldn't relax.

We tried visiting in Don and Lori's home in Tulsa, but the children had even more latitude there; and since Dexter couldn't seem to fall asleep on a water bed, he missed his afternoon naps.

After Gil and Peggy banished meat from their diet, Dexter didn't like visiting in their home either. "I never thought my own son would turn into a weirdo," he told me as we drove home.

"You don't like spaghetti with walnut and orange sauce?" I teased.

"Damn right," he said, "but that's not the worst of it. The worst of it is when you fix my steak. She looks at you like she thinks you're barbecuing the family dog."

Now that Dexter was gone I realized how much I had worried about hurt feelings and how hard I'd worked to keep the grandchildren quiet around him. I shouldn't have bothered. For all his gruff ways his family had adored George Dexter Gilpin.

Even after several of my visits Sara Jane did not give up on her grandfather's promise. Hugging her and Chet I told them, "It's too cold to go to the zoo today, kids. The animals will be hiding in their warm houses, but I'll take you skating if you like."

I hadn't been skating in years. Lori looked at me skeptically.

"Well, maybe I'll take them to play miniature golf at that new indoor amusement park," I told her.

Sara Jane rode my hip the last half of the course. Chet knew a little about golf from watching Don practice putts on a portable green. He strode alongside me as if he were playing The Masters, and I were his caddie. After I hit a lucky shot which caromed into the clown's mouth, my grandson seemed to view me differently.

"Grandma knows how to play golf too," he proudly told his dad. "She hit a hole in one."

When the weather warmed, I took my grandchildren on outings to the zoo and to museums. Chet and Sara Jane knew I was always good for at least one Disney movie, replete with

generous amounts of popcorn, soda, and candy. I often took
them to McDonald's and rewarded proper table manners with
an extra half hour on the playground. To Lori's horror I once
spread a king-sized sheet on her living room floor and poured
fifty pounds of cornmeal into the center of it. The children and
I spent a rainy afternoon building roads and rivers and castles
in our cornmeal city, then I packed everything into a new gar-
bage bucket and vacuumed Lori's carpet.

I baby-sat with Skip, giving Gil and Peggy evenings away
from home.

Not a day went by I didn't think of Dexter, but I no longer
wept at the sight of gray sideburns beneath a western hat, or
broad shouldered men who walked with gliding grace and held
doors open for me. I told myself, you're going to be okay,
Maggie. My life—not unpleasant—a mix of church and
nursing home duties, and helping with my children. I just
needed to concentrate on what I had.

And then my delicate balancing act would crumble.

Spring arrived early in Oklahoma that year, and the grass
grew tall by mid-April. I dragged our gasoline-powered mower
from the storage shed and poured fuel into its tank. Proud of
myself for the courage it took to invade the musty, spider
infested domain of arcane tools, spools of wire that Dexter said
were too expensive to give away, and dusty jars of assorted
nuts, bolts, and thingamabobs, I pushed the mower onto the
drive. I pulled the cord with all my strength. Nothing. I tried
again, slamming energy into a rapid extension and release of
the cord. I was rewarded with a brief sputtering noise. I kept at
it for twenty minutes. It was a pleasant seventy degrees in full
sun, but sweat poured into my eyes, and my arms felt as heavy
as lead. The machine stood mocking me. Panting, I sat on the
steps of the side porch and insulted the ancestry of that mower
until I was sobbing. Then I went inside, changed clothes, and
drove to the local hardware store.

"Give me your best electric mower," I told the salesman,
"and enough outdoor cord to ring City Hall."

A voice close beside me said, "Going into the landscaping
business, Mrs. Gilpin?" Ron Patrick, wearing a knit shirt

beneath bib overalls, was examining the price tag on a riding mower.

"I need something to do between soap operas and game shows," I told him.

He helped me load the new mower into Dexter's old truck. Why, I wondered, did men look so virile in work clothes while my paint-stained shirt and faded denims transformed me into frump of the year. I pushed limp hair behind my ears as I thanked Dr. Patrick for his help, then drove home to tackle my yard.

A few weeks later I began to sort and box Dexter's clothes. He had a habit of throwing all sorts of odd mementos into his dresser drawers—doubloons from a New Orleans Mardi Gras parade, a faded program from the Broadway production of *Evita*, a box of horse apples Orin had given as a gag on Dexter's fiftieth birthday. I consigned odd keys and key rings and outdated licenses to the trash, pruning Dexter's things from my house.

And there was so much to learn about living alone.

Dexter always paid our bills. I procrastinated. One summer day as I sat in his den and began to sort bills for payment, something—Dexter's handwriting, the faint odor of pipe tobacco, the collection of family portraits on the wall—triggered my memory, and I had to quit. I wanted only to weep for the lover no longer present to comfort me. I thought of his skin, his coarse mustache, his tongue coaxing me, his lips urgent with kisses, and his gentle caresses teasing my body to a ripeness of desire and surrender. I lingered over every detail until I brought them into sharp focus. Release eluded Maggie Gilpin. There was only the weight of loss.

When she called I thought about telling the lady from *Visa* to get a life. "When can we expect payment?" she wanted to know.

Much as I enjoyed feeling sorry for myself, I knew I'd feel worse if, in addition to sex, I had to forego the convenience of charge cards. So I told her, "The check's in the mail."

"Mr. Gilpin always paid by computer, but I notice you've been mailing your payments. I take it you'll be paying by mail from now on?"

"I've had trouble with my drive," I told her. Not to mention my motivation.

I drove to the post office to mail the checks. When I returned I made a pitcher of lemonade and forced myself to sit in Dexter's chair in front of his desk. I still didn't know ROM from DOS but I did know how to boot our software. I flipped a switch and the machine began its electronic gyrations. When the screen quieted I found icons for the word processor and the spreadsheet. I read the booklet that came with the modem. I fed data disks into the computer. The drive hummed and beeped as a chronicle of the past decade marched across the monitor.

Dexter had been thorough. He had neatly labeled each disk as to content and date. The information lacked emotion—it provided "just the facts, ma'am." It proved easier to look at the entries if I concentrated on taking control of the computer. From dreading the experience I soon advanced to confidence. I spent several hours each week poring through the information on the disks.

I accessed a computer network and nearly shouted for joy when I punched the correct keys. Screens revealing the latest stock quotes appeared at my command.

Our portfolio seemed to have lost several points since Dexter's death. How would he have responded? Tentatively, I sold two hundred shares of farm equipment stock and bought three hundred in a recycling corporation *Wall Street Week* had favorably reviewed.

A few abbreviations on the balance sheets were puzzling. But since Dexter had prepared last year's tax file months before the deadline, I'd let our accountant take care of everything. "Could you give me a crash course in investments?" I'd asked.

He laughed. "Afraid there's no such thing, Mrs. Gilpin. But I'll be happy to review your situation periodically and make recommendations. I don't have Mr. Gilpin's touch, but I can keep you on an even keel."

One entry among Dexter's bookkeeping raised flags. The yearly payment for his life insurance had been somewhat excessive. I read an article about purchasing insurance so I knew costs and benefits varied greatly. But, even taking the variances into account, our premiums topped the charts. I felt justified in having removed my funds from Lester Quinn's guardianship. Too bad I had missed the opportunity to explore Quinn's greed with Dexter. "It's a business decision," Dexter had said, but it seemed he had expended money needlessly. I wondered if my husband was as infallible in business as I'd believed. It was a new and jarring thought. I must have been getting along in the grief process. Elsie told me I would have to admit that Dexter had faults before I could begin to make a life without him. At least that's what she'd learned while listening to Oprah.

Occasionally I would hear whispers about the stranger who'd attended the funeral—I'm sure it choked Flory and Amelia not to ask me about him. But there was nothing I could tell them if they had asked. Word searches consistently failed to locate Wilmer Darling in the computer files. I rifled through receipts in various folders too but found no trace of the man and no hint of Dexter's relationship to that mourner. Weird Wilmer remained an irritating mystery which seemed to have no resolution, but it troubled me no more than a thousand other questions which came in the middle of the night.

The most persistent one: what had Dexter been trying to tell me the night he died, and why had he been so worried?

"I think Dexter had some sort of premonition," I told Ron. I'd dropped by his office to get the next week's schedule, and he invited me to stay and share a cold drink with him.

"It happens," he said. "I've seen it more than once with nursing home clients. Of course, most of them aren't like Dexter... that is, they don't have so much to live for."

When I mentioned the man Lori and I called Weird Wilmer, he said, "It's a dull man who dies without a few secrets."

"You don't understand. It wasn't like that between us. Dexter and I shared everything."

"Then your daughter's right. The man probably attended the wrong funeral."

But Weird Wilmer had sobbed as though his heart were broken, and somehow I believed those sobs had been for my husband.

Seven

Elsie continued to drop by my house every few days. Most of the time she was a welcome guest, but I was flabbergasted when, some months after Dexter's funeral, she insisted I should be "ready to shop for a new husband."

"I don't want a new husband. The idea of marrying somebody else scares me to death, Elsie. I think I'll always feel married to Dexter."

"Even if you don't marry you ought to date. According to a guest Sally had on, you took a giant step toward recovery when you got rid of some of Dexter's clothes. That's one of the signs to look for in the grief process. I think you're definitely ready to socialize with a nice man."

"I do socialize with nice men."

She arched her eyebrows. "You do?"

"Sure. Orin and J. Ronal Patrick and half the men at church."

Elsie continued earnestly, "It's no joke, girl. A few more years and you'll be too old."

We were having our second cup of coffee that morning in my kitchen. Once Elsie made up her mind to pursue a subject, it would have been easier to reroute the Mississippi than to distract her, but I tried. "Did I tell you Mother Wickfielder called me "Elsie" last week? She thought I was you the whole time I bathed her."

Old Man River continued toward the Gulf, and Elsie smiled coyly. "Orin and I have a widower friend in Tulsa who is quite a catch."

Her disloyalty to Dexter angered me, and I raised my voice, "No, Elsie. Absolutely not."

"You're lucky to have friends like Orin and me who can get you a date."

"If I want to date maybe I'll just call one of those professional dating services."

"You wouldn't. Really?"

"Not unless I thought it would stop you from offering to fix me up with Orin's friend."

"Well, as a matter of fact I was going to suggest the two of—"

Anger and tension welled up inside me. For weeks I had endured her hovering kindness and nosy intervention but I would not allow her to attack Dexter's memory by insisting I needed another man in my life. I picked up an open jar of jelly and rolled it in my hands.

Elsie looked at me tentatively, then continued, "Maybe the two of you could—"

I hurled the glass toward the kitchen sink, nailing the chrome spigot dead on. Glass shards sprayed over walls, cabinets, and floors. Grape icicles hung from the ceiling.

Elsie gasped and stared open-mouthed at the mess I had made. "Whatever made you do a thing like that, Maggie?"

I hoped I hadn't ruined the spigot, and I thought I might have to repaint the ceiling. But the look on Elsie's face was almost worth it. "I didn't want to go to jail for hitting you, for trying to get you to listen to me."

"You could have just said no."

"That wouldn't have convinced you."

She stood slowly, placed freckled hands on her narrow hips, and thrust her jaw forward. "Well, you needn't think I'll clean it up for you." She shook her head, then picked her way toward the door that led to my carport before turning to face me. Sounding as normal as if she hadn't had to step over slick globs of jelly, she said, "I'll call at six this evening to take you to choir practice. You can ride with me to pick up Louella Finney. You remember, she moved here from Tulsa a few months back, after her doctor-husband died." Elsie's tone became confidential. "You and her are in the same boat. Of course, Dexter wasn't a doctor, and she may be more refined than us, but I think we need to extend her the hand of Christian fellowship."

I considered telling Elsie to count me out. But my real anger was at losing Dexter, not about her bumbling efforts to ease my pain. She tried to help me as best she could and didn't deserve my childish tantrum.

"I'll be ready at six," I said.

"You don't mind if I give Louella a chance at Orin's friend in Tulsa, do you? She has undergone the most pitiful case of depression and heartbreak I have ever seen."

In the months since Mrs.-Doctor Finney had returned to Redbud, I'd heard gossip about her family. The founding Watson had made a fortune in real estate and oil before retiring to Redbud near the turn of the century. Once, at Circle, Amelia Crabtree had read us articles which featured socially prominent Louella Watson Finney. "Mrs. William Finney and Mrs. Sara Gladstone Host this Year's Medical Wives' Club Extravaganza," and "Doctor's Wife Sews Toys for Homeless Tots." With her busy schedule in Tulsa, it was no wonder she seemed to have visited Redbud only rarely before her husband died.

After Elsie left and I cleaned the jelly mess, I retrieved Dexter's high school annual from Mother Gilpin's trunk. I found Louella Watson's full page picture, captioned "Football Queen." Her lashes were long. She smiled less mysteriously than Mona Lisa, more as if she were anticipating another delicious romp in bed. Her bosom spilled above a strapless gown. She'd signed, "For Dexter, Captain of the team, Captain of my heart. Love, Lulu." Lulu? Captain of my heart?

In a collage of snapshots there were photos—Louella washing cars with a grinning young man, marching in her majorette uniform at the head of the band, building a snowman with another swain, in the arms of a boy at the prom, having a soda with yet another admirer at Crabtree's Drugs. The only student featured more prominently was Dexter. I smiled. Was I destined to meet one of Dexter's old flames?

When Elsie arrived to take me to choir practice, she wore an olive and magenta plaid skirt and jacket of polyester. The heavy colors did not flatter her pale, lined skin. I noticed the jacket fastened with velcro underneath the buttons and knew

Elsie had made the ensemble. She has never been able to make a decent buttonhole. The roll of the collar wasn't quite right, and some of the seams were puckered. At the thrift shop, which our church runs with the Methodists, there are always dozens of similar garments—Wickfielder originals.

"You still got jelly stains on your ceiling," she said.

"It's a test patch. I'm thinking about redoing the colors in here."

"Are you ready to go?"

"Maybe I should change," I teased. I wore slacks and a casual top, the customary uniform for ladies in our choir on Wednesday evenings.

"You don't have time. I don't want to be late to pick up Mrs.-Doctor Finney."

When I opened the front door of Elsie's Buick, she frowned, "Would you mind sitting in the back this time, just in case Louella prefers the front seat?"

"Shall I hide on the floor?"

"Louella used to be a Watson before she married her doctor-husband."

"I know. She graduated from high school with Dexter. I looked her up in his annual. LuLu was voted 'The Girl You'd Most Like to Live Next Door To' and she was the Class Secretary her senior year."

"She's always had money but she's still down-to-earth."

"Good for her."

"But she's extremely cultured."

"You probably hadn't noticed, but I quit slurping through my straw and I no longer saucer my coffee."

"I don't think Louella knows anyone in Tulsa who pitches fits just because a friend is trying to help her," she said.

The Watson house sat far back from the road, and mature oaks and pecan trees shaded the yard. Elsie drove the circular drive to the front of the old Victorian. A wide porch wrapped around three sides of the structure. A shadowy figure waited behind a leaded glass entrance. Elsie stepped from the car and tried to open the front passenger door for the sorrowing widow, but Louella Finney hurried from her house, crossed to the driver's side and opened the back door and settled into the seat. Then she turned to me, smiled, and stuck out her hand.

"Hi, I'm Louella Finney."

She had on orange and green striped sweats and a pair of Nikes. A spangled headband adorned her forehead. She smelled of vanilla, citrus, and gardenia. The entire effect was delightfully appealing and slightly wild. *So much for sophistication and gentility,* I thought. *Even though she was Dexter's age she looked nearer forty. Good genes,* I thought, *or a face lift.* By the time we arrived at church, Louella and I found we enjoyed the same movies and books and we both liked to sew and to garden.

"You'll have to admit I was right about the two of you," said Elsie as she pulled into the church parking lot. "You ought to be good company for each other."

"I'm not sure I'm such good company," said Louella. "I have times when I fight the blues and I'm still angry that Bill died, but I'm not as cuckoo as I was. When Bill went into a coma I promised God if He let Bill live we would go to India and help Mother Theresa's organization." Her laugh filled the empty lot. "I don't think the Lord thought that was much of a bargain. So I took Bill's death as a sign God didn't mind if I cashed some of our investments when I refurbished Grandma Watson's house. But I sent Mother Theresa's people a contribution, just in case I had misunderstood Him."

Elsie said, "Speaking of misunderstandings, I hope you won't misunderstand my intentions, Louella. I just want to help out. I wouldn't want you to get upset or to think I butted into your personal business."

Louella looked puzzled.

"She's going to ask if you'd like to date one of Orin's friends. I didn't react well when she offered to play matchmaker for me."

Elsie laughed nervously. "She pitched jelly all over her kitchen. It was the doggonedest mess you ever saw."

"Well," said Louella, "Bill has been gone nearly a year, so I'd consider dating. But I won't go out with anyone older than fifty. I won't date a recent widower, a fellow who expects me to clean his house or do his laundry, or any man who watches professional wrestling."

Louella had declared virtually all Orin's cronies ineligible. We had arrived early so we were still waiting for the director to open the back door that led to the choir room. Halogen lamps lit our faces, and I saw Elsie frown.

"I don't know why you'd want to narrow your chances that way. Some of the nicest men enjoy wrestling matches on TV. And at your age you'll have to settle for an older gentleman."

"But before Bill died I gave him my solemn promise not to date anyone like that."

I don't know if that explanation satisfied Elsie but it did shut her up, and it fed my growing admiration for Louella Watson Finney. I was delighted when she asked Elsie and me to accompany her the next morning to shop for a new bathtub.

"Of course, I've already talked to Orin about installing it. He said for me to find what I want and let him know. I'm looking for a marble tub with water jets, maybe with its own heater." She briefly closed her eyes and smiled. "I loved our whirlpool tub in Tulsa. A warm bath is such a sensuous way to relax. I thought maybe you could show me how to get to the plumbing supply place, Elsie."

"I thought you could find your way around Tulsa wearing horse blinders."

"Except for the industrial area. I've never been on that side of town."

Elsie shook her head. "I can't go tomorrow, but Maggie's been there with us before. She knows where it is and she's not busy."

Eight

A dozen chores cluttered my list, but I easily persuaded myself to postpone cleaning the oven and re-hanging the bedroom
curtains. Louella was different from my other friends—
sophisticated and a bit worldly. Her personality intrigued me.

The next morning I dressed, heaped a can of tuna on
Schlegg's plate, backed my Mercury from the carport, and
arrived for Louella by eight. She met me at the door and asked
me in for coffee.

I had last been in the Watson home when Louella's grandmother invited me there with Dexter. "It's a little like Queen
Elizabeth summoning us for a royal visit," Dexter had
explained.

At the time Mrs. Watson was ninety and in a wheelchair,
pushed by a pleasant, middle-aged black man. After dinner
she'd directed us into the drawing room where "Uncle Fred"
produced an old photo album. Dexter's parents smiled from the
brittle pages—black and white moments of people so carefree
and different from the stodgy pair I remembered, I wondered if
I had known them at all.

Mrs. Watson removed several snapshots and gave them to
my husband, telling him, "They went to Yellowstone that year
with Ken and La Nelle. Your grandmother on your mother's
side kept you, and we kept Louella. They were gone a whole
month." Her eyes fixed on a distant past and she sighed. "I
used to think you and Louella might...." Uncle Fred, standing
behind Mrs. Watson's wheelchair, had shrugged and rolled his
eyes.

Now as I followed Louella through the living room and

down the hall, the house sang with color. Floral chintzes and tapestries seemed to bloom in light which flooded through opened draperies. Real cut flowers, scattered among pots of greenery, perfumed the entry.

"Oh my, Louella. I wouldn't have believed this place could be so lively. It's beautiful."

She smiled. "When I used to come here as a child, I pretended I owned this house. I think I started decorating it, in my mind, way back then."

She led me into the kitchen and directed me to a table. We sat by bay windows overlooking the garden as Louella poured coffee.

"We could have moved here right after Grandmother died, but Bill didn't want to relocate his practice. So when Grandmother's servants, Uncle Fred and Aunt Flossie, agreed to stay on, I offered them the house. But Aunt Flossie said it was too grand—the quarters were just fine. They kept an eye on things for me, and Bill and I stayed here as often as we could."

"Are they still in the quarters?" I asked, remembering the pleasant cottage at the back of the lot.

"Uncle Fred died last summer. He kept the yard looking like a golf course up until the last few months. I don't prune a rose but what I think of him. He and Aunt Flossie were so good to me. And Aunt Flossie—well, she got a bit addled. After Uncle Fred died their kids and I moved her to a nursing home. Nowadays I hire help where I can find it, but nobody knows as much about gardening as Uncle Fred did."

"Aunt Flossie's not at Happy Heart," I said, thinking of the half-dozen African-American women I knew there.

"No. There's nothing wrong with Happy Heart, but this place is a bit nicer—Blackwood Retirement Home. She tells me she's well-treated. I don't get to see her as often as I would if I still lived in Tulsa, but she's nearer some of her children."

I knew Blackwood by reputation. Ron said he could never match their standards because they operated on private funds. "If you outlive your time Blackwood's the best place to be," he told me. "Only, their budget rivals the national debt."

I smiled thinking of Aunt Flossie living such a rich life among the elderly upper crust of Tulsa. It had to cost somebody a small fortune. Perhaps her children had prospered, but I suspected Louella was a generous benefactor.

As if reading my thoughts, she said, "We all loved Aunt Flossie and Uncle Fred. Grandmother left me a trust fund, and I promised her I'd use it to take care of those two. They earned it, the way they looked after this house, this family." The Southern Belle speaking about her duty, but I decided not to read a patronizing attitude into her words.

She refilled our coffee cups. "Sorry I can't offer you anything to go with the coffee but I don't cook much anymore. If you like we can grab a bite to eat at a drive-through before we go to the 'Plumbing is Us.'"

On the way to Tulsa, Louella asked me about people I knew in Redbud. Although she'd grown up in our small town, she seemed as removed from it—as distanced from genuine friendships—as I felt. In her case it was probably because she'd had little contact with old acquaintances during her marriage to Dr. Finney. There was an undercurrent of sadness to her stories as she told me of her childhood in Dexter's home town. Every word about him and his friends was welcome illumination:

"When the high school team won a game, we'd all sneak into town in the middle of the night and put soap powder and green dye in the town fountain. All the next day the copper tree would rain green bubbles on the courthouse square. Chief Johnston would bluster and scold, saying how we were desecrating the town symbol, but he never tried to stop us." She grew pensive. "He could be very understanding."

Understanding wasn't a word I would have used for Chief Johnston, now an addled old man at Happy Heart.

"Charley, Chief Johnston's son, had been crippled with polio. The March of Dimes didn't pay everything, so my folks helped out. And the boys would usually include Charley in their outings, so the Chief cut us a lot of slack."

We crossed the bridge that led from Main onto the state highway. Louella pointed to the trashy ravine below. "The creeks and ponds weren't polluted like they are now. We swam in them." She chuckled. "One time a bunch of us girls followed Richard Mitchell's truck to Indian Lake. He had a truckload of boys, and we knew they were all going skinny-dipping. We

sneaked to the creek bank, took their clothes, hightailed it to
the school yard, and ran as much underwear as we could up the
flagpole." She seemed to read my mind. "Yes, your husband
was with them."
"He never told me about it," I said. "Did the boys know
who'd done it?"
Her voice was full of satisfaction. "It wouldn't have been
much fun if they hadn't seen us, would it? By the time they
managed to swim to shore and scramble to the truck, we were
locked in my car and I had the truck keys." She grinned as she
maneuvered into the passing lane. "I backed a safe distance and
threw the keys to Richard. He uncovered himself when he
reached to catch them. All the girls screamed, and he blushed
beet red. Of course, most of us were still virgins that year,
except for Flory, so it was pretty shocking."
"Flory?"
"Bible thumping Flory. She didn't get religion till she
started going with Ray Santos."
"Flory?"
"Yeah. It's funny. Some of us turned out about like everyone thought we would, and others are real surprises. I'd have
bet Flory would have gone through a string of men by now
instead of settling down with Ray.
"And I always thought Richard Mitchell would be a vet like
he planned. He used to find baby skunks and bring them to
school and he always had a sick bird or a wounded raccoon he
cared for. I don't know if he couldn't make the grades or if he
just didn't have the money. Anyhow, there's Richard, running
the hardware store for his uncle, and I don't think he and
Shirley even have a pet dog."
"What did you think Dexter would be?" I asked.
"Oh, Dexter's one of those guys who stuck to the script,
except I thought he might marry a local girl. Anna Travis was
her name. I think she married some guy from Minnesota."
"Elsie's mentioned her to me once or twice."
"And there were plenty more who set their cap for Dexter.
But I guess he waited for you."

Not that I'd been seriously jealous, but her words comforted me. "Meanwhile," I said, "I understand he kept busy courting the girls of Redbud." I didn't mind. He'd married me. "In a town this small there were a lot of romances that bloomed and died. Half the fun of the necking parties at the cemetery was to see who'd broken up and who the new couples were."

This was a feature of Redbud dating Dexter had never mentioned. "You necked at the cemetery? How creepy."

"It didn't seem like it at the time. We'd park our cars on the drive that runs along the ridge. You could look down on the town. It was quite charming, especially during the holidays when all the colored lights were strung."

Had she and Dexter "necked?" She seemed to read my mind. "Dexter and I were an item in the eighth grade, before any of us were into necking parties, but then he threw me over for Linda Collingsworth." She laughed. "He broke my heart."

"I envied Dexter his childhood," I said. "The wholesomeness of small town living appealed to me, and I wanted to raise Lori and Gil here."

"Just remember, the old days always sound better when you look back on them. I dreamed of living in a town with more than one dress shop, a city where you could sneeze without getting a call from your grandmother or your doctor."

"I guess the grass always looks greener."

"Elsie says you grew up in Oklahoma City."

"In Capitol Hill, not far from Packing Town. And my high school was nearly as large as the whole town of Redbud."

"How did you meet Dexter?"

My eyes misted as I remembered. "I was in my senior year at Central State, planning to marry a boy named Robert. He called me one night from some little town in Texas, to tell me he'd eloped with a friend of his mother's. Robert said he regretted the way things turned out and he'd love me forever. It was so bizarre—he said he had to marry her because she was pregnant."

I laughed to cover the catch in my throat. "I knew I hadn't loved Robert and I'd been thinking of breaking it off, but he'd

shattered my pride. And so my college roommate arranged for
me to date her brother's friend from O.U."

"And the friend was Dexter?"

"It must have been shortly after he broke up with Anna. He
told me he planned to stay away from any serious commit-
ments for a long time, and I certainly didn't expect to fall in
love."

I remembered how understanding he'd been when I told him
about Robert, calling Robert a jerk and a fool. We went to the
movies, and afterward Dexter bought us strawberry cones. We
ate them while walking hand in hand across the campus under
the stars, and I said a million prayers of gratitude that Robert
married somebody else.

"Yes," I told Louella. "That's how I—" I cleared my throat.
"We were so much in love."

She looked at me and said softly, "They say you'll get over
it, Maggie. They just don't say when."

Louella picked out a marble tub half the size of my guest
bedroom, then we went to the mall. We each tried on outland-
ish clothes that I would never have bought. We looked at
antique hats and vintage dresses. Louella wore a size ten so she
tried on outfits from Swing and Sizzle. I hadn't laughed much
since I'd lost Dexter, so I was startled to hear myself cackling
with amusement. We had barely managed to stagger outside
the store before we both burst into laughter.

"Did you see the look on that poor salesgirl's face?" asked
Louella. "She tried to think of a nice way to say, 'Dear, don't
you think you're a bit old for tank tops?' But she couldn't do
that because she would have lost a sale for sure."

"I thought you looked pretty good."

"Liar. I used to lift weights—they were little pink barbells—
and I had progressed to three pounds for each arm. I exercised
religiously every morning for three months, and all that
happened was I developed something that looked like a golf
ball inside here." She pointed to the upper part of a tailored
sleeve. "If surgery weren't so painful I'd have some of that
wattle whacked off."

At Dillard's she talked me into a pink and aqua jacket she
assured me would add pizzazz to my black sheath. "If you

insist on wearing such boring clothes, at least punch them up with a little color," she told me.

"Haven't you ever heard of mourning clothes?" I asked, not half serious.

"A custom invented by wives to keep good-looking single women like us from stealing their husbands."

"You know, Louella, that's just how most women I know act—like I'm trying to seduce their men. Can you believe they'd suspect us of flirting with their husbands?"

"Hey! Flirting's fun. I may have to give up sex and chocolate, but don't tell me I can't wink at Clayton Crabtree or notice Richard Mitchell's aftershave. I ain't dead, you know."

From that day, outings with Louella Finney became a regular part of my life. We drove to the mall, ate lunch, shopped, and took in an afternoon movie nearly every week. Sometimes I felt like a hypocrite because, when I was with a friend, I could compartmentalize my grief. I noticed it less. Fun was like a narcotic. When I was with Louella or Dr. Patrick, I sometimes laughed until my sides ached. And when I was alone I wondered if I had been disloyal to Dexter.

Several weeks into our friendship, Louella and I were eating lunch at *El Sombrero's* in the mall. Perhaps the movie we'd seen made her introspective. "My psychologist says I have unresolved feelings about my marriage and Bill's death. Dr. Mulvaney thinks I'm just postponing the inevitable breakdown."

"You go to a psychiatrist?"

"A psychologist. You're the only one in Redbud who knows, Maggie." She hadn't needed my promise to keep that secret. Her fingers drummed on the hard table top, jangling turquoise bracelets. The usual lilt left her voice. "I don't want people like Orin and Elsie Wickfielder thinking I'm crazy, but I've seen a therapist for years."

"I imagine it helps, especially now."

By that time I thought I knew Louella fairly well. On the surface she was worldly, wild, outspoken, and apparently a shallow soul. But in unguarded moments she displayed kindness, depth, and sensitivity.

Elsie had been sure that, "Living in Tulsa has probably given Louella some refinement. You don't move in medical circles and stay a small town girl." But some of Louella's language and attitudes jarred Elsie. "She told the Reverend Pierce she didn't see anything wrong for a man to wear an earring. And she says damn and hell just like the fellows at Orin's poker parties."

Having been around my children and their contemporaries, I sometimes found Louella's language disagreeably earthy, but not shocking. I discerned a fragile soul in need of my friendship. Learning she saw a therapist gave me one more piece of the puzzle to her personality.

"What do you do now, Maggie, when you need a shoulder to cry on? You're not keeping a man in the closet, are you?"

"Good grief, no. I just wear out you and Elsie." I saw no point in mentioning how much I enjoyed my visits with the director of Happy Heart Nursing Home, and it didn't seem fair to complain of how little solace I received from the rest of the women in Second Thursday Circle whose sympathetic words seemed to hide distaste for my lingering grief. "And I talk to my kids, but I don't want to burden them. Gil and Lori are sad enough about losing their father. Sometimes I hug Dexter's cat, but Schlegg has an attitude, and...."

"And?"

"This may sound strange, but I get a lift these days from volunteering at the nursing home."

"Hm." She wrinkled her nose as if she'd discovered a bite of jalapeño in her salad. "I had enough do-gooding in Tulsa to last me a lifetime."

"Handling Dexter's investments helps take my mind off things too." I grinned at her. "And I eat chocolate bonbons and watch TV and go to silly movies with other dilettantes."

"I suppose I could get involved in volunteer work again, like I did in Tulsa. But I'm not sure I could do anything that would be useful in Redbud."

"Nonsense. You sew beautifully, and your gardens are the prettiest in town."

"That's just about it, a complete catalog of my talents." She took a compact from her purse and powdered her nose. "That, and I know how to have a helluva good time. It's not the same without my beautiful man, but when I move real fast I sometimes forget he's not there."

"That sounds like me," I said. "Only, at first I acted like a woman with the emotional maturity of a fruit fly. After Dexter's funeral I went to bed and tried to forget the world. Elsie was afraid I was becoming agoraphobic. If she hadn't pulled me out of bed, I'd probably have died there."

"Elsie's been awfully sweet to me too, but just between you and me, she can be a pain in the ass. If anything, she's worse than when we were in school. I gather you two have been friends a long time and... well, I wouldn't have put the two of you together."

"No?"

"Oh, come on. You know what I mean. You're so... so proper and well-spoken."

I did know what she meant. But, unlike many of Redbud's citizens, Elsie didn't let my "proper and well-spoken" style get in the way of our friendship. Uncomfortable with Louella's criticism of Elsie, I tried to explain my penchant for correct grammar. "I taught high school English for three years."

"It's more than that. You and Elsie are like... well, it's as if Miss Manner's best friend was... a shock jock."

I grinned, "Then, who are we?"

"I don't know about you, but I'm Sharon Stone in a dark wig." She playfully patted her hair. "But seriously, did you know Elsie's joined a book club? And she's trying to read a classic a week."

I hadn't known but I wasn't surprised. I said, "Elsie has always wanted to make something of herself, but it's only been the past few years she's had the luxury of serious study."

"Trying to make a silk purse from a camel's rump, I guess."

Soon after I'd met Elsie, Dexter had pointed out that correct speech doesn't guarantee intelligence or a good heart. Elsie had both. Poverty and her family's attitude toward higher learning had saddled her with the facade of a country hick. But, Dexter warned, Elsie's malaprops and mispronunciations should never be interpreted as a lack of intelligence. I tried to keep my voice level. "Elsie's nobody's fool, Louella. And surely you can appreciate how far she's come from being a sharecropper's daughter. Much as she can annoy me, I admire her. She was the first woman besides my mother-in-law to welcome me to Redbud, and she's always been my friend."

"Aren't you ever bothered by how much she exaggerates?"

"I guess, if Elsie feels insecure, she does sometimes stretch the truth."

"Till it snaps," said Louella. She took a final swallow of tea, then gave me her share of the bill. "Would you mind paying the check? I'd like to go back to Dillard's and pick up that scarf I looked at earlier. I'll meet you in the lot."

Nine

Once Louella and I became friends I didn't miss the latest movie or give up restaurant dining, because she was usually available to go with me. But much as I enjoyed her company, I didn't want to neglect older friendships. As Dexter's wife I'd had many friends, and most had stood by me when I'd lost him. I worried especially about the widening gulf between Elsie and me.

At one time Elsie and I had a standing appointment for Sunday evenings. Orin worked with the young people's group at church, and Elsie didn't like to stay alone. Dexter, who had great affection for Elsie but appreciated her most in small doses, used to hide in his den until she went home. After Dexter retired and curtailed his out of town excursions, I spent Sunday evenings alone with him. Elsie never complained, but I think she felt I had abandoned her.

After she had refused several invitations to shop with Louella and me, I spoke with her after services one Sunday. "We used to have such fun," I said. "Why don't you come over this evening?"

She hesitated only a moment. "Will anyone else be there?"

"It will be just the two of us," I said. "Like old times."

When I opened my kitchen door to her, she stood in the carport, holding two grocery sacks. "You haven't got any pecans from the old Watson house yet, have you?"

"No, Elsie. You know Louella. I doubt she's thought about gathering her pecans. She probably buys them shelled from the grocery store."

"We've had these a while, and I was going to give half to

you." She set the sacks on the table. "Orin took them to market and had them run through the automatic sheller, but you still have to pick out the nutmeat."

"It's so much easier when the shells are cracked," I said. "Tell him thanks for me."

"I almost didn't bring them because I figured maybe you had plenty already from Mrs.-Doctor Finney." She fairly spat the last words.

"You mean Louella? It seems a shame for hers to go to the squirrels. Maybe we should ask her if she'd like to donate them to the thrift store. The three of us could gather them some afternoon."

Elsie smirked. "Maybe you should ask her the next time you two have one of your social outings."

"Why don't you go with us?"

"I wouldn't want to be a fifth wheel. You two remind me of a couple of high school kids where one of them can't sneeze without the other one catching cold."

Her words surprised more than offended me. "Why, Elsie, I've never done anything to make you feel like a fifth wheel. Besides you're the one who introduced me to Louella."

"I thought she might be different than she was in school, but she's as disturbed as ever."

"What? I thought you held her in high regard—you told me she was so cultured. And she told me you'd been very kind to her since she moved home to Redbud. How can you call Louella Finney disturbed? What's going on here, Elsie?"

"I have to admit it—I've got a heart as big as all outdoors and I'm a sucker for a hard luck story. I took her to the bosom of my friendship, never looking for her to slip into degradation. But, if I was you, I'd watch her like a hawk."

Louella's language hardly qualified as degradation, even in Elsie's book. "Are we both talking about Louella Finney?" I asked.

"Let's do ourselves a favor and talk about something else."

"Fine," I said. "I agree, we should drop the subject."

"I thought we might watch *Tootsie* again tonight," she said, taking a video from her huge purse.

"Great. I love *Tootsie*."

"It's hysterical."

When the butter melted on the popcorn, we started the movie and the pecan shelling. The first time I laughed aloud—at Hoffman's unsuccessful auditions—Schlegg left the room to protest the noise. I could count on Elsie to giggle with me as Tootsie adjusted to female clothing and thwarted lecherous passes. And when Bill Murray feigned disapproval of Hoffman's slutty behavior, we were into a steady rhythm of shelling, punctuated by chuckles and guffaws.

When the movie finished Elsie wiped her eyes with the back of her hand. "That Dustin Hoffman is hysterical."

"Witty, talented, funny, and amusing."

"High-larious and hysterical."

"You're not making some sort of obscure pun, are you, Elsie?"

She frowned. "What are you talking about?"

"Hyster, you know, the root for hysterical. It means woman. It originally had to do with the idea the Greeks thought women had less control over their emotions than men do over theirs."

She looked at me over the top of her bifocals. "I'm not one of your high school English students, Margaret."

"Of course not. I'm sorry. Sometimes I can't help myself."

"Well, you ought to try. I don't think you realize how much Dexter toned you down, and now you're getting to where you sound like you speak a foreign language." She sniffed. "I said Dustin Hoffman was hysterical, and that's what I meant."

"Very hysterical."

"Which reminds me—the plumbers have their costume party the thirtieth. Orin and I are going as Cone Heads dressed up like we're going to a prom. I took Orin's tux to the cleaners —the one he bought for Candace's wedding—and I'm wearing a pale blue formal that she wore to the prom her senior year." With a thumb she pushed an errant bra strap beneath her blouse. "Your sapphire and cloisonné brooch would be the perfect assessory."

"Accessory," I mumbled.

"What?"

"Elsie, I hope you understand. If I were going to lend it to anybody, it would be to you. But since Dexter died I've kept that brooch in my shadow box. If I lent it to you or if I wore it myself, one of us might lose it."

"I'm not in the habit of losing things."

"I know that. But Dexter gave me that brooch. I'm very sentimental about it."

Her mouth hardened into a straight line. "Please, just forget I asked for it."

"Isn't there something else I could lend you instead?"

"I'm sure I'll get along fine without you loaning me a thing, Margaret. I'd best be going. Orin will be expecting me."

"Wait while I divide the pecans." I poured Elsie's half into plastic bags and gave them to her. "I'm glad you came over tonight. I really enjoyed watching *Tootsie* again."

But all she said as she took her pecans, squared her shoulders, and walked to her car was, "Good night."

I could have brushed off the incident had I not felt so guilty about neglecting our friendship. The more time I spent with Louella, the less I saw of Elsie. And remembering some of my conversations with Louella made me feel worse.

On one of our shopping trips Louella had asked me, "Did Elsie ever tell you about the time I stole her boyfriend?"

"Not Orin?" I asked, thinking what an unlikely pairing it would have been.

"No. I never considered Orin much of a challenge. It was before Orin. His last name was Truman, so the guys nicknamed him Harry. He asked Elsie to a party our junior year. I arrived with another boy but I flirted shamelessly with Harry. I invited him to my folks' country club. Elsie and Harry were history after that."

"She's never said a word," I told Louella. "I didn't suppose she'd ever dated anyone but Orin."

"I'm embarrassed to remember how I must have hurt her. I was young and I acted without thinking. But she was always such a tempting target."

Louella shook her head. "Has she told you yet how she would have been a star at the Grand Ole Opry if she hadn't married Orin?"

"She doesn't mention it more than once a week."

"In my opinion," said Louella, "she probably did have an

outside chance. But I never met anyone with a worse habit of tooting her own horn. I overheard her tell Flory Santos she could still fit into her wedding dress if she hadn't had to cut it up to make curtains, back when she and Orin were first married."

Though I often found Elsie's behavior irritating, Louella was being too rough on my friend. "Elsie's a dear and she's been wonderful to me since I lost Dexter. We'll probably both rot in hell if we don't quit saying ugly things about her."

Now I wondered if Elsie still harbored a grudge against Louella for stealing Harry. Why had she warned *me* about Louella? I had never seen Louella flirt with married men, but even if she had, I had no husband for her to steal.

As I recalled Louella's revelations, I watched Elsie's headlights swing into the street. Then I picked Schlegg up, went into the living room, sat on the sofa, and pushed the channel changer to CNN.

I needed Dexter. He could have put it all in perspective for me. "Elsie's temperamental," he would say. "And you're younger, prettier, and smarter—no wonder she's jealous. But she'll come around, Maggie. Just don't let her get to you."

He'd grinned the first time he'd tried to explain Elsie to me. "Granddaddy had a horse named Old Blue," he told me. "Old Blue would eat the corner posts on the fencing, ran like she was wearing three shoes, and puffed up her belly when you tried to saddle her. But she came when you whistled and she never once threw a kid or kicked a dog. You make allowances for a horse like that.

"Elsie's sort of like Old Blue—she does a lot more good than she does harm."

There wasn't anyone else I could talk to—it would sound so silly to Lori—and I didn't want to fuel Louella's negativity toward Elsie.

"Schlegg, old boy," I said, my face buried in his neck, "I need a friend tonight." He sat on my lap, kneading his paws into my stomach. When I drew back, I could have sworn I saw sympathy in his eyes.

Ten

Monday morning my kitchen drain stopped up. It was evening before Orin came.

"Your air gap was clogged. I found popcorn kernels in the pipe," he said accusingly.

"I always put them in the disposer."

"Women."

"Next time I'll throw them in the trash. How's Elsie?"

He wiped a hand on his coveralls. "Right as rain. All worked up about the Christmas cantata."

"I suppose she'll be doing one of the solos again?"

"If Doc Finney's widow don't beat her out of it. She'll know a week from Wednesday at choir practice."

"Louella doesn't have nearly the voice Elsie does. I'm sure Brother Lee will have Elsie sing the solo again this year."

He cleared his throat loudly.

"What do I owe you?"

"Five dollars will cover my cost, the truck and all."

"Orin, you should charge me just what you'd charge anybody else."

"We ain't that hard up yet, Maggie."

"I guess all I can say is thank you."

Orin looked away. "You're more than welcome," he mumbled.

"I understand you and Elsie will be going to a costume party. Elsie wanted to borrow a piece of jewelry, but I turned her down." I shook my head and tried to explain. "I'm sorry, Orin. I know I'm too sentimental, but with Dexter gone I couldn't bring myself to lend her my brooch."

He wiped his hands on a paper towel, and threw it under the kitchen sink. "They always throw a benefit for Halloween. Elsie already picked up some stuff so she can make herself an artificial corsage to wear with Candi's dress."

"That sounds nice."

"Maggie, Elsie has a firecracker temper but she don't hold grudges for long."

"I know. Thank you, Orin."

All that day Elsie remained stubbornly unavailable for my phone calls.

"I dropped by the house to see her," said Louella over the phone. "She said she had to work on the books at Wickfielder's Plumbing and Electrical tomorrow. Then Orin was going to help her wire her bleach bottle lamps."

"Bleach bottle lamps?"

I thought of the winter Elsie crocheted two hundred catsup bottle covers. In six months we sold two. Then I secretly unraveled the yarn and made some pot holders. We hadn't wanted to hurt Elsie's feelings, so Amelia, Flory and I created phony sales receipts. Elsie bragged about being the top seller at the Thrift Shop. Now it seemed we might need to manage another subterfuge.

We'd do it because we loved Elsie, because she was first among us to visit a sick friend or comfort the bereaved. Because she was like that horse, Old Blue.

Louella interrupted my woolgathering. "You'd better get ready to sell twelve lamps. She had Orin make her some wire frames and she's gluing craft sticks on them to make the shades."

"Oh dear. What do they look like?"

"Like something the Cub Scouts might make, especially if Andy Warhol was their den mother. You know me—I usually say what I think. This time I held back, but I couldn't bring myself to show much enthusiasm for them. I hope I didn't hurt her feelings. Maybe you can admire them when she brings them to your house for Second Thursday Circle."

I told Louella about the year I entered a candlewicked pillow at the county fair. "Elsie filled a coffee can with sand, covered it with macaroni and daubed metallic paint in what she called a free form design. She entered the can as a door stop. After the fair we collected our entries. Mine won a blue ribbon, but Elsie's...."

"Elsie's had been mercifully overlooked, I bet."

"Right. On the drive home in my car, she spilled a thermos of coffee on my cream colored pillow. She was terribly upset about it, and I couldn't be angry. 'Let me take it home and wash it for you,' she said. Months later I'd insisted she return it. The pillow form was in shreds from the bleach she'd used on the stain."

Louella clucked her tongue. "All that work...."

"Elsie uses bleach like some people use water. She could probably make several dozen lamps."

"Twelve seems more than enough."

After church on Sunday, while we were hanging up our choir robes, I invited Elsie to drop by for the evening.

"I'd love to but I have plans. Sorry."

I barely stopped myself from asking her, "What plans?" Elsie and I each had friendships outside our Redbud acquaintances, and my twinge of curiosity and jealousy was unfair. I didn't want Elsie to think I had taken her company for granted.

"Oh, well," I said, "I'll see you next Thursday at Circle. Don't forget it's at my house."

On Monday morning the handyman arrived to paint the jelly stained walls and ceiling in my kitchen. By evening all traces of the sticky incident were gone. Monday through Wednesday I sandwiched an orgy of cleaning in between work for the thrift shop and the nursing home. For the first time in a great while, I skipped choir rehearsal. I changed Furr Schleggener's litter box so often he threatened to move. I fluffed my draperies in the dryer. I washed windows inside and out. I vacuumed beneath the sofa cushions. I brought the ladder in from the storage shed and stood on it to polish my collection of cloisonné plates.

When Gil and Lori were small and I first hosted Circle, Dexter tried to help by hiring a cleaning lady. I wore myself out getting the house ready for her to clean.

"I don't want her to think we're dirty," I told Dexter.

He said, "Dirt's part of the human condition."

Dirt did not belong to the world of the Second Thursday

Circle. Dust bunnies multiplied beneath refrigerators and beds, and mildew grew in the cracks of shower stalls the rest of the year; but on Second Thursday a pristine condition of antisepsis settled on the house of the hostess while she pretended spotless ovens were a normal circumstance of everyday life.

In the guest bathroom I took mementos from the shadow box in which I kept my cloisonné jewelry. I vacuumed the velvet background, then I carefully returned my treasures, treasures which included the heart-shaped brooch Dexter brought back from Korea. The sapphire gleamed against the cobalt blue of the enamel.

"Blue sets off your eyes," Dexter said when he gave it to me.

I paused from my work, remembering the night he'd put the brooch in my hands. After welcoming Dexter home Mom and Dad Gilpin volunteered to keep Lori for us over the weekend.

"I'm not letting either of my girls leave our house without me," he'd told them.

I had looked forward to, had expected his romantic ardor, but was surprised and pleased the way he instantly bonded with the baby. When Lori cried he took her from me and held her to his shoulder while he walked her. He seemed to know just how to quiet her.

"You'd think she wasn't his first child," I said to Mother Gilpin. We both marveled when Dexter—tough, macho, manly Dexter—wept with love for his tiny daughter.

My mother-in-law had followed Dad Gilpin from my house, shaking her head. "We would've brought her back to you, son."

After Lori fell asleep Dexter still held her awhile. Then he laid her in her crib and came to our bed. Our marriage had been so fragmented by the Army, I felt I barely knew the returning soldier. He seemed not to feel my shyness, and a new dimension sparked our love-making. He was very sure, very skillful. When we had spent some of our passion, he drew back and took my face in his hands, staring at me like a lost traveler who has found his way home.

"They're blue," he'd said. "Your eyes are so wide and blue."

The den was the last room I cleaned Wednesday evening

before Circle. A spider unwisely dropped from a single strand attached to the bottom of Dexter's desk and landed on the carpet. I crushed the spider and stooped to see what webs might remain. There, taped beneath the desk, was a small manila envelope. I opened it and found a receipt for a safety deposit box in a Tulsa bank, and a key.

I sat on the carpeted floor and turned the key over in my hand. I wanted to be at that bank the moment it opened to explore whatever mystery the box might hold, but a wave of frustration swept over me as I realized there wouldn't be time Thursday morning to drive to Tulsa and back before Circle. I could not escape my duties tomorrow. I would have to wait until Friday morning to inspect whatever Dexter had thought important enough to place in a bank vault.

Eleven

Months have passed since that Circle meeting in October, but I can recall it the same way one remembers details of a car accident or the searing pain of touching a hot stove.

At ten thirty Elsie arrived with her bleach bottle lamps. She carried decals of snowmen and Santas to glue onto the white plastic, and packages of craft sticks from which to fashion lamp shades. Among collages of glitzy Christmas decorations, I thought Elsie's lamps might seem festive. They were, after all, no more garish than plastic Santas and garlanded, nose-blinking reindeer.

We greeted one another warmly. Elsie didn't seem the least standoffish to me, but she didn't speak to Louella until Louella called out, "Hi, Elsie. Congratulations on getting the solo for the cantata."

Louella had to say it twice before Elsie answered. "Why, thank you. I'm sure I don't know why Brother Lee wanted me to sing it again this year, but maybe it's because I do know the part already."

Louella smiled. "It's because you don't shriek on those high notes."

"I've been drafted to direct the children," said Shirley Mitchell.

I was sure she had volunteered to take charge of the young-sters so she could ensure her grandson a starring role. Shirley's daughter Lindsay had moved home after her divorce from Big Carter McCoy, bringing Little Carter with her.

"We're doing our program right before the cantata. I need help with some of the costumes and the makeup."

Little Carter, who closely resembled Alfalfa on *Our Gang Comedies*, was six years old and had been labeled hyperactive by tactful professionals. With some justification his grandmother said, "Carter is precocious. He gets bored because he's so bright." Five minutes after Little Carter entered a room, bedlam erupted.

Elsie looked at me pointedly as if expecting me to volunteer with the children, but I'd determined to extend my hours at Happy Heart. Corralling other people's children had never brought me closer to their parents or been as enjoyable as my conversations with Dr. Patrick.

Sharla Sanders, whose daughter was cast as Mary, had no choice but to volunteer. Conversations about the children flew back and forth. Flory Santos agreed to make some of the costumes, and Amelia Crabtree offered to do makeup.

Elsie set her supplies at the end of the sofa and called us to order. "Now that we're all here, let's get started with the lesson."

I joined Second Thursday Circle soon after Gil was born, the same year I resigned my teaching post at the high school. The men at church liked to think of us as a benign group who accomplished little more than baby showers and gossip. But we took pride in having begun a "Meals on Wheels" program and Mother's Day Out, and in our various philanthropies such as the Community Thrift Shop. Except for yearly business meetings, we long ago dispensed with minutes. Sometime in the eighties we decided to dispense with the recitation of the "Apostle's Creed" and hymn singing. We patterned ourselves after the Virtuous Woman of Proverbs so we emphasized crafts which we could use to benefit others.

We always had a brief lesson. Elsie was serving as Lesson Chairman for the quarter. She handed Louella a piece of paper. "These verses are all from *The Living Bible*. Please read them, dear."

Louella read, "Exodus 20:15: 'You must not steal.' "Leviticus 19:11: 'You must not steal nor lie nor defraud.' She paused and looked at Elsie before continuing. "You want me to read all the rest?"

"Please, Louella, read every word."

"Jeremiah 7:9 and 10: 'Do you really think that you can steal, murder, commit adultery, lie, and worship Baal and all of those new gods of yours, and then come here and stand before me in my Temple and chant, "We are saved!" —only to go right back to all these evil things again?'"

Louella cleared her throat. Her voice had a tentative quality as if she expected Elsie to cut off the reading at any moment. "Romans 13:9: 'If you love your neighbor as much as you love yourself you will not want to harm or cheat him, or kill him or steal from him.' Ephesians 4:28: 'If anyone is stealing he must stop it and begin using those hands of his for honest work so he can give to others in need.'"

"Thank you, Louella." Elsie paused, looking from one to the other. Her words were loud and delivered in the fashion of a televangelist. "Let her who hath an ear to hear, hear." She sat down.

We waited for some sort of expository, but none came. It was the shortest lesson ever heard from Elsie Wickfielder, and Second Thursdays seemed stunned into silence.

I cleared my throat. "Is that it, Elsie?"

"There's power in the Word to convict the sinner and to bring her to repentance."

I wondered about suggesting to Louella she apologize to Elsie for stealing Harry Truman.

Lisa Beach chuckled. "Well, you certainly found a den of iniquity here, Elsie."

Elsie started to say something, but it was as if a referee had blown a "time-in" whistle. The meeting filled with sounds of small talk, rustling fabric, and clicking needles. I stood and began to arrange the living room for craft work. I set up a card table with a plastic cover for those who would be painting the Christmas angels.

Lisa excused herself to visit the bathroom. On her return she told me, "Your jewelry is beautiful, Maggie, but I'm wild about those miniature cloisonné plates. Maybe someday when the kids' braces are paid for, I can start a collection like that."

"I prefer ceramic plates myself," said Elsie. "I've got a plate from every state and the District of Columbia. My Christmas plates alone are worth a fortune."

Ceramic plates lined the rail, high in my dining room. All members of Second Thursday Circle had some sort of plate collection. I looked at Amelia Crabtree. She seemed to be struggling to keep silent about her Spode and Wedgewood. While arranging craft sticks on the wire frame of a lamp shade, Elsie chewed and sucked noisily on her lower lip. "Orin has my plates insured for ten thousand dollars."

Elsie's plates included *Gone with the Wind* china from The Bradford Exchange and a plastic plate with Elvis and Priscilla's picture pasted under seven layers of white glue.

"Ten thousand dollars?" I regretted the abrupt way the question had popped from my mouth, but I had found myself wondering if the Wickfielders also did business with Lester Quinn.

"Why, Maggie, as you might expect, we had to get a rider on our homeowner's. You could do the same thing if you had a mind to, only you don't need riders if all you have is little trinkets." The smile on her face was so sweet, it would have done credit to the first serpent.

I suppose Louella thought she needed to defend me, but it would have been better if she'd kept quiet. "I would love to show you the slides of our Paris trip sometime. Of course, I'd have to edit them because some of you might be offended—the French are so sophisticated and worldly." She grinned wickedly. "Lots of European women go topless on the beaches. Anyhow, when Bill and I were in France, we saw a collection of cloisonné at a museum. Some of Maggie's souvenirs would be right at home there."

Elsie sort of shrugged. "Margaret's stuff is nice. I certainly didn't mean to say it isn't... nice."

Louella looked directly at Elsie. "Yes, Maggie has a wonderful sense of style and understated elegance."

Louella might as well have called Elsie an unpolished clod.

The tension in the room was palpable. I busied myself with spreading newspapers on the floor, finding scissors and a size three crochet hook. I assisted wherever I could. I gave Elsie a damp rag so she could clean the glue from herself and from my coffee table. I located trash baskets for scraps and thread. Then I finished preparations for refreshments. I was sure more conversation passed between Louella and Elsie, but I didn't want to hear it.

The week prior to Circle I had baked petits fours. Before Circle started I removed the perfect, small cakes from the pantry refrigerator. I had frozen distilled water in ice trays, and each cube held a melon ball. I floated the ice in what my Grandmother York had called her secret punch which I served in Mama's crystal and ruby glass bowl. I cut crusts from slices of bread and made chicken salad sandwiches. I served fresh vegetables with dip. Along with the petits fours I served home-made peach ice cream, using peaches I'd frozen earlier that previous spring.

I could never explain to Dexter's satisfaction why the refreshments were so carefully prepared. "I like the compliments I get," I told him.

But it was more than that. No matter I'd lived in Redbud most of my life, I was a "city girl." I'd learned to pickle cucumbers with the best of them, had memorized pertinent pedigrees and histories, yet I still felt the need to prove myself. Intellectual accomplishments were fine, but in our town a woman's real success lay in her homemaking abilities. In Redbud, Oklahoma, I always felt the need to overcome my "foreign" upbringing.

In the dining room I surveyed the table, pleased with the results of my hard work. As the girls took their dessert plates, there were numerous compliments.

Amelia said, "I don't believe they serve fancier stuff at the Governor's mansion."

Sharla said my chicken salad had her mama's beat six ways to Sunday.

Elsie didn't say a word until she took a sip of punch, her little finger bent pretentiously. She contorted her face into squinting disapproval and made small smacking noises. "It's tart, Maggie. Do you have any sugar?"

I pointed to the sterling bowl on the table. "I thought someone might want sugar in her coffee," I said.

The punch tasted deliciously sweet to me, but Elsie's face still twisted in a sour grimace, and all stopped talking so they could hear what she'd say next.

"You probably doubled the lemons without doubling the Kool-aid," she said in a whisper that carried across the room.

Amelia and Lisa looked at me, keenly interested now in the punch ingredients.

Anger crawled my neck and flushed my face. Elsie had managed to irritate me to the point of what Dexter would have called "biddyness." "Sometimes when you women get together, you sound like old biddies in the chicken yard. I could swear I can look at you and see when one of you has had her feathers ruffled," he'd say.

And I would tell Dexter about the times I'd seen him and his friends poke "good ole boy" fun at each other. "If you had a chaw of tobacco, you'd sound like Gabby Hayes."

But even as I heard myself speaking, part of me had agreed with Dexter's assessment.

Now, with Dexter not there to give me his quiet approval, it suddenly became very important that everyone know how hard I had worked on refreshments, that I had squeezed the juice myself. I allowed all who wanted to copy my recipe—the "secret recipe" my mother had found pressed in the Bible Grandmother York left her. Grandmother's pride in the concoction had always caused me amusement, but now I was furious for having disclosed the ingredients.

Lisa drank her third or fourth refill of punch. "I hope you girls don't expect anything this wonderful when it's my turn. You'll be lucky if you get iced tea."

"It's not supposed to be a contest," Elsie scolded. "And after all, Margaret doesn't have little ones running around getting in her way."

Whatever Elsie's problem, and by now I was convinced there was a problem, I was determined not to argue with her. I took a deep breath. "You're right, Elsie. I never worked so hard in my life as when I hosted Circle while my kids were small. I'd dust and vacuum and Lori would decorate with peanut butter while Gil tracked mud on the carpet."

"It wouldn't be so bad," said Lisa, "if they'd stay well. We all took our flu shots, so at least they shouldn't get the flu this year."

Flory thought Lisa had acted sensibly. "I take the shots

every year now, since two years ago when I was in bed for five days. And I was puny for weeks."

The mention of influenza was encouragement enough for Elsie to tell of her bout with the illness, an illness which had grown more serious with each recitation.

"You're lucky you could get up after just five days, Flory. You may recall that I took sick the same year. Both lungs were full of corruption and I nearly died. My fever was so high, Orin said it was off the thermometer. I don't think anyone could have had a worse case and lived."

"How long were you in the hospital?" asked Louella.

"The doctor and Orin wanted me to go, but I refused. Orin needed me to answer the phones when he went on calls."

"You mean you worked while you were that sick?"

"We have an extension to the shop, so I answered the phone from my bed."

Louella sounded incredulous. "How remarkable. If I'd ever been that sick, I'd have made Bill get me a hospital suite and bring in a dozen specialists to fuss over me." She smiled, as if suppressing a secret. "I wouldn't have passed up the chance to be pampered."

"Orin says I've got more grit than any woman he knows."

I heard Phoebe Kearny whisper something to Sharla about Elsie's being full of grit.

We filed into the living room, and the conversation turned to childhood memories. Like Elsie, Amelia Crabtree grew up in a family whose stark poverty outlasted the Great Depression.

"Suppers were usually nothing more than milk and cornbread, and sometimes we had a little side meat."

Flory said, "Our cupboard was never bare, but money was tight. We picked lambsquarter. It grew wild in the fields next to our house, but I hated it."

Elsie's circumstances were leanest. "I was just a toddler but I remember my daddy trapped one rabbit and a possum the whole winter of thirty-nine, and that's all the meat my mama had to feed the twelve of us for six weeks. The cow dried up, and we'd have thought we were in heaven if we could have afforded cornmeal."

Phoebe cleared her throat, and Amelia shook her head. I

knew from Dexter that some of what Elsie said was true. If she embellished her stories... well, I could think of no one who didn't add a detail to make history more entertaining. Elsie just embellished more than most people. But today she not only "stretched the truth till it snapped," she came dangerously close to being a laughingstock.

Flory jumped into the breach. "I wish I had my Christmas shopping done."

At the mention of Christmas Sharla grew enthusiastic. "I can't wait. Kevin is buying me a microwave oven. I'm trying to talk him into giving it to me early so I can use it for Circle in December."

"They have proven that microwaves will cook your brain," said Elsie. "Orin wanted to buy me one, but I told him I'd rather have a crock pot."

Our prayer leader, Amelia, remembered to inquire about prayer concerns. It was as though we all sensed a storm coming, and hoped against hope to find shelter from it.

Lisa asked us to pray for her, as she was scheduled to have a hysterectomy.

Gynecology is a favorite topic of Elsie's, and before others could announce prayer requests, she said, "One time Montel had a panel of doctors on who said that hysterectomies are the most overdone surgeries in the U.S. But having had female surgery myself, I can assure you that sometimes they are absolutely lifesaving. The point is, not everyone who has a few fibroids needs a life threatening procedure. Are you sure you really need the operation, Lisa?"

Poor Lisa started to explain she had a lot of confidence in her doctor, but Elsie talked over her.

"I would hate to see you go under the knife without consulting a really good O.B.-G.Y.N."

"Was your hysterectomy life saving, Elsie?" asked Sharla. As our newest member she hadn't yet learned not to provide that sort of opening, especially when Elsie was in one of her theatrical moods. It was a bit like telling our pastor the back row was full of lapsed alcoholics.

Elsie set her dessert plate on the floor. She looked at Sharla, folded her hands piously, sighed, and closed her eyes with the pain of remembrance.

Lisa had shrunk back in her chair, probably wondering if she should have a third, maybe even a fourth specialist examine her womb.

I sensed the patience of the others growing thin so I spoke before Elsie could launch into her story. "Ladies, I think we need to pray for our world leaders too—everything's in such a mess." Forbearance went only so far, and I was not in the mood to hear about the medical trials of Elsie Wickfielder.

She acted as if I hadn't spoken. "As a matter of fact, Dr. Combs referred me to a specialist in the City. My condition was so perilous that a few more months would probably have meant cancer." She lowered her voice. "The specialist operated and told Orin he had never seen a uterus with so many fiberoids in a woman who had managed to walk into his office under her own power. He kept it and sent it to the medical college."

Louella and I exchanged looks. I remembered her saying she wished she had a nickel for every one of Elsie's organs that had been sent to the medical college so the poor students could marvel at them. "To hear Elsie tell it, her gall bladder had enough stones for Orin to have paved their driveway."

There was more to Elsie's recitation. "The surgery threw me into menopause, so of course I had hot flashes. Terrible, smothering things that estrogen supplements didn't faze. Fortunately, I didn't lose any of my womanly passion. Orin says—"

Louella spoke in concert with Elsie, as if they were a chorus. "There's snow on the roof, but there's fire in the furnace."

The room plunged into silence. Elsie stood. She glared at Louella, then turned to me. "I'm sorry. Some people here are far too cultured and tasteful to want to hear anything I might have to say." Tears filled her eyes. "I'll continue my story sometime when they're not around so I won't bore them."

I reached for her, to calm her, to apologize. "Oh, Elsie, Louella didn't mean anything by that. Please don't go away mad."

She shrugged and gathered the plastic lamps and her other craft materials into a box before flouncing out my front door. We stood there, the sound of the slamming door lingering in our minds.

Flory Santos spoke first. "Nothing like this has happened since the time old Mrs. Smith accused Olene Goff of trying to seduce married deacons."

"I'll stop by to see about Elsie on my way home," said Amelia. "Do you suppose there's something wrong with her? She's been so... so—"

"So much more Elsie-ish," said Flory.

"It's as if she came here today just to play one-upmanship," observed Lisa.

A dejected Louella expressed remorse. "I've heard that story a dozen times and never said a word. I wish I'd kept my mouth shut today."

Sharla told her not to worry. "Call Elsie and apologize," she suggested.

All the girls held hands while Amelia prayed for Lisa's surgery to be successful. I tried to gather my thoughts as we asked for guidance, for blessings for our missions in South America, for our world leaders to be moral and wise, but it was no use. All I could think about was Elsie.

Amelia finished, "Forgive us for harsh words and misunderstandings, Lord."

Louella too was on the verge of tears. She excused herself, staying in the guest bathroom while the others left. When she came out she was dry-eyed but glum. She looked every one of her sixty-two years.

After Louella left I cleaned up the mess of papers and crumbs in the living room. I wanted to settle into a chair and bawl, but I knew the activity would help me sort my thoughts. When I'd finished cleaning the kitchen, I went into the guest bathroom to replace the towels. That's when I saw the empty space in the shadow box. My brooch was gone!

Twelve

Only the women who had been in my house for Circle had the opportunity to steal from me, and I would have trusted every one of them with the keys to Fort Knox. We were a community of unlocked doors who collected our purses and set them in our hostess' bedroom, a town where one's word was taken seriously.

But I had entertained a thief in my home—one who stole what I prized for its sentimental value even more than its considerable monetary worth.

I thought of how I had polished the jewelry on Wednesday, then carefully fastened the pin to the black velvet. I looked throughout my house, knowing all the while no object could have been removed from the closed display except by a deliberate act.

When I returned a third time to the empty glass case, I sat on the edge of the tub, defeated.

Elsie's strange lesson came to mind. I wanted to call her to ask why she had selected the Scriptures about stealing, why she had been so hostile and accusatory. "Let her who hath an ear to hear, hear," she'd said. Did she know something? Had been speaking directly to a thief in my home?

And why did she seem fired with self-righteous pomposity? But in spite of Orin's assurance she didn't carry grudges, I judged it best to give Elsie a few days to settle down.

My mind reeled with possibilities. Elsie embroidered the truth, but that was one of her few vices. Yet she coveted my brooch. Her preoccupation with Scripture might be a reaction to her own guilt. Had she taken it to punish me for not lending it to her?

And then there was Lisa who had paid special attention to my cloisonné. I went into the dining room and counted the plates on the wall, feeling silly about it. The plates were in full view, and nobody could have removed one without being seen. The Beaches were rumored to live beyond their means, but I did not believe Lisa was a thief.

Even Louella had the opportunity—when she'd gone into the guest bathroom to cry. But Louella, probably the richest woman in the county, could buy all the jewelry she wanted. My brooch would be nothing to her. And she was becoming my closest friend.

I ran through a list of my guests. Not a woman among Second Thursdays seemed to merit my suspicion, but it was eerie to know that one I'd welcomed into my home could no longer be trusted.

Amelia Crabtree called that evening. "What on earth has gotten into Elsie? Are she and Louella involved in a feud or something?"

"If they are, I think it's one-sided," I said. "I don't know what Elsie's trouble is."

"When I stopped by her house after Circle," said Amelia, her voice incredulous, "she said she didn't want to talk about it. And did you ever hear such nonsense as Elsie's lesson today — all that talk about thieves?"

"Did you ask her what she meant by that?"

"You'll never believe this, Maggie." Amelia spoke softly into the phone. "Elsie says one of the Second Thursdays has been stealing things."

This was more confirmation Elsie was the thief or knew who had taken my brooch. *Maybe,* I thought, *she took my keepsake to cast doubt on Louella's character.*

Amelia rattled on, "She said for the time being she would pray and hope the perpetrator falls under conviction."

While she was on the phone, I fleetingly considered trying to sneak Amelia's oversized carpetbag from the choir room next Wednesday and examine its contents. I blushed with shame. What was I thinking? It was preposterous to consider pious Amelia being tempted by worldly treasure.

"Did Elsie say what had been stolen?" I asked.

"No, she stayed real close-mouthed, Maggie."

After we'd hung up, I called Louella. "Is there more to your quarrel with Elsie than you've told me?"

"No, you know all about my relationship with Elsie. As far as I'm concerned, there's no problem." She paused, seeming to consider the situation. "I think she's just jealous of our friendship, Maggie. But I'm sick that I said what I did about the 'fire in her furnace.' She treated me with such kindness when I first moved back here, and I wouldn't have upset her for the world."

"Have you tried to talk to her since Circle?"

"Of course. I want to apologize and to see if we can be friends again. Orin promised she'd return my call, but she hasn't, and I don't know what more I can do for now."

I had known Elsie all my married life but I had no answers for Louella. "What did you think about the Scripture lesson?"

"Except for her having me read all those Bible verses, I thought it was rather brief. You have to wonder if Elsie ran out of time before she got a lesson prepared."

"Amelia says Elsie thinks there's a thief in Circle."

Louella gasped. "What makes her think that?"

"I don't know how she found out. I guess I'll give her a chance to cool off before I ask her. But however Elsie knew, I think she hit the nail on the head."

"Maggie, whatever do you mean?"

"My cloisonné brooch—the one with the four carat sapphire —was taken from the shadow box in the guest bathroom."

"Oh my. That's a hell of a note," she said, clucking her tongue in sympathy. "Is it insured?"

"I checked. My policy doesn't cover mysterious disappearances. No breaking and entering. Besides, it's more than the money. Dexter gave it to me—," my voice broke, "and it's my favorite keepsake."

"Oh. I'm so sorry, dear." She paused, as if looking for ways to comfort me. "When did you miss it?"

"Right after Circle."

"I'm sure it will turn up, Maggie. I'm always misplacing things around here."

"I didn't misplace it, Louella. I remember dusting the shadow box on Wednesday."

"Maybe it fell into a trash can, or something. I always go through my bathroom trash before I put it out, ever since the time my daughter sent a new pair of shoes to the city dump."

"I wish I were only missing a pair of shoes," I said, irritated by her suggestions. "I've been through all my trash. Louella, it's gone. Someone took it."

"Maybe it was stolen before Circle."

"I'm sure it wasn't. I'm absolutely positive."

"Oh. Well, do you have any idea who it could have been?"

"Until today I was sure I didn't know anyone that low. It gives me chills to think I have a thief for a friend."

"Isn't calling her a 'thief' a bit harsh?" Louella scolded.

"That's what she is."

"Now you're going off half-cocked. You sound like Elsie."

"All I know is someone stole my brooch, and that makes her a thief. I'd like to search every house in Redbud until I find it."

"Don't do anything rash, Maggie." Louella's words were rapid, her tone urgent. "If I were you I'd keep a lid on it—wait and see if it doesn't turn up. Otherwise no telling how many people you'll offend if you start talking about a thief among the Second Thursdays."

I sighed. "Of course you're right. Maybe whoever took it will bring it back. Goodness knows she won't be able to wear it in Redbud."

"If one of the Second Thursdays took it, she'll probably return it."

"There's no 'if' about it. One of the Second Thursdays took it, and I'd sure like to know why."

"Am I under suspicion?"

"Good grief," I said, feeling the heat in my face. "I must be purple with embarrassment. I won't be able to mention this to anybody without sounding as if I suspect them. I'm sorry, Louella. Sometimes I speak without thinking. I hope you didn't think I accused you."

She laughed. "We both know I like good cloisonné."

Just talking to her made me feel better. It was nice to have someone with whom I could be completely unguarded and honest. "I wasn't going to tell you, but I guess I'd better. As angry and jealous as Elsie is," I said, "I've wondered if maybe she took it."

"Hm. I wouldn't say that to anybody either."

"I don't intend to. I only told you because I didn't want you to think I thought you took it."

"I understand. I know you feel terrible about this, but try not to worry, dear."

I wanted to take Louella's advice but I felt more vulnerable than I had since Dexter's death—as disillusioned as a wakened child who catches her parents putting presents under the Christmas tree. As I lay in bed that night, I prayed for guidance and serenity.

As if in answer to prayer, I remembered the safety deposit box. The brooch was gone, but perhaps Dexter had left me another remembrance.

I enjoyed concocting scenarios to explain his hiding the key beneath his desk. My favorite had Dexter leaving me another expensive piece of jewelry to add to my collection. He would have stored it in the Tulsa bank, saving it for my next birthday or for our anniversary. I would drive to Tulsa and retrieve whatever my husband had placed there for me.

Unable to sleep I got out of my bed. Schlegg hurried after me. I picked him up, carried him to the window and opened the blinds. A gibbous moon glowed through moving clouds, and I watched as the wind bent the trees from north to south. An autumn storm was pushing its way into Redbud.

We had buried Dexter nine months ago, and I still drove to the cemetery every few weeks. Spikes of undisciplined green poked from the red dirt atop his grave, vying to cover the earth with a carpet of grass that would blend with other mounds in the Gilpin family plot—a gray and green pattern of stone and lawn hiding the clay and its secrets. The cemetery gates were locked at sunset now, and no lively couples sparked or courted on the ridge overlooking town. Overnight, frost would nip the tender roses I'd planted in the box which marked the section's boundary.

Thirteen

The bank officers didn't even look at the copies of Dexter's death certificate and will. They led me into a vault where I took possession of the contents of the box—two large manila envelopes, each bearing my name. They were numbered one and two, with directions to open them in that order. It seemed further confirmation Dexter had known about his heart condition.

His treasures needed a special setting. I left the bank and drove to a park on the outskirts of Tulsa, my pulse racing with anticipation. Through the paper of one of the envelopes, I could feel the outline of an audio cassette tape. Thoughtful husband that he was, Dex had left me another comforting memento.

I sat in my car while sheets of rain washed plastic ponies and filled the sandy holes beneath the empty swings. A lifetime ago I'd watched from a bench at the edge of the playground while Dexter romped with his children. I'd believed my little family could teach the likes of June Cleaver and Carol Brady to covet. Dappled sun had washed the golden trio, as if to show me the perfection of my life.

Now, with cold bullets pelting the windows, my car served as a warm bastion against the world. I ripped the sealed flap of envelope "one," and withdrew the tape. On "Side A," Dexter had printed my name. My hands were trembling as I slid the tape into the player, eager to hear the voice of my husband.

In my sleep I still reached toward his side of the bed, sometimes found myself listening for his footsteps. I collected anecdotes before I remembered he would not be home to share dinner with me. So his voice, coming from the car's sound system, held me in a moment of welcome unreality.

"Hello, Maggie. If you're hearing this confession, I'm dead, figuratively if not literally."

In a cajoling tone I knew well, he laughed, trying to interject humor. I ached to reach my arms around his manly neck, to cling to him, to hide myself in his embrace.

"Since the den is my sacred lair, I'm betting you won't be hearing this tape until long after my demise."

Demise. Unpretentious and brilliant, Dexter liked to mock me with what he called "highfalutin" words. He said the older I got, the more I sounded like an English teacher.

"I was an English teacher," I would remind him, "not an ignorant Okie." My calling him an Okie guaranteed a sham confrontation which often led to a genuine truce, the terms of which were forged in lovemaking.

But he sounded more apologetic than playful, as if he had spilled something on the carpet or forgotten to return the ice cream to the freezer. I smiled. Tears flooded my eyes, but Dexter's words still had power to comfort me.

"I've no doubt, great little housekeeper that you are, you'll eventually find the key to the safety deposit box, and then you'll find this tape. You're a strong woman, Maggie darling, and somehow I think you'll handle this tape better if... if I'm dead before you play it."

His speech wasn't exactly slurred, but Dexter's usual crisp cadence was ponderous. I thought, *he sounds the way he did when he had to tell me about my parents' boating accident—* having downed a few whiskey-sours, he'd gently led me into our bedroom, his face full of sorrow, and told me the news.

Now, too, he spoke gently, reluctantly. "I have this compulsion to confess to you, Maggie. I don't expect anyone to admire me for my honesty in spilling my guts, but one of those fancy specialists in Tulsa says my ticker is on borrowed time. He's going to do what he can, but...."

I burst into tears. "Why didn't you tell me?" I whispered to the car's dashboard. "I could have helped." I would have been more understanding. Hugs and kisses without physical exertion were all I really needed.

"So part of the reason I'm doing this is I want to set things in order, to tie up any loose ends while I still can." He paused, and I could picture Dexter clenching and unclenching his fists in a gesture that matched the deepening intensity of his voice.

He made a false start, "But it, uh, it—oh hell, Maggie." Dexter almost never swore unless he battled fear. His discomfort jarred me with a sudden premonition of tragedy, and I pulled the tape from the player as though I could reverse his illness, prevent his death.

In spite of warm air blasting me from the heater, I shivered and settled farther into my coat. After regaining my composure, I restarted the tape.

"There's only one way to say it. Honey, I wish I didn't have to tell you, but I guess I haven't been one hundred percent faithful."

A low moan escaped my throat.

"It happened in Korea, Maggie. You were so far away. And I was so lonely."

Dizzy. My throat went dry and I felt dizzy. I rode in a car with failed brakes, heading for a steep precipice.

"There was this Korean girl, and uh—it just happened."

Air emptied from my lungs. I'd forgotten how to breathe. And still he went on, "I don't want to die with it on my conscience, Maggie, and I don't want you hearing about it from someone else. I guess maybe God is giving me this one last chance to get it off my chest."

I croaked through tears, "You filthy s.o.b.!" I slammed the steering wheel with my fists.

"I lived with her for a while and she... she got pregnant." Oh, God, no, I pleaded, as my last shred of comfort evaporated.

His voice broke, and the tape made a click as if it had been turned off, then restarted. I wanted to stop listening, but I sat paralyzed in horror.

"I want you to know the truth, Maggie, yet I can't face you. God knows, I've tried. Once, when Gil and Lori were small, I started to tell you. I knew you'd leave me. I knew you'd take the children, and I couldn't stand the idea of losing any one of you."

There were snorting sounds as Dexter blew his nose. The

handkerchief was probably one of the bandanna types he favored in his retirement, and I would have washed and ironed it before folding and stacking it in his dresser.

"Maggie, sweetheart, this secret has been like a cancer, but I couldn't risk losing you. Oh, baby, try to understand." He cried now, his choking sobs echoing my own. "I won't bore you with the sordid details. I guess I deserve to burn in hell," he blubbered. "But we both believe in forgiveness, so I'm hoping you can forgive me. It's important that you know I never loved Lee An... well, not like I love you." He blew his nose again and somewhat recovered his composure. "I didn't even think she was very pretty. Hell, I'm not facing you, and this is tough."

He paused again. I screamed at the stereo speakers, "You son of a bitch, you lousy, selfish son of a bitch." He'd called her Lee An. He'd said it with such easy familiarity.

"I don't know if you'll want to tell Gil and Lori. But if you do, please tell them I loved their mother, and, except for one rather... significant error, I was faithful to her."

My late, lamented husband was no better than a panting cur jumping a bitch in heat—that's what I wanted to tell his children. And so self-absorbed he would rob me of all my treasured illusions.

"I tried to make it right, Maggie. I did the best I could. I supported her and the baby until she could get a job."

As if he'd acted generously. Dexter, the soft-hearted benefactor of widows and orphans.

"One of the guys knew a fellow at the American Embassy, and they had an opening for a translator. Lee An's English was pretty good, so she got the job. And one of the State Department guys fell in love with her. They got married, and he brought her and the baby to the States. That's when Lee An's husband adopted our baby, Jo Ann.

"They were in D. C. for a while. After he retired they moved to a little farm near here. It was so pitiful, Maggie. Jo Ann's mother and step-father were killed in a car accident her last year of high school. So I decided I ought to step in."

He went on and on, telling me how he'd carried his "burden" and tried to atone for past "mistakes." From the time she was seventeen years old, there had been a secret filial relationship between the child and my husband.

At the end of the tape, Dexter sounded almost optimistic. "I know you can't be like a mother to her, Maggie, but I hope someday you'll meet her and that you two can be friends."

I pushed the car door against the wind and stepped onto the parking lot. Bile forced its way into my throat, and I vomited on the pavement. My head hurt. I couldn't breathe through my nose. While writing me letters of undying love, he'd lived in an illicit relationship and fathered a bastard. He had the gall to suggest I might, when revealing his filthy secret to our children, emphasize how much he'd loved their mother.

I, the dutiful patriotic wife, had been proud of my soldier husband. If my heart held questions, they'd gone unasked. I'd subdued every hint of suspicion. And though I had been young, attractive and vulnerable in my loneliness, I never, never broke my marriage vows.

I remembered how incensed Dexter had been when he learned Gil lived with Peggy before their wedding, how he bristled when Lori arrived home past her curfew. Significant error! Forgiveness, indeed! If I hadn't already buried George Dexter Gilpin, I'd have forgiven him, forgiven him just as soon as I'd taken a dull knife and cut off his balls.

I got back into the car, wet, rumpled, and shivering. I found a mint to take the acrid taste from my mouth. With trembling fingers I ripped open the second envelope. It held pictures of a little girl in the arms of a Korean woman. By some accident of genetics the child looked more Mexican than Korean. It was small comfort she did not look like anyone in our family. My mind reeled, wondering if Dexter could have loved her as he loved Gil and Lori.

Together with other documents were more pictures, including one of Dexter with his arms around his college-aged daughter. Hoping I could manage a case of instant and permanent amnesia, I lowered the window to toss everything into the wind and rain.

Fourteen

Rain blew in the open window as I gathered pictures and documents to deliver to the storm, but my gaze was arrested by the likeness of a gap-toothed, smiling child in a school uniform. Her dark hair needed combing, as if she'd just returned from recess. Over and over the thought assaulted me—this child is part of Dexter, his very flesh. She shares a heritage with Gil and Lori.

And she is no part of me.

According to the date, the little girl's picture was twenty years old. Jo Ann was near the age of our own Lori.

I put everything back and stuffed both envelopes under the car seat. I would need proof when I exposed Dexter to his children and friends.

Somehow I drove home, though I don't remember a moment of the trip. I flopped into a kitchen chair, exhausted.

Schlegg whined in complaint—his dish was empty. At the sound of the can opener, he cried more insistently, arched his back, and rubbed against my legs. I put his dish, heaped with tuna, on the floor. When he'd finished, he belched, flicked his tail, and headed for the sofa. I intercepted and lifted him, cradling him like a baby. He had a word for such occasions. It sounded like *"Ptrdurp."*

"Dexter probably kept a Rottweiler in another town," I told Schlegg. "At the very least I bet he kept another cat."

Of course Schlegg wouldn't have minded if Dexter had kennels full of other animals, just as long as there was tuna in our cupboard. But I was not magnanimous. My pain felt as fresh and unbearable as the night my husband died in my arms.

Not only did I grieve, I was disoriented. My situation was foreign to the public mourning I'd seen others endure. How does one behave when her heart is such a mixture of wounded pride, revulsion, grief, frustration, and love as my heart was?

Had I learned of Dexter's infidelity before he died, I would have had options: I could have divorced him, killed or maimed him, forgiven him, borne my cross like a true martyr, gone insane, or held my reactions in abeyance and had the pleasure of torturing him with thoughts of what I eventually might do.

Emotions pulled me this way and that. I had been married most of my life, and Dexter's betrayal invalidated those years. As soon as I had knowledge of his adultery, I called into question my entire system of values and beliefs. Had I wakened from a nightmare to find Dexter alive, I would have been the happiest woman in the world. At the same time I felt an emptiness only revenge could fill. It was as if each eye saw into different worlds, and I could not meld them into focus.

From the attic trunk I took stacks of his letters to my bed and read them, searching for clues.

"I miss you so, sweetheart. How are you feeling? Tell the little one you're carrying his daddy loves him. (Or her.)"

And, "The months can't pass too quickly for me. I want to take you in my arms and hold you forever. I'd say more, but who knows who else will be reading this?"

Dexter's affair with Lee An must have begun shortly after his arrival in Korea, perhaps before he knew I was pregnant with Lori. When had it ended? Before his next furlough home? After his discharge?

There had been no ongoing hostilities while Dexter served in Korea. He was not a frightened young man searching for some sort of immortality when he shacked up with his Korean paramour. And when he wasn't... fornicating or pushing papers for the Army, he'd written to me. I could find no gap in his declarations of love. The words he used, the pledges he gave were no different than those he gave me when he returned home. He'd played me for a fool almost our entire marriage.

How he must have worried over each phrase, lest he give himself away! When we made love, did he guard his words to keep from calling me by her name? Did he slip and call her

Maggie? What did he tell her about me? How did he choose between the two of us? If Lee An had been pregnant a second time, if his parents had the capacity to accept his marriage to someone not Caucasian, would he have chosen her? And the most dehumanizing thought of all, which of us did he prefer in bed?

Had there been other dalliances after he left Korea? I would have been willing to swear to the contrary. Now I called everything into question: the secretary who occasionally phoned him at home to discuss an office problem; the young divorcee he'd helped when her car wouldn't start—he drove to the store for a car battery and installed it himself, and he'd removed a dead tree from her yard; his out-of-town trips with Lester Quinn, reputedly to attend ball games; seminars in Vegas; travel for his clients. Hell, I could even imagine him having a romp with Louella in the back seat of her car at the cemetery.

And yet his "dying confession" declared there'd been just "one significant error" and that he'd loved me.

I remembered how he'd bridled with disgust when we'd run into Bob Beach in the French Quarters in New Orleans. Drunk, Bob had been in the company of a scantily clad woman. "Don't tell Lisa," he'd begged. And, after Dexter had extracted a promise from Bob that he'd shape up, we hadn't told. But we never socialized as couples with them again, and I... I'd pitied Lisa. From my lofty secure pedestal I'd wondered how Lisa could fail to see the signs everyone in town talked about.

Dexter had been a Scoutmaster. He'd been a deacon in our church. Repeatedly, friends and acquaintances remarked what a fine, virtuous man he'd been.

I had so many questions and nowhere to go for answers. Pain threatened to overwhelm me, but I fought to keep my balance. As I lay in bed that night, snuggling an overfed, clawless feline and blubbering sobs into his tiger-striped fur, I told myself that my children, my friends, my work, and my church were valid reasons not to lose myself in another orgy of grief or anger. I had withstood Dexter's death and somehow I would withstand his betrayal. Maybe.

I thought of no excuse for skipping my scheduled shift at the nursing home the next day, and it was easier to show up than to concoct an alibi. Lacking enthusiasm for a discussion of Shakespeare with J. Ronal Patrick, I tried to slip past the office. I'd forgotten his view of the employees' parking lot. The director's office occupied space originally intended to serve as a dentist's examination room—the former owner's son had briefly provided free dental care to the residents. A sink had been transformed into a small bar, and the dark one-way glass window overlooked a pretty garden by the edge of the parking lot.

Ron must have been following my progress because when he saw me in the hall, he beckoned me inside.

"The coffee's hot, Mrs. Gilpin, and you look like you could use a cup."

I thanked him and tried to smile amiably.

"Sit down, Maggie. You look depressed enough to play Lady MacBeth this morning."

"Your professional charm never ceases to amaze," I said, trying to keep my voice light, but sounding more like a scolding fishwife. "I'll bet that line goes over big with all the old ladies of Happy Heart."

"Or maybe you should play one of the witches."

I thought if I kept up the banter, I might be able to pull it off —to finish my coffee without an embarrassing torrent of tears. I forced my mouth into a wide smile and tried to be clever.

"Don't you dare be nice to me, Dr. Patrick. Don't give milk to starving children, and don't give me kind words. I just might regurgitate and die."

He joined my rough game. "Holy shit. What's wrong with the Widow Gilpin today? Let me see. You wouldn't be volunteering here if you had money problems."

I swallowed coffee and peered at him over my cup. I thought I detected sympathy behind his gruff manner, and just as I can't stand for someone to ask me if I'm all right after I've extracted my fingers from a closed car door or banged my head against the sharp edge of an open cabinet, I knew I couldn't deal with his pity. He could help Betsy Todd accept the loss of a breast, and he could calm Miranda Chase's concerns about her son's rare visits to see her, but I didn't think he could help me. I would tell him only part of the reason for my depression. "Someone stole my cloisonné brooch."

"Oh, hell, that's awful, Maggie. Real ball-busting break. German cockroaches are tough to kill, but what the hell is a Gloss-in-Abe roach and why would anybody steal it?"

"Cloisonné," I said. "Enamel painted on metal... oh, forget it."

"Maggie," he said, softening his voice, "this is serious, isn't it? I mean, you look like you're about to cry."

"Big girls don't cry," I said. "You know, like the song. You're not too old to remember the song, are you?"

"The song wasn't about jewelry. It was about girls who got jilted."

"Yes."

"You've told me you don't care to date, so I doubt you've had the chance for some fool to jilt you. You're not reacting to that sort of hurt, are you?"

His intuition touched me even more than sympathy could have, but I didn't want to show it. "Men are... dung heaps. Cretins. Devils." I forced a smile as if I'd made a clever joke.

"Except, of course, George Dexter Gilpin."

"Especially George Dexter Gilpin."

Ron's eyebrows shot up in surprise. "Maggie, what are you saying?"

That's when I cried, sobs choking my throat and bursting forth in a wail. I covered my face with my hands.

He came to me and took my wrists, gently pulling them from my face. "Maggie, what's wrong?"

"He cheated on me."

He sighed, and let go my hands.

I shoved some papers to one side and rested my arms on his desk. I lowered my head to muffle the moans.

He walked around and turned the chair, forcing me to sit upright. He took my face in his hands and shook his head, his eyes suddenly filled with warmth.

"I'm sorry, Maggie. Do you want to tell me about it?"

I took his offered handkerchief, and he stepped into the outer office.

"I'll be in conference for a few moments," he told the wide-eyed receptionist.

My face flushed hot with embarrassment.

He sat across from me, his broad face personifying interest and sympathy, his body language indicating professional distance. He was no longer a friend, but had metamorphosed into a skilled counselor willing to guide me through the maze of my emotions.

"He... betrayed... me," I began. And from there it was surprisingly easy to tell him everything.

When I'd finished he got up and walked to the window, frowning. "You've got to realize Dexter never meant to hurt you, Maggie."

"I don't know how it is with others, but the sanctity of our marriage was special to me. I never so much as looked at another man."

"Would you be feeling better now if you had?"

"The question is irrelevant. I believed in my marriage vows."

"I bet Dexter did too. All of us do when we're standing up there at the altar, fresh and ready for the adventure of marriage. But not many of us make it to the end without a stumble."

"If you're telling me lots of men and women stumble or that you've stumbled, I don't care. All I care about is Dexter, and he cheated on me."

"Yes. With one other woman, he said. Shit, Maggie, there's preachers and priests who can't stand before Judgment and say that."

"I don't see it the way you do," I said.

"Bitterness is a killer. Let me help you work it through or let me recommend a therapist who can—"

"Not now," I said. I stood and walked to the bar, rinsed my cup, and put it into the cabinet. "If I'm to continue working here, I'd appreciate your forgetting all about my little outburst."

"No can do," he said. "We don't have to talk about it again if you don't want to, but neither of us will be forgetting."

"I'm sorry," I said. "I hadn't meant—"

"There's nothing to be sorry for, Maggie."

I walked into the hall. I'd never intended to tell J. Ronal Patrick about Dexter.

Or had I? I told myself that if I had to blurt the scandal, at least I'd turned to a trained professional for understanding. As I walked toward my first assignment, I blushed, remembering how warm Ron's hands had been on my face. It was such a revolting thought to the righteous woman I thought I was, fresh tears came to my eyes.

Fifteen

Over the weekend I tried to behave as though everything was normal, but my lack of concentration must have been apparent.

At church a decidedly unspiritual revelation swept over me: My husband left an annuity to Jo Ann, and Lester Quinn knew all about it. I knew from the tape that Darnold was her last name. Quinn's secretary had almost let the cat out of the bag, and I now had an explanation for the high insurance premiums Dexter paid. I wondered how much he'd robbed his family to provide an inheritance for his love child. I thought how Quinn must have joked all these years about Dexter's double life.

I didn't notice when the choir stood for the anthem. Sharla nudged me, and I finally became aware of the director's exasperation. While Brother Lee waited for me to adjust my music, I dropped the church bulletin. It went fluttering over the pew onto the head of one of the deacons. Elsie gasped, and someone (probably Louella) reduced a giggle to a noisy snort.

At the last of the service, as Brother Pierce intoned the benediction, I realized I had been too concerned with the re-evaluation of my marriage to profit from prayers, Scripture, or preaching.

Don and Lori had driven over with their kids to attend church with me. They stayed for lunch. I made biscuits without salt and I forgot to put any sugar in my apple pie.

"You seem preoccupied," said Lori. "Is everything all right?"

"I don't cook much anymore. I think I'm out of practice."

Chet, ordinarily a quiet child, said, "The pie tastes like puke, Grandma."

His parents wanted him to apologize, but I came to his defense. "Chet's being honest, and I don't believe in punishing children for truthfulness."

His sister was emboldened to say, "Real barf-o, Grandma."

"A little honesty goes a long way, Sara Jane. Come help me, and I'll make everyone banana splits for dessert."

When Lori was small she had asked me once if we could trade Gil for a sister. I wondered how she might have felt if Dexter had introduced his other daughter to Lori, if she would have liked knowing her half-sister.

Late that evening as she prepared to leave, Lori said, "I'd worry less if you'd come home with us."

"Don't worry about me at all. I'm okay. I promise to let you know if I start losing it."

"I didn't mean you were 'losing it,' Mom."

"Whether you meant it or not, I must have seemed goofy when I dropped the bulletin on Brother Blackard."

"Hey, Effie," said Don, addressing me by a weird pet name he has never explained, "I stayed awake the rest of the service just to see what would happen next."

Sara slept on the sofa, so Don lifted her and carried her to their car. He fastened her in, and she slumped in her car seat while I helped settle Chet next to her.

"Grandma," he said, "do you have to sell the camp?"

"Chet!" scolded Lori. In the floodlight on my driveway, she looked sheepish. "I guess he heard Don and me talking about Grandpa and Grandma's camp."

"Don't be embarrassed, Lori. I haven't decided yet whether or not I should sell it. With your daddy gone I'm not sure I can keep up with it. What do you and Gil think I should do?"

"I haven't talked to Gil about it, but Don and I just hope you don't have to sell it."

"I guess we all need to get together to decide what to do."

I remembered how she'd enjoyed the tire swing Dex had hung in the woods. The camp had been our weekend and summer retreat all her life, and I knew she couldn't think of the place without remembering how Dex had loved it.

"You miss your dad a lot, don't you?"

"Of course I do, Mom. I think of him at least once a day."

"I always thought he was a good father to you and Gil."

"The best. I wish my kids could grow up knowing him."

"Here, take my handkerchief. I didn't mean to make you cry."

If my thoughts were distracted by day, they were focused at night. I fell asleep examining the few choices open to me. I could expose my husband's secret to his children in such a way they would be robbed of respect for their parent. It would hurt him not at all, and I would take no satisfaction in marring the memories they had of their father.

I had no plans to forgive Dexter. I didn't want to be Christian enough, as he'd suggested, to be a friend to Jo Ann.

It would humiliate me to reveal Dexter's infidelity to our minister and our friends, and I needed all the self-esteem I could muster.

I wanted to spare our children, to shield them from the truth. But there might come a time when they'd hear something, when Jo Ann would confront them, when they'd turn to me for answers. I couldn't think about that until I had come to grips with her existence myself.

I thought how I had divulged the scandal to J. Ronal Patrick, a man I liked and respected, but had known less than a year. What had led me to trust him with Dexter's reputation? Why did I feel better for having told him? *Maybe,* I thought, *I spoke so freely to him because Ron hadn't known Dexter.* Maybe because he was kind and sympathetic. Maybe because some friendships, like mine and Louella's, were so rewarding they took shortcuts to a level of trust where you felt you'd known the other person all your life.

My woolgathering continued Monday. I was in Mr. Johnston's room at the nursing home, applying lotion to his roughened elbows, when he caught me off balance and pulled me onto the bed. He succeeded in planting a kiss. Right on my mouth.

We did not slap the clients, so as I freed myself from the disgusting lecher, I scolded, "You old pervert, behave yourself, or I'll call the orderly."

I had loosened the restraints on his blue-veined hands when I clipped his nails and I had forgotten to reattach his wrists to the bed rail. I secured Mr. Johnston, then wiped the drool from his mouth. He verbalized a suggestion of the kind that had horrified his poor wife and daughters and led to his being a "guest" of Happy Heart. I had to will myself to recall he'd been a fine gentleman and the Chief of Police when I'd first moved to Redbud.

"Get in bed with me," he leered. "I want to show you my credentials."

"Promiscuity will loosen your teeth and make your hair fall out," I told him as I left his room.

People like Mr. Johnston always called forth an automatic prayer that I die while my mind is unimpaired and before I become a burden or an embarrassment to my children. However, with my heart so full of vengeance, I was sure I went unheard that day. More dismal was the crack in my faith which entertained the possibility there had never been a God to hear me.

Passing by the desk I called to the nursing supervisor, "Better withhold Johnston's vitamins."

"Is he getting frisky again?"

"Still," I replied.

"The last time I saw his credentials, they looked to me like they'd expired." She laughed uproariously at her own joke.

At home I scrubbed myself in the shower, always cautious lest some trace of institutional odor cling to me. Dressed in gown and housecoat I popped open a diet drink. Then I played Dexter's tape again.

When the tape had ended I was dry-eyed and much clearer about my feelings. It helped that I had lost weight and had begun to feel more attractive. Since losing Dexter I tended to eat healthier meals (except for the days immediately following the funeral when I had tried to find comfort in chocolate and sleep.) At Louella's suggestion and behind closed doors, I routinely donned leotard and tights and exercised with either Fonda or Simmons. Again, thanks to Louella's influence, I used flattering make-up and wore my newly tinted hair in a becoming, short style. I dressed with more care. I paid more attention to color. I knew my appearance had improved.

To assuage the pain, I yearned for confirmation of my desirability. Libidinous sex could soothe my ego, and there was very little of that around. The chance of finding Brad Pitt lusting for an older woman, of finding him or someone like him in my bedroom roughly equaled the chance of finding Dexter there.

No matter the deceased could not be cuckolded in the conventional sense, Maggie Gilpin made a sudden decision to shop the singles scene.

"Elsie," I said when Orin had persuaded her to take my call, "I wondered if your offer is still good."

"Don't think I'll go pick pecans with you, not after the way—"

"Would you be willing to get me a date with Orin's widowed friend in Tulsa?"

No sound came through the earpiece for a moment. Then, "Hold on, Maggie." Elsie forgot to be aloof as she rose to the challenge. I could barely detect her breathless voice explaining my request to Orin. A few minutes later she returned to the phone. "I wish you had come around sooner. Slappy got married last week to one of the ladies on the mixed bowling team. But give Orin and myself some time, and we'll come up with someone."

"Not just anyone, Elsie. Someone really nice."

"One of the experts Oprah had on said you should lower your expectations the second time around, and then you'd have a better chance of success. Unfortunately, there's a lot of beautiful young women out there, so it's hard for people like yourself to compete."

"I'll wear a girdle and support hose."

"Orin says you should plan on going to the Plumber's Association party next Friday. We're going as Cone Heads. Maybe we could find another Cone Head outfit for you."

"I remember you telling me about the party. Thanks, Elsie. Don't worry about my costume. I'm sure I can find something to wear."

"Orin says be ready at five o'clock. We have to drive clear to the other side of Tulsa, and Orin doesn't like to be late."

After I hung up, involuntary spasms seized me. I had made

arrangements to go to a costume party for plumbers and their significant others with Orin and Elsie Wickfielder. And, knowing Elsie, I would probably have a date. Slappy had been grabbed by a member of the mixed bowling team, but Happy, Dopey and Grumpy were, so far as I knew, available.

I sank into the sofa, and Schlegg jumped onto my lap and settled into a steady purring mode. I tucked his head under my chin and scratched his chest. "Old boy," I told him, "there are limits to my desire for revenge, and I'm afraid I'm destined to exceed them."

Sixteen

Having recently lost much sentimentality for Dexter's wedding tux, I trimmed the pants legs and hemmed them. Rummaging through boxes in the attic, I found an old bowler hat and a cane that had belonged to my father-in-law. A pair of black patent leather oxfords from Gil's junior high days, little worn, fit me. I paid six dollars to a costume shop in Tulsa for the perfect mustache.

I lacked the dexterity to twirl the cane in Chaplinesque fashion, but carrying it lent an air of authenticity to my costume. It was the Friday before Halloween, and I practiced my "Little Tramp" walk in view of the full length mirror on my closet door. There was not enough time to master the distinctive, rolling gait, so I decided I wouldn't attempt it at the party.

I viewed myself in profile and head on. What I saw in the mirror startled me. The clothing made my sexual identity less apparent, but it didn't totally obscure it. I saw a weird looking woman in male clothing.

I looked almost as weird as Weird Wilmer.

My knees weakened, as if I'd been pummeled, and I sat on the floor. Wilmer Darling had been none other than Dexter's daughter, Jo Ann. The revelation made so much sense I was surprised I hadn't thought of it when I'd first learned of her existence.

Of course Jo Ann had attended her father's funeral. To preserve Dexter's reputation she'd disguised herself in masculine attire. I recalled her look of anguish at the church, visible as she'd briefly turned from the casket to look at us. "Weird Wilmer's" distress had been genuine, indeed.

And she knew who we were, knew our names and where we lived. Had she secretly observed family events—Lori's and Gil's graduations, their weddings? In the months since Dexter's death Jo Ann had not tried to contact us. I could wait for her to drop the other shoe, or I could mount a preemptive strike by observing her in secret before she decided to approach my children. At the very least I wanted to meet the young woman and take her measure—to adjust to the situation before allowing her to blindside my children as I had been.

Her aloofness aroused my curiosity and gave one more reason to "know my enemy." Then I would decide when and how I should introduce her to my family. She had existed in secret. I would do my research clandestinely. For the first time since I'd heard Dexter's tape, I felt a sense of relief. Perverse pleasure, to be sure, but the prospect of spying on her seemed ...sort of delicious. It would restore the feeling of control and confidence I'd lost.

Louella would help me. I didn't need a professional. All I wanted was to know something about Jo Ann's lifestyle and values. It couldn't be that hard. Now that she had thawed toward me, I could have asked Elsie for help instead. She would plunge into the task with all the enthusiasm of a spaniel chasing squirrels, but I needed a friend more worldly and experienced than Elsie Wickfielder.

Louella would be surprised and titillated by my predicament when I told her, but she wouldn't be scandalized or judgmental, and she was sure to enjoy the excitement of the search. While still reeling from the latest revelation concerning Dexter's daughter, I called Louella.

"Can you come over tomorrow morning? I'll have a pot of coffee ready any time after eight. I need your help."

"Of course I'll come. What's the problem?"

I put her off. There was too much to explain over the phone, and the Wickfielders were due momentarily.

It was fortunate our call was over by the time I saw Orin and Elsie at my back door. I could not suppress a scream that sent Schlegg from the room at warp speed. As I jumped my cane went clattering across the floor. Above the Wickfielder eyes were high expanses of skin that ended in grotesque, cone-shaped baldness. Orin's elegant tux contrasted with a Lilliputian, orange beanie perched on the pinnacle of his head. Elsie had a mammoth, shocking-pink ribbon fastened to the peak of her bald head. Her dress was deeply cut, almost to cleavage, exposing the crinkled texture of her fair and aging skin. Puffed sleeves did not completely hide bra straps. Her orange corsage was appropriate for Halloween.

"You two look out of this world," I said.

"And you—" said Elsie, frowning. "Do you have to wear a mustache?"

"I'm Chaplin's 'Little Tramp.'"

"Well, I hope Mickey isn't put off by your get-up."

"You found me a date?"

"Couldn't you change into something more lady-like?"

"You're the one who suggested I go as a Cone Head. I can't think I would have looked better. You found me a date?"

"At least you would have looked like a woman."

"Elsie, it's five o'clock. I don't have time to change."

"It wasn't easy, but we got you a date. He's meeting us at the party and he'll drive you home. I don't know what he'll think about going out with a transvestite, though."

I started to argue that wearing a Chaplin costume did not equate to cross-dressing, but Elsie's wry smile told me I had risen to her bait.

Orin looked pointedly at his watch.

"Take lipstick with you," said Elsie. "You can take that fool thing off your lip after they judge the costumes."

At the curb Orin held the door for me, then my hosts eased themselves gingerly, bodies first, into the front seats of their Buick, their mountainous heads tilted toward their respective doors in order to accommodate their domes. Then, as if they had rehearsed a dance, each lowered and swung upper bodies in arcs until mounds nearly joined at apexes. Even from the rear they looked like silhouettes from *The Far Side*.

"You just watch," Elsie said as we turned onto the highway. She held her neck muscles rigid and twisted slowly from the waist to face me. "Every time Orin goes out of town, a basement floods or some kid flushes a load of laundry into the toilet."

Orin craned to see me in the rear view mirror, his peak brushing Elsie's in a parody of intimacy. "Half the people in town don't know where their shut-off valve is."

I giggled. "Orin, do you know how hard it is to take you seriously when you're dressed this way?"

He smiled and settled back for the drive to Tulsa. Elsie pushed in a Willie Nelson tape and turned the volume high, making further conversation difficult.

I closed my eyes and pretended Dexter sat opposite me. Any moment he would put his hand on my knee or give my arm a squeeze. Orin was his good friend, and Dexter always made an evening with the Wickfielders fun. I wondered if they noticed the emptiness in the car.

And I wondered if either of them knew of Dexter's infidelity.

Busboys were still setting up tables when we walked into the Conestoga Room. "The bar will open in about fifteen minutes," said a hotel employee. He examined our costumes and grinned. "Looks like you're all set for a good time."

"I guess we're a little early," said Orin. He watched the door hopefully.

"Not at all, sir. Please make yourselves comfortable." He led us to a table near the platform.

"Charley Bobbitt's going to emcee tonight. He's hysterical," said Elsie.

"You know, Elsie, it's all right if your friend doesn't show up. I'm sure I'll enjoy the evening with just you and Orin."

"Mickey will be here," said Orin. "He's on one of them new asthma medications, but he said he wouldn't miss this party if he had to crawl through goldenrod to get here."

"Oh. He's asthmatic?"

"It kept him out of the army."

"You've known him a long time?"

"He used to work for me before he got married and went to work for his father-in-law."

"He's a widower?"

"Twice widowed, twice divorced," said Orin.

"He caught his last wife (her name was Marlene), he caught her in bed in flagrant delectus," said Elsie.

"I beg your pardon?"

"In flagrant delectus. It's a French phrase. It means she was in bed with another man, and Mickey caught them doing 'it.'"

Having imparted this distasteful information, Elsie sat frowning at me, her brow furrowed beneath the mile high forehead.

Orin warned, "He doesn't like to talk about it."

I wondered if catching a spouse "in fragrant delectus" was more unsettling than hearing about it on tape. "I can understand his not wanting to discuss it. Believe me, it's not a subject I would mention, but the poor man sounds unlucky in love."

"Don't get the wrong idea," said Elsie. "He was married to Gladys for twenty-two years. She had a double mastectomy and died on the table. He married her in between his first divorce from Karla and his third wife Annabelle. Poor Annabelle crashed into a concrete overpass on the Turner Turnpike."

"They figure she hit doing about one-twenty," said Orin. "Probably fell asleep at the wheel and never knew what happened."

I shuddered, "That's terrible."

Orin straightened his bow tie and sighed. "He's had his share of misery, but you'd never know it. Mickey's always got a smile on his face."

Others arrived. Some wore imaginative costumes, but most wore street clothes. I began to feel conspicuous. A quartette of costumed figures walked over to greet Orin and Elsie.

"Oh, leave it to Elsie to come up with something so outstanding," gushed a woman introduced to me as Ruby Taylor. Her hair was styled in tight curls and forehead ringlets. She wore a toga that would have been at home on the set of *I, Claudius*.

"This here's our friend, Maggie Gilpin," said Orin. "She's supposed to be Charlie Chaplin."

"Charlie, the Chaplin?"

I thought perhaps she'd confused Chaplin with a spokesman for tuna fish. "Er... Chaplin was the silent film star," I said, "and his signature character was 'The Little Tramp.'"

"Oh, how funny. You really do look just like a man. Do you guys have room your table for all of us?"

"All of us" included Ruby's husband, Tray, dressed as Nero, and their friends, Roy and Jeanne Palmer.

"Just so we save room for Mickey Holden," said Orin. "Keep your eyes peeled for a skeleton."

"Oh, how funny," said Ruby. "Mickey's so thin, he won't even need a costume."

My stomach tightened as I tried to imagine my date. An image of Ichabod Crane filled my mind.

Ruby sat between Orin and Roy, Roy sat across from me. He produced bottles from a tote, then removed a Nixon mask from his head.

"Anybody ready for a drink?" A map of capillaries decorated his own bulbous nose. "We've got Scotch, gin and vodka."

"I'll buy the first round," said Orin, meaning he would order set-ups from the bar, a bar which (by law) took the customer's liquor, mixed it in drinks, then accepted a fee for the service.

"What a cute liquor tote," said Ruby. She held up a canvass bag emblazoned in psychedelic lettering which said, "Bootleg Libations."

"My Uncle Harry used to be a bootlegger," said Roy. "He took to selling liquor satchels when the 'wets' overturned prohibition." He slapped Tray's wife on the back. "Ruby, I can see by your face you don't believe that, but it's the truth."

"Really?" Ruby's high pitched laugh sounded forced. She batted her lashes, flirting. "Oh, Roy. You're a caution."

"Baptists sure make life complicated for drinking men and women," said Tray, taking one of Elsie's hands in his. "Elsie, wouldn't it be a lot simpler if you and I went out to my van and got snockered? You don't need no club membership to buy a soda and a cup of ice from Seven-Eleven. We could tie one on a whole lot cheaper out there in the parking lot."

"Margaret and I don't drink alcoholic beverages." Elsie's voice had a touch of holier-than-thou as she jerked her hand from Tray's and turned toward her husband. "Orin, get Margaret a Coke and you can just get me a Dr. Pepper."

"Well, if my husband looked as spooky as Orin, and I didn't drink," Jeanne wryly observed, "I'd have to take it up."

She wore a pointed hat and a rubber nose covered with warts. I thought Tray probably drank a lot.

Jeanne reached across the table and playfully removed the beanie from Orin's bald dome. "Ooh, it feels so real," she said, running her hands up and down the mound above Orin's face. "Ruby, just touch the top of Orin's head and see how real it feels."

Ruby pushed her chair back and stood behind Orin. "It doesn't feel all that real. Rub the top of Tray's head and you'll see what I mean."

Ruby leaned across the table to demonstrate, and Tray imitated a wolf howling at the moon. He looked at me, winked, and howled again.

"Elsie," I said, "I'm going to find the restroom."

"I'll go with you, Maggie."

"Which restroom are you two looking for, Elsie?" Tray Taylor asked. "I think your friend will probably get thrown out if she tries to go in with you."

"Orin," I said, "please order me a set-up for a screwdriver."

In the restroom I studied myself in the mirror. I saw Elsie looking at me.

"Yes, Elsie, I brought something to remove the mustache glue, and I have a tube of lipstick."

Elsie took a compact from her purse and furiously powdered her nose.

"I can't wait to take this itchy thing off and comb my hair."

"It doesn't look comfortable," I said.

"Maybe I'll take it off after the parade. Charley always starts the judging by having everyone march across the stage."

Elsie crammed her makeup into her purse. Turning from the mirror to face me, she settled her mouth into a tight line. Her narrowed eyes were smaller beneath the expanse of flesh-colored rubber.

"Maggie Gilpin, what's gotten into you?" she asked. "You know what Brother Pierce thinks about alcohol. He says alcohol does wicked things to a man but it's ruination for a woman, and here you are asking Orin to order you a set-up for a screwdriver."

From the moment I ordered a drink, I had braced myself for

Elsie's temperance lecture. "Mama and Daddy used to have homemade wine all the time," I replied, pleased there was something about me she didn't know. "And every year Dexter and I made eggnog at Christmas."

"But that's not real drinking. How come you ordered a screwdriver?"

"If you're a teetotaler, that's your business. But I thought a screwdriver might settle my nerves tonight."

"You aren't nervous about meeting Mickey, are you?"

"A little."

"Well," she said, obviously relieved, "in that case, drinking comes under the category of medicinal. But don't get nervous about Mickey. He's real easy going... for a plumber."

I straightened my suspenders and patted my mustache. "Elsie, will you tell me what you know about a thief in Second Thursday Circle?"

She didn't flinch. "Not until I get the goods on her."

"Then you do know who she is," I said, turning to her expectantly.

"Yep."

"Well?"

"Soon as I can prove it I'll let you know."

"But she stole my cloisonné brooch."

"Oh. Oh, Maggie, I am sorry." The high forehead made her look insincere, even though I could hear sympathy in her voice. "I'm not surprised she took something from you."

"You didn't see her steal my brooch?"

"If I'd seen her I'd have stopped her."

"Then how did you know about the thief in Circle?" She smiled and put a hand to her lips, circling her fingers as if turning a key. "Elsie, I deserve to know," I said.

"Like I said, Maggie. I'll let you in on it when I can prove something. I'm not even going to say you deserved to get that pin stolen after you refused to loan it to me." She started for the door, stopped and frowned. "But don't lose any sleep over it. I bet it will show up."

"It's not in my house. I looked high and low."

"Just be patient, Maggie."

"That's what Louella said."

"Louella? She said be patient?"

"She said it would probably turn up. I hope you're both right."

By the time Elsie and I returned to the table, Mickey Holden had arrived. He stood six feet tall and was about one hundred forty pounds of charm. Iron gray hair lay incongruously atop his skull. Introductions were made, then we sat to enjoy our drinks.

"You're 'The Little Tramp,'" said Mickey. Make-up obscured his face, and I couldn't tell if he approved of me.

I took several sips of the screwdriver, clumsily coating my hairy lip with orange liquid. "I guess I should have brought a mustache cup," I said. "Elsie wants me to remove this after the parade."

"I'm a Chaplin fan," said Mickey His breath smelled minty sweet.

"Then I've probably desecrated the memory of one of your heroes."

"You look too much like a woman, but I don't mind."

"What a line," said Ruby.

"Go for it, Mickey," said Tray.

"Pardon my friends, Maggie. They spent their lives in the sewer and they got no class."

The emcee announced the parade. "Come on," said Elsie. "It's time for the judging."

I said, "Elsie, I'll watch from here."

But a chorus of protests loudly urged me to join the line. As costumed figures assembled for a march across the stage, I swallowed the last of my drink. I reached for my cane, and followed with the Wickfielders and their friends.

"Can you walk like 'The Little Tramp?'" asked Mickey.

"Not too well."

"You *have* to do the walk."

The line moved toward the stage, and a harem girl gyrated to accompanying hoots and whistles. A honey bee wiggled his posterior and "stung" the emcee. Two pairs of Ed and Trixie Nortons strolled arm in arm, carrying "plumber's friends." Inside jokes and insults were yelled at crowd favorites.

I had never felt more like an outsider.

I closed my eyes briefly. When I opened them, I was still in the ballroom of a Tulsa hotel. As I watched, Orin and Elsie bowed to the applauding crowd. Tray and Ruby were received with enthusiasm, and Roy and Jeanne drew polite applause. I took a deep breath, bent my knees, turned my toes out, and tried to walk like Chaplin. I twirled my cane and dropped it. I was on stage just long enough to hear loyal clapping from the Wickfielders and my new friends.

As soon as I stepped down Mickey took center stage. He moved his body in rhythmic pelvic thrusts and fancy footwork that would have put Elvis to shame. He looked like a cardboard skeleton dangled from the end of a string. The room went wild with applause.

"And he's single again, ladies," cooed the emcee. "If you ask me we ought to turn a hose on him."

Moments before it happened I knew I was going to be sick. I fought my way through the crowd and managed to stagger into the ladies' lounge before splattering the floor with recycled orange juice and vodka. I was disposing of the last of the paper towels when Elsie walked into the room.

"Elsie, I feel rotten."

"You're just not the type to drink hard liquor." She walked to the mirror and reapplied her lipstick. "You missed the announcements. Mickey won first prize for the men, and Orin and I came in first for couples."

"You all three deserved it. Elsie, could I borrow your car and maybe Mickey could drive you home later?"

As it turned out Mickey did not feel well either. Exercise and smoke had combined to plague his breathing.

"Perfume. Too much perfume," he rasped. He swallowed some pills. "Come on. I'll drive you home."

Seventeen

Orin and Elsie walked us to Mickey's truck. Elsie looked quite pleased, as if she had deliberately maneuvered Mickey and me into an early departure where we could be alone together. My "date" still labored to breathe. He wobbled on his feet and didn't have the strength to operate a motor vehicle.

Orin helped me into the driver's seat. "Take Mickey in his truck to your house, Maggie. He ought to feel better by the time you get there, but if he don't, leave a message on our answering machine. Elsie and I'll come over and get him."

The vents on the truck's heater were covered with home-made filters. By the time we were on the highway, Mickey began to breathe easier, but an occasional gasp punctuated his speech.

"I think I'd have been okay if I hadn't tried to show off. My medication has been working pretty well the past few months, but I ought to know better than to strut around like a damn fool teenager."

"How long have you had asthma?"

"All my life. Some people outgrow it, but not me."

"Maybe I should take you to an emergency room. We aren't far from a hospital."

"No, I'll live now that I'm away from all that smoke and perfume. By the ti—the time we get to—to your—house—" He coughed violently, then removed an inhaler from the glove box. In a few minutes, he tried again. "By the time we get to your house—I hadn't ought to be dizzy anymore, and it's not much farther—down the road to my place in Oak Flats. I told Orin—I wouldn't have minded stopping for you on my way in, but

Elsie—said you'd probably be more comfortable going with them—this being your first—date since your husband died."

"What more did Elsie tell you about me?"

He smiled, showing teeth which looked yellow against the chalkiness of his facial makeup. "That she about had a heart attack—when you gave her the go ahead to get—you a date."

My hands tightened on the steering wheel. "I'll bet she did."

He yawned. "My eyes sure are tired. Doc says it's a side effect—of the medicine. I'm sorry to do this to you, but I'll—probably feel better if I try to get a little catnap. I hope you don't—mind if I don't talk for a while."

"That's fine with me. I have a splitting headache and my stomach is still a trifle unsettled." I could have added that my upper lip felt raw from the discarded mustache.

As I drove I tried to imagine a sexual relationship with the man nodding beside me. *I thought, can you see us, Dexter?* Would it be a larger insult to Dexter if I became intimate with a man for whom I had no romantic inclination? I wasn't sure. All I did know was it was much easier to think about than it would be to accomplish. Dexter and I were together so many years, I felt completely comfortable in our intimacy. Still deeply in love with my flawed husband, I yearned for his embrace. But when I thought of another man's touch, my neck muscles tightened and hammers pounded inside my brain.

Mickey Holden was offbeat looking, but nice. His appearance reminded me of Jimmy Stewart. If he recovered long enough to stay awake and if he got his asthma under control, I wondered if I could feel passion for him. He wasn't Dexter, but he was... he was probably clean. A clean and pleasant package of aging masculinity. He wouldn't be able physically to sweep me off my feet and carry me to Dexter's and my bed. I did not expect to partake of a memorable romantic or erotic experience, but revenge did not require ecstasy. Any sort of romp in bed would betray my marriage to Dexter.

Elsie wasn't the only one ever to watch a talk show. According to the "experts," rules of dating had changed since I was a girl. On that first encounter I might let Mickey kiss me good night. He might ask me for another date. The second time we would neck a while before I sent him home. I remembered the woman on the panel saying, "Most mature men and women get together in bed by the third date."

All my life I'd followed the teachings of my church. I had guarded my virginity, then offered it in love to my husband. And look at my reward. First, widowhood was thrust upon me, then all those years of faithful marriage called into question by Dexter's affair. It was enough to make me angry with God. Forget the old rules, I told myself. If I wanted to avenge the injustice Dexter had committed, I needed to grow up. I couldn't get pregnant, and Mickey didn't seem like a drug user. With so many marriages, he probably didn't pick up hookers. AIDS didn't seem a likely consequence, still it had to be considered. But if I could calm the bile gathering in my throat, I might not wait until the third date to let Mickey Holden take me to bed.

I parked in the carport to the side of my Mercury. Mickey opened his eyes and yawned. "Part of my problem might be the makeup. Honest, I'm not trying to pull anything, but I think it would be a good idea if I take a shower before I head on home. Otherwise, I might go to sleep at the wheel."

I remembered poor Annabelle running into a concrete abutment on the Turnpike. "I wouldn't want that on my conscience, Mickey. You could very well be allergic to all that makeup on your face." It took effort, but I smiled agreeably, showed him to the guest bathroom, and told him where the towels were.

Now that I was home I could try to get rid of my headache. I hadn't taken the sedative prescribed for me when Dexter died, but I took one now. I hung the heavy tux jacket on my bathroom door and threw the bowler hat onto my dressing table. The shoes had rubbed blisters on my feet, so I changed into slippers.

I ran a brush through my hair. I covered my reddened upper lip with foundation and applied fresh lipstick and rouge. My eye makeup still looked okay. I took a wash cloth to my neck, hoping to erase traces of my favorite perfume. I considered changing into something more feminine than a man's ruffled shirt and baggy trousers, but drew back, not wanting to be too obvious in my pursuit. Moreover, my sleeping libido could not possibly revive until my head quit hurting.

I went into the kitchen and started a pot of coffee. Under the circumstances I thought the caffeine would do us both good. We'd left the hotel before dinner, and although food did not appeal to me, I realized Mickey might be hungry. I took ham from the refrigerator and sliced it. I had half a loaf of Elsie's homemade bread, so I heated it in the oven. I thawed a package of frozen fruit in the microwave. Mama always said the way to a man's heart was through his stomach. It wasn't a bad meal on such short notice, and besides, I had slices of chocolate cream pie I could serve for dessert.

Mickey's shower lasted a long time, long enough for the sedative to blur the far edges of my headache. But my stomach was still uncertain.

The brewed coffee smelled almost inviting, and bread was warming in the oven when Schlegg sauntered into the kitchen. Nothing would do but that I feed him a can of tuna. I held my nose while I piled his plate high with cat food. He was chewing noisily when Mickey came to stand in the doorway.

"A cat!" he yelled, pointing at Furr Schleggener. "You've got a damn cat!"

"Whatever is the matter?"

"Cat." he rasped.

"Well, yes. He was my late husband's cat. Now he's my cat."

"Get him out of here before he kills me."

I scooped Schlegg up in one arm, his dish in another, and set them in the carport. Schlegg didn't like loud noises. He seemed happy to be away from the screaming stranger.

I turned to look at Mickey. He had not re-dressed in his skeleton costume, but had fastened one of my beach towels around his waist. I wondered if he wore shorts beneath the towel. To my surprise the idea of his unclothed "credentials" repulsed me.

"What are you doing?" I asked. "Where are your clothes?"

A mat of black hair covered his narrow chest. When his breath sucked in I could see ribs beneath the hair. His respiration was rapid and shallow. Wet strands of gray were combed smooth and straight back on his head. There were tattoos on both his skinny upper arms. I had my first real look at the man's face. Panic spread across it almost as quickly as the blue tinge. He croaked something. I didn't hear him clearly, but I ran to the truck for his inhaler. He grabbed it from me.

"Call nine-one-one," he instructed before he fainted.

Nine-one-one was the number you dialed in the City. In Redbud, every house seemed to have a calendar hung near the phone, courtesy of Santos' Funeral Home and Ambulance Service. Their seven digit number was printed in large red letters beneath a picture of the newly remodeled Hope Chapel. Flory's brother-in-law, Albert Santos, picked up on the ninth ring.

"Albert, this is Margaret Gilpin, and I need an ambulance at my house right away. A man can't breathe. He's having an asthma attack."

The phone system may not have been as modern as Tulsa's, but Albert didn't have to think about where I lived. And he was only minutes away.

After making the call I covered Mickey with an Afghan from the sofa and put a small pillow under his head. While waiting I alternated between checking his pulse and respiration, and looking through my front window for any sign of the ambulance. Mickey labored to breathe but he rallied enough to ask the whereabouts of my cat.

"Don't worry. Schlegg is outdoors."

I kept praying, "Please, God, don't let Mickey Holden die. If you let him live I promise I won't commit an act of fornication, only please don't let him die."

I could hear its faint siren from the time the ambulance left the funeral home. It grew louder as it approached my neighborhood. Houses lit up. Porch lights up and down my street blazed in the dark. The neighbors across from me, and those on the east, donned jackets and came to stand on their lawns. On seeing the red lights, small children jumped up and down. Their parents stood on tiptoe, concerned and curious. A police car followed. Albert gave the siren one last blast as he came to a stop, all four wheels cutting deep ruts in my yard.

The officers held the door while Albert and the attendant carried the cot into my living room. "Go back home, folks," I heard one of them yell. "We got it under control."

"Thank God, you're here. Come this way." I led them

through the dining room to where Mickey lay half in and half out of my kitchen. "He's having trouble breathing."

Albert and the younger man with him took Mickey's vital signs. One of them placed the pressure cuff on Mickey's arm, and the other listened through the stethoscope. "What's your name, sir?"

"It's Mickey Holden," I said. "M-I-C-K-E-Y H-O-L-D-E-N," It was hard to not sound like one of the Mouseketeers. "He lives in Oak Flats and he's had asthma all his life. He seemed to be getting better, but all of a sudden he came into the kitchen where my cat was, and he just turned blue and fainted."

I could hear myself rambling on, but was powerless to stop. "I suppose he's allergic to cats. I know he can't stand smoke and perfume, but he never told me about cats. I gave him his inhaler, but it didn't seem to help much. He had washed all his makeup off, and I thought that would make a difference, so he could drive on to his home. He lives in Oak Flats."

Albert held a hand up for me to be quiet. I picked up the inhaler from the floor and handed it to Albert's assistant.

"You had these attacks before, sir?"

Mickey nodded weakly.

"We're giving you a little oxygen, then we're going to transport you to County Memorial. What's the name of your doctor?" Albert detached a speaker from his belt and relayed Mickey's breathless information to the hospital.

"All right, sir," said Albert's assistant, "you just rest easy while we take you for a little ride."

As he spoke he tossed the Afghan aside to strap the patient onto the cot. Mickey's long legs and bare chest were exposed, and contact with the Afghan had brushed the towel to one side. The attendant's expression changed ever so slightly, but he did not drop his professional demeanor as he straightened the towel, then fastened the straps. He covered Mickey with a sheet and blanket stamped "Santos Ambulance Service."

I ran into the guest bathroom and brought the skeleton costume, shoes, underwear, and Mickey's billfold to the officers.

"I guess I'll keep his truck keys so the Wickfielders and I can bring it to the hospital tomorrow."

"You can follow us now if you'd like," said Albert.

"I'm too shaky to drive." I thought of the medication I had taken. "Besides, I'm feeling sort of doped up."

One of the policeman eyed me curiously. I recognized him as the son of a young man in one of my English classes years ago.

"Prescription drug," I said, as he held the door for me.

After they settled Mickey into the back of the ambulance, the other policeman asked, "Ma'am, would you care to ride with him to the emergency room?"

"Oh, I don't think so. I don't really know him that well."

Albert was preparing to step up into the front of the ambulance. The break in his stride was unmistakable, though he couldn't have looked at me more than a second or two before he strapped himself in and started the engine.

"He's a friend of the Wickfielders," I yelled to Albert. "We met at a party tonight, and he wanted to take a shower before he drove home because he thought the makeup gave him a reaction, and then Schlegg walked in—"

Albert pushed the siren button.

I looked around. I could feel neighbors staring at me from darkened windows.

"I don't think I'll tell you why I'm wearing men's trousers," I muttered, walked into my house, and slammed the door.

Eighteen

In my dreams Dexter held me. I reached the point of ecstasy when, within the dream, I opened my eyes. The broad face and straight brown hair of George Dexter Gilpin melted into the features of a skeleton. I thought I screamed, but it may have been only the phone on my nightstand jarring me awake.

Louella called to tell me she was on her way. It was nine o'clock, Saturday morning, and I'd been in bed less than five hours. If my brain had been functioning, I'd have canceled the invitation for coffee. Instead, I threw on a housecoat and staggered into the kitchen.

About half the brew had trickled into the glass coffee pot when Louella arrived. I hadn't yet combed my hair or "put on my face." Lack of sleep painted dark circles under my eyes. Louella hung her coat in the pantry. She grinned conspiratorially. "How was your date?"

I burst into tears.

"What in the world—"

"Louella, I feel so ashamed."

She grabbed a box of tissues from the telephone desk and thrust it into my hands. "Maggie, your reputation's safe. Everyone knows Albert Santos is the world's biggest gossip. No one believes half what he says, even when he sticks to the truth."

I drew back, my tears checked by surprise. "You mean you've already heard about last night?"

"Yeah, Flory called me this morning to dish the dirt." She grinned. "There's nothing more threatening to an aging, reformed wild woman like Flory than an attractive widow on the loose. I expected to see you sporting a romantic glow or special twinkle, but you look more like I feel when I've baby-sat my grandkids."

"I haven't had time to put on makeup."

"The last I heard your date was still alive at County Memorial, so this isn't grief I'm seeing, is it?"

I blew my nose, and Louella hurried to pour us coffee.

"You'd better sit down and talk to me."

I sat. "I'll sell my house and leave town."

"Because your lover nearly expired from an asthma attack?"

"Mickey Holden is not my lover!"

"Whatever. Did he get an attack during or after?" She leered with interest.

I bit off my words. "Louella, if I told you I had jumped into bed with a man I barely know, and we had a romp fit for a soap opera, you wouldn't be a bit disappointed or surprised, would you?"

"Not at all, dear. You're only human."

"Well, if I had gone to bed with him, I would never be able to look at myself in a mirror again."

"Why not? Was he that unattractive?"

I tried to remember which of Mickey's features had reminded me of Jimmy Stewart, but all I could recall clearly were his chalk-colored nose and pale yellow teeth.

"He was attractive enough. But I don't believe in sex outside of marriage."

"Believe. I can produce evidence."

"I mean, I think it's wrong. All my life I've known it was a sin."

"And Maggie Gilpin is a sinless creature."

"Oh, come on. You know I don't think that. But I should never have considered having an affair with that man. I don't know him well enough to say I even care for him. And there I was, thinking about... about sex, just so I could get even with Dexter. Louella, *nothing physical happened.*"

"What are you talking about—getting even with Dexter?"

"I'm not saying I'm innocent. The intent was there, so I'm as guilty as... as guilty as David when he lusted after Bathsheba. But nothing happened between Mickey and me."

"My condolences. But what did you mean about Dexter?"

It took four cups of coffee, but I told her all about Jo Ann and my plans to betray my marriage vows. Then I recounted every pertinent detail of Mickey's and my activities, to the point of Albert Santos' arrival.

When I finished the story we sat looking at each other across my kitchen table. Louella started to speak. "This would be so sad, but—" I watched her lined fuchsia lips quiver, then start to curl. She snorted, trying to suppress a giggle.

"It must seem like a hoot to you, but I feel terrible."

"Oh, of course you do. I'm sorry." She came around the table and gave me a hug. "But, honey, I hope you're not going to go around in sackcloth and ashes over something that only almost happened."

I stood up and put the dishes in the sink. "I can't help feeling ashamed."

"Maybe I should get you an appointment with my therapist. She doesn't believe in guilt."

"Believe. I can produce evidence."

"You know, if you'd dressed Mickey before the ambulance arrived, it wouldn't have looked nearly so risque."

"Albert and the police were here minutes after I made the call. Besides, I don't think the make-up residue on his costume would have been good for his asthma."

"So, how did you wind up at the hospital last night?"

I dried my hands and looked at Louella.

"I wasn't going to go, but when Orin and Elsie got my message on the answering machine, they called County Memorial to see how Mickey was doing."

He could have been dead, but I hadn't cared enough to call the hospital. Or, more precisely, I hadn't wanted to compound my embarrassment with too much show of interest. Of all the self revelations of the "sinless" Maggie Gilpin, the knowledge I had put my reputation ahead of any concern for Mickey engendered the most revulsion. With no thought for his welfare I had planned to use him, then toss him aside.

I sat down and toyed with a paper napkin. I searched for words to make Louella see my guilt, but I knew she wouldn't understand.

"He was in intensive care, so the Wickfielders decided the

three of us should go to Mickey's bedside to hold a prayer vigil." I began folding the napkin into a fan. "When we arrived at the hospital Mickey had rallied and was out of danger. But wife number four was with him."

"His wife? I thought he was divorced."

"So did the Wickfielders. But when Mickey thought he might be dying, he had the hospital call Marlene. They're reconciling. She came to the waiting room to meet us."

"That had to be interesting."

I remembered the diminutive Mrs. Holden, clad in tight jeans and a knit shirt that read, "Divers Do It Deeper." She'd introduced herself and handed me my bath towel, neatly folded. To my relief Marlene had seemed grateful we'd come to the hospital. "Thank you for saving Mick's life," she'd said, giving my hand a squeeze.

"She looked so much younger than Mickey," I told Louella. "She borders on being pretty, but she's had her eyes tattooed— permanently lined with black. She said her eyeliner aggravated Mickey's allergies. Elsie thinks Marlene looks like a hooker. She kept saying 'How could Mickey Holden be married to someone like that? Gladys would have a fit.'"

"Gladys?"

"Mickey's first wife."

"What's so awful about Wife Number Four?"

"Well, she has hair out to here." I put my hands out to indicate a teased hair style. "And her nails were longer than yours. She had painted them in rainbow colors."

"Tight clothes and lots of cleavage?"

"No cleavage. No bra either. And to quote Elsie, 'That woman's jeans are so tight, they look like she's been screwed in them.'"

"Mm. Sounds impossible, but who am I to argue with Elsie."

"What impressed me about Marlene is I think she really does care for Mickey. And she was cordial. She thanked me for calling the ambulance."

"That was nice of her, considering her husband had been your date for the evening."

"Please don't call him my date."

"A rose is a rose. The man brought you home." While still talking, Louella bent down and lifted Furr Schleggener into her arms. "He took a shower in your bathroom and he made a move to take you to bed."

"He did no such thing—try to take me to bed, I mean. And you're laughing at me again."

"It's a funny story, Maggie. But don't worry about your reputation. The Wickfielders will put Albert in his place." She returned to her chair and sat down. She rubbed Schlegg with one hand and held the other to the light to check for chips in her nail polish. "Besides, everyone knows you're about as wild as cookie dough. You won't even jaywalk. Nobody will believe you were about to violate one of the Ten Commandments."

"Thanks for not embarrassing me, Louella. I couldn't stand for you to call me wholesome or devout. Wild as cookie dough is higher praise, I'm sure."

She grinned. "So, what are you going to do next? Advertise in the personals columns for a lover?"

"Not unless you'll let me use your name. No, I'm going to forgive Dexter."

"Oh, really? You're actually prepared to forgive your late husband for being a lonesome, randy soldier whose major crime was acting like a healthy male animal?"

Schlegg leaped from Louella's arms onto a vacant chair. I scooted him over and put my feet near his ears.

"That's the whole point, isn't it? He did act like an animal— like a rutting beast, instead of a faithful married man."

"I'd bet being lonely and so far away from home had more to do with it than hormones."

I looked at her. "Well, I can't ask him, can I? I can listen to his damn tape and read his damn letters a hundred times over and I still won't know why our marriage meant less to him than it did to me."

"What about the girl?"

Our coffee had cooled, so I poured two more cups. "Jo Ann? I'm going to find her."

Louella reapplied her lipstick before taking another sip of coffee. "Yeah. I can understand that. I'd be curious."

"Do you want to help me?"

She looked at me and smiled, her brown eyes lively with mischief. "This could be exciting."

We went into the living room where I dumped the contents of Dexter's envelopes on the floor. I played the tape for Louella and watched her reactions as she listened. A sober, troubled look replaced her merriment. Her eyes grew round and her lower lip quivered. After the tape finished she said, "I feel as if I've been through a bout of chemo."

"I know what you mean. I wish he'd told me while we had time to work things out."

"He thought you would leave him."

"Maybe I would have. I don't know."

I picked up a picture of Jo Ann taken at her high school graduation. "She's pretty, isn't she?"

"Not as pretty as Lori, but she's pretty." Louella sounded as if she meant it, and I was pleased my Lori would be considered prettier than her half-sister.

We found a return address on the back of a letter Jo Ann had written to Dexter in care of a Tulsa post office box just weeks before his death.

"She's surely known about me for a long time. Whenever I think of it I feel so... so creepy knowing this person was seeing Dexter, hearing about me, hearing all about Lori and Gil. Now I'd like to know something about her before I call her up and say, 'Bye-the-bye, this is your father's wife, and I'd very much like to meet you.'"

"Which is why you want my help. You want me to snoop around and tell you what I find so Jo Ann won't know you're investigating."

"Will you do it?"

"I'll drive to Okmulgee County next week and find out what I can," said Louella. "There's a clothing outlet on Highway Fifty-six I want to shop, and Highway Fifty-six cuts right through Okmulgee."

Nineteen

I sat across from Ron and drank my coffee, declining a slice of cranberry bread he offered me.

"Helen's mother made it," he told me. "Mailed it all the way from Boston in case the stores here in the hinterlands don't carry cranberries."

Helen was his wife. I wondered if she would understand my growing friendship with Ron, what she would think of the innocent mornings we spent together. Had she been a fly on the wall, she couldn't have found a flaw in our conduct, so why did I feel guilty when I thought of her?

Ron wore a pullover sweater patterned in forests and antelope and Mallard ducks. He laid an unlit pipe in a pristine ashtray. He exuded understanding and solidity. I imagined Helen at home knitting him another sweater, baking his favorite dishes, hearing about his problems at work.

While I told myself not to reveal my reckless and tasteless behavior to this man I so respected, I heard my voice, tentative and small. "I tried to cheat on Dexter," I said.

He rested the butter knife on his plate and looked at me.

"I didn't intend to say that," I said, standing

"Why not? What's so wrong with Maggie Gilpin admitting her humanity to a friend?"

"Do you have a container for the cranberry bread? I can take it to the refrigerator in the cafeteria's kitchen if you like."

"Please," he said, rising, brushing my shoulder with one hand, then folding both hands together. "Please don't go yet."

I set my cup on his desk, my hands trembling, wanting to tell him all about Mickey Holden because it hadn't been enough to confide in Louella. I sank into the chair. This fine man, this psychologist, this friend would understand my guilt, my need for confession that was stronger than my fear of his disapproval.

"I should be talking to my pastor, I guess. But I don't think he'd understand."

"Just what is it he wouldn't understand, Maggie?"

"I made plans to go to bed with another man... but I didn't do it."

He took a paperclip from his desk and straightened it. "Going to bed with another man would be less bizarre at this point than going to bed with Dexter."

I bit my lip, stung by his cavalier response, thinking how foolish I'd been to mistake his camaraderie for friendship. I struggled with self-control, determined not to give him the satisfaction of seeing me cry again.

He flinched, his eyes reflecting my own pain. "Sorry, Maggie, that was a lousy remark. I guess you took me by surprise—not your behavior, just the way you chose to announce it. Do you want to talk about it?"

I nodded, and he stood and walked to the door of his office, closing it to the questioning glance of the receptionist. He came close and sat on the corner of his desk, so near I could smell the scent of *paco rabanne.*

I began haltingly, but his quiet acceptance gave me courage. I told him everything, hoping he wouldn't laugh as Louella had. And the second recitation seemed somehow easier than the first.

When I finished he sat looking at me, not speaking. I asked him, "Aren't you going to say something?"

His hands were up as if he wanted to reach me and hold me, but he stood and turned so quickly I thought I'd been mistaken. His fists were clenched tight. I waited, expecting to hear him tell me how badly I'd behaved, but that I should put the incident behind me and get on with my life.

When he spoke he faced a bookcase jammed with classics that crowded against texts on nursing home management. I heard a husky quality in his voice. "I can't."

I caught my breath. "Please say something. Say how awful I

was to want to use Mickey—to want to fall into bed with a man who means nothing to me. Tell me how tacky—"

He turned and our eyes met. Returning to his chair, he sat, drummed his fingers on the desktop, studied me, and I could not read his expression. I looked away from his gaze, took our cups to the sink, rinsed them, dried them with a paper towel, and set them in the cabinet. From the corner of my eyes I watched as he turned to answer the phone in his professional, comforting manner. Without glancing his way I headed for the room of a favorite patient to play our weekly game of checkers.

When she saw me Bella said, "My, my, young lady. Is it that cold outside? Your face is so red it looks like you've been shoveling snow."

"No snow, Bella, but the parking lot's half-flooded with rain. How've you been?"

"Well as can be expected, dear. But if I didn't know better I'd swear some man put that blush on your face."

Was I so easy to read? I had been wondering how the evening would have ended if Ronal Patrick had been my date. I determined to behave more circumspectly while in the company of married men. I respected the institution of marriage too much to play games, and I hoped I hadn't changed the quality of our friendship by burdening Ron with Dexter's affair.

Now that I'd decided to find her, Dexter's daughter was never far from my mind. Considering the commotion among the Second Thursdays when they learned about my date with Mickey Holden, I wondered how they would react if they learned about Jo Ann.

I shopped in Thompson's one day where I saw Amelia Crabtree ahead of me in the check-out line. I called to her, "Amelia, how you doing?"

She stared resolutely in another direction, her sharp nose tilted upward to indicate distaste. I felt as if I wore a scarlet "A" on my forehead. Amelia wouldn't change deodorant brands or vote for dogcatcher without asking Flory's advice, so I knew who'd shared unsavory gossip with her.

Someone, probably Flory, anonymously mailed me a book on Christian widowhood.

On the second Wednesday following Mickey's hospitalization, I entered the choir room. People greeted me with their usual warmth. It was as if no one had told them a naked man had nearly died while sprawled between my kitchen and dining room. Amelia was especially solicitous. I thought Louella was correct—the Wickfielders' efforts to restore my reputation were precisely the character endorsements needed.

Brother Lee expressed delight with the progress the choir had made on our Christmas program. And Shirley Mitchell reported the children were rehearsing well. "They are the cutest things," she said, "absolutely darling."

We finished rehearsals, and I walked to my car which was parked next to Shirley's. "My, that's a pretty blue sweater," I told her as I slid behind the wheel. "I used to have a cloisonné brooch just that color."

"I picked it up at Wal-Mart," she said, regarding me with a strange expression. "Thanks."

Elsie's turn for Second Thursday Circle arrived during the frenzy of Thanksgiving preparations. Sharla Sanders took her children to California for the holidays, and Shirley and Richard Mitchell traveled to Arkansas to visit his brother. But most of us would find ourselves at Elsie's, knowing we had five more days to clean houses, shop, bake, and otherwise prepare for Thanksgiving.

Although the temperature dipped into the thirties, there was no wind; so I packed my craft project into a large tote and walked the six blocks to Elsie's. I passed houses I'd seen nearly every day for thirty years, but this time I wondered about the dramas unfolding inside.

At Elsie's it wasn't easy to keep my mind on craft work. Flory asked me about Gil's dental practice three times before she broke through my personal fog. When I wasn't speculating about the thief who stole my brooch, I thought about finding Jo Ann Darnold.

And more and more, thoughts of J. Ronal Patrick intruded

into whatever tranquility I had left. As a trained counselor he seemed to know and understand my struggle to forgive Dexter. We didn't speak again of Mickey Holden; but there was a new gentle quality in Ron's attitude, as if he sympathized with my inner struggle to rebuild my trust. To an outsider our banter, as we continued our morning coffee sessions, might have seemed rough and hurtful. But there was a teasing quality to it. On my part sexual tension lurked beneath each insult. I was like an impossibly flirtatious teenager who, knowing she cannot attain the desired prize, hurls gentled barbs at the object of her hidden affection.

I thought how repulsed Ron would be if he knew I found him attractive, if he knew how I fantasized a convenient death for his wife and his turning to me for comfort. Maybe I had betrayed my marriage vows simply by lusting after a married man. If lusting was the same as adultery, why not enjoy the benefits of my sin? Maybe I'd get to the point where I wouldn't feel guilty.

No, I reminded myself. I'd learned from my date with Mickey Holden how unprepared I was to take a lover, even a man I'd thought unmarried. I vowed again to keep my friendship with J. Ronal Patrick untarnished and to banish impure thoughts.

Flory asked each of us to contribute to a "prayer of gratitude." I had mixed feelings. These women had given me emotional support after Dexter's death for as long as they perceived me to be a grieving widow. Although my friendship with Louella grew stronger all the time, and Elsie still hoped to mold me, I thought the other Second Thursdays were trying to make up their minds about me, whether to trust me around their husbands. They would never know how safe they were—as the victim of a home-wrecker I wasn't about to enter into a relationship with a man married to one of my friends.

Besides, none of their husbands interested me the way Helen Patrick's did.

I couldn't pray honestly in response to Flory's request. My secret sins were becoming too sweet to forfeit, and I thought God might strike me dumb if I mouthed a string of empty platitudes.

"If I haven't told each of you," I said, "I want you to know I'm immensely grateful for the trouble you took to comfort me when Dexter died."

But I hadn't deterred Flory. She urged, "Why don't you close our prayer circle, Maggie."

"Thanks, Flory, not now," I said.

I knew my refusal stirred curious minds. Thoughts and gossip would churn around me like stinging insects; but I've never wanted to lie to myself, and I knew there was no point in lying to God.

Flory turned to Louella and smiled, "Then will you do us the honor, dear?"

For one who didn't believe in guilt, Louella's prayer sounded quite sincere and contrite. "Lord, I'm a sinner," she prayed. "A miserable sinner. Please forgive me. Forgive us all."

After the devotional we adjourned to the dining room where Elsie poured Kool-aid and told everyone it was my secret punch. She tried to atone by explaining to one and all how she and Orin contributed to my embarrassment by arranging a date for me with a still-married man.

"It was a mix-up, of course, but Maggie has been so sweet not to hold it against us," she told the women at Circle.

Their looks indicated they'd heard the whole story.

Elsie served an elaborate buffet. Cardboard and crayoned Pilgrims, apparently wrought by Elsie's own hand, decorated a plaid table cloth. The plaid was in shades of purple, lime, and brown, best described as overwhelming, and matched the pant suit she wore. Her gold vest was two years out of style, but was nearly the same shade as her suede sandals and toenail polish.

I looked for something to admire. "I've always loved your sterling coffee spoons," I told her.

"I used to have twelve of these little spoons," she said, looking around the room. "I am down to eleven. But I don't intend to lose another."

Elsie has always been proud of those sterling spoons. When she stepped into the kitchen to refill the coffee pot, I followed.

"Are you telling me someone stole one of your spoons?" I whispered.

"Call me up sometime, Maggie." Her smile was as condescending as it was secretive. "We'll have a nice chat on the phone."

When I began work on my project, an embroidered queen-size bedspread to sell at the thrift shop, I couldn't find my thimble, so I asked Elsie if she had an extra one.

"You mean you're missing that gold plated Betsy Ross thimble Gil, Jr. brought you from D.C?" I saw her exchange a look with Amelia.

"I expect it fell under one of my sofa cushions, Elsie. I used it last evening, and I'll find it when I get home."

She brought me another one. "If I was you, Maggie, I wouldn't wear myself out looking for a thimble. Chances are you'll be having more important things to look for."

I wanted to tell her she should stop being coy—that I had a right to know the name of the thief since she obviously did. But if she wanted to play games, so be it. "Whatever are you talking about?" I asked.

I thought Elsie would burst with smugness. I looked at Louella whose face was a mask of forbearance, raised my eyebrows, and gave my shoulders a slight shrug.

When Circle ended Louella drove me home from the Wickfielders. "Elsie seemed to be bursting to tell me who took my brooch," I said.

"Forget Elsie. One of the leads you gave me finally panned out, and I think I've located Jo Ann. Do you want to drive with me to Miracle Creek Springs tomorrow?"

Twenty

As she drove me home from Elsie's, Louella withdrew a strawberry-blond wig from a paper bag. "It's an Eva Gabor. Your own mother wouldn't know you. And I brought these, too." She produced a pair of dark glasses. "They're Christian Dior."

"Do you think they'll work? I don't want to confront Jo Ann until I know more about her."

"Try on the wig and we'll see."

I settled the curls over my salon-colored brown tresses and pulled down the mirrored sun visor to study the effect. The style didn't flatter, but Louella was right. No one would recognize me.

"You look different too. It must be your new contacts. I like them." Her brown eyes appeared turquoise, and I thought she looked quite attractive without her bifocals.

She acknowledged the compliment with a nod. "I spoke with the school principal in Amberville where Jo Ann used to work." She giggled. "I think he wanted to go to bed with me. He would have told me everything in the bedroom."

"Louella, that's disgusting."

"Yeah. He wore white socks, and I didn't care for his after-shave."

"Be serious," I said in frustration. "What else did he tell you about Jo Ann?"

"Killjoy," she said, exaggerating a pout. "He says she left Amberville at the end of the last school term without renewing her contract. It seems her grandmother is trying to raise one of

Jo Ann's siblings by herself, and she decided she wanted Jo Ann to move home to help her."

"Did you find out where 'home' is?"

She shrugged. "Somewhere near Miracle Creek Springs, which is a wide spot on old U. S. 66. Jo Ann's address is a rural route on Mulberry Road."

"Did you get her phone number for me so I can call her?"

"I called the number the principal gave me, but it's been changed. The operator said it was unlisted."

I slumped against the car's headrest. "Were you able to talk to anyone else?"

"I cornered a couple of teachers in the lounge. They said Jo Ann was a good teacher, but they didn't know her too well socially. So I'm afraid she's still a mystery woman."

"Louella, how did you... I mean... do they know why you wanted to find her?"

"Sweetie, there are some things you really don't want to know. Just trust me on this. I found out where she is, and nobody got my real name."

"Hot dog," I said, snapping my fingers. "Watson, you did well."

Louella looked pleased. "No one's called me Watson since I was in school." She studied my face. "You'll need to adjust your make-up to match the wig. Do you have any orange lipstick? And why don't you pull your hair back with rubber bands before you put it on. You don't want all those brown wisps sticking out."

She pulled into my driveway but did not turn off the motor.

I paused a moment before opening the car door. "Louella, I'm not sure I'm cut out for this sort of clandestine activity."

"Don't worry about a thing, Maggie. Nobody will give a second look to two middle-aged innocents like us. Women like us could carry off half the county and the dogs wouldn't even bark."

Fields stretched across the rolling plains on either side of the two-lane highway. Now and then a wash of red clay or a stand of winter-bare trees streaked among the stubble of harvested wheat. Smoke curled from farmhouses, homey two-story structures mostly painted white and flanked by rows of cedar trees. Between the houses were miles of farmland. Cattle stood on ridges against the brittle sky, and hawks, solitary in their vigils, perched on utility poles looking for easy prey.

Louella left the highway and parked her Lincoln alongside an ancient gasoline pump. "Maybe they'll know where Mulberry Road is," she said, indicating the mom and pop store. She went to find a restroom while I fueled the car.

I crossed the drive and stepped into Barber's Country Store. Shelves of cans, jars, and boxes covered weathered walls. The gray floor had been recently oiled. I smelled a mixture of bologna, pickles, and propane in the oxygen-starved room, and the flames in the free-standing stove baked the air, threatening my sinuses.

"Howdy," said the man behind the meat counter. "Kin I hep you?" He rolled a toothpick in his mouth.

I smiled and laid a small bunch of overpriced bananas on the counter. "I'd like to fill my Thermos with coffee too, if that's okay."

"Be four dollars, all together. Cream and sugar?" He took his hands from his overalls and walked to the counter for a handful of packets. He stuffed the packets into a bag with the bananas and poured a scorched looking brew into my container. "Be anything else?"

"Can you tell me how to get to Mulberry Road?"

"Whatcha wanna go out there for?" asked a woman, emerging from what must have been an attached residence. She looked as if she understudied Auntie Em—her salt and pepper hair was ratted in a bun, and she wore a red-checkered apron.

I gave her my prepared cover story. "My friend and I are doing research about the children of men who marry Korean women. I understand the Darnold family used to live around here, on Mulberry Road."

She looked at me over her bifocals. "Is this for the gov'ment?"

"Goodness, no."

"Cause if you ask me, they waste too much of our money already on boondoggles."

"I'm sure you're right. But this is privately funded."

"That's good," she said. "But we can't help you much. The

Darnolds—the woman he married was definitely one of them Orientals—was both killed a while back when they pulled in front of a cement truck on the highway. The truck driver never even braked. Squashed that car right into itself. Pitiful, wasn't it Lamar."

"Pitiful, Irene honey, just pitiful."

"How about their children?"

"Oh, the youngest child got killed with them. I couldn't rightly say about the rest of the family."

Louella came inside. She straightened a silk paisley scarf so that it hung in neat folds over her clinging jersey jump suit. The frown on her face told me the restroom had been disappointingly inadequate for the fastidious. "Do they know anything about the Darnolds?"

Irene started to say something, but Lamar stopped her.

"Nope. We sure don't." He smiled in satisfaction. "'Fraid you ladies have wasted your time. But I guess it all goes on an expense account."

"It would be enough if I could just find the oldest daughter, Jo Ann."

"She used to teach over to Amberville. You could try there."

"We did, but they said she gave Mulberry Road in Miracle Creek Springs as her last address," said Louella

"I guess you've run into a dead end here," said Irene.

Louella bought a candy bar, and we returned to the car. "Your turn to drive," she said. Only at that point did I realize I hadn't learned how to get to Mulberry Road.

"Surely those people would know if any of the Darnolds still lived around here, Maggie."

"Probably. But since we're this close to where she used to live, I'd at least like to see the neighborhood."

I went back inside. "I never did find out how to get to Mulberry Road," I said.

"Ain't nothin' down that way," said Lamar.

"Then you won't mind if we waste the afternoon taking in the country."

He shrugged. "You can't miss it. Go up to the next section line. It's just before the Baptist Church. Turn west and go two miles. You'll cross a little bridge just before you get to an old silo. After the silo, keep going on up the hill. The road will curve to the right. After it curves, it makes a fork. When it forks, you go left about a quarter of a mile. You'll see an old red, falling down barn. You can't miss Mulberry Road. It's just spittin' distance past that barn."

"Much obliged," I said.

Irene and Lamar looked at me with blank faces. They still had little use for government employees.

When I got back to the car, I began to search frantically for pencil and paper. "Did you find out anything?" asked Louella.

"Hush a minute, so I won't forget." I scribbled the directions, hoping I remembered them correctly. I put the pencil back in my purse and turned to her. "Yes, Louella. I think I can get us to Mulberry Road; either that, or we're driving into the country to be bushwhacked."

"I live in hope, dear."

Twenty-One

Once we were "spittin' distance" past a decrepit barn, official signs became as rare as camels in Redbud, Oklahoma. We followed a road which cut through acres of plowed fields. Gravel crunched beneath the tires; dust plumed behind us, obscuring the view through the rear window. We had driven about twenty minutes on Mulberry Road, past a few dozen farms, when the gravel petered out. Grassy ruts stopped at the edge of a creek bank. Cattle had left their calling cards on the landscape, but not another breathing soul was visible.

"I think you've driven right up to the edge of the world."

"If the Darnold's farm is on Mulberry Road, we must have passed it," I said.

"Brilliant deduction, Holmes," said Louella, still playing the game.

Although many of the homesteads had painted wooden signs above closed gates, ("Alteizer's Rocking A" and "Dulce's Hill") we'd seen no clue to the Darnold place. "I'm ready to go home and do some more sleuthing by telephone." I backed the Lincoln, turned, and headed from the creek.

A loud bang startled me. I sensed the heaviness in the steering column before I heard the slap against the damaged tire. "Oh no," I said. "Louella, you better call road service."

But we seemed to be in some sort of no man's land where her cell phone wouldn't work. "How's your spare?" I asked.

"Fine, I guess. If I've got one. "Can't we just drive it until we get to a service station?"

"As flat as it is and as far as we are from the highway, I don't think so."

I pulled to a stop, set the parking brake, and pushed a button which popped the trunk lid. Then I walked back to retrieve the spare. My "winter-white" slacks quickly acquired dark streaks from brushing against the tire. Louella stepped from the car and joined me to assess the situation.

"Those damned tires. I've never had a flat in my life. Why couldn't this have happened when we were in civilization?"

I thought of the lecture Dexter had given Lori the first time he'd let her drive her car to the university. "Before you take off you have to show me you know how to change a flat. You can't expect a blimp to land out of the sky to do it for you. If you're capable of driving, you should be capable of a few simple repairs."

I smiled at Louella. "I'm just grateful you have a good spare and a jack."

"Do you know how to change a tire?"

"I think so." I ran through the procedure in my mind. "There can't be much to it. Racing crews change all four tires and dump gas in the tank in seconds."

"Maggie, that's TV. This is real life. What are we going to do?"

I felt as uncertain as her shaky voice, but I knew giving in to panic would solve nothing. I gave her a withering look, hoping to engender confidence. "Wedge some rocks beneath the rear wheels," I told her. I assembled the jack, set it under the car, and began to pump.

In spite of her reluctance to rumple her clothing, Louella offered to help. "I don't have a lot of upper arm strength, but I could move that handle up and down as fast as you're doing it."

We both knew it was my problem which had taken us onto Mulberry Road, and I felt bound to decline her tepid offer.

Even in the afternoon chill, perspiration dampened my brow, and I breathed heavily; but after what seemed like ages, I'd raised the tire inches from the ground. Once I'd removed the hub cap, I took the wrench and started on the lug nuts. Each time I gave the wrench a spin, the wheel would begin to move. I made little progress.

"I don't think that's the way you're supposed to do it," said Louella.

I thought about how hard I'd worked to get the tire off the ground, then I walked to the jack and tried to ease the car down. It settled heavily onto the road. With a weary sigh I returned to the task of removing lug nuts. "Put them in the hub cap so we won't lose them, Louella."

I was a disheveled wild woman by the time the pick-up pulled beside us. I sat squatting, both legs numb, my hands blistered from the effort of trying to loosen the last stubborn nut.

"Oh, thank God," said Louella.

I tried to stand, but my legs wouldn't support me. I sat back on my haunches, millions of needles stabbing me from thigh to toe as blood rushed back to my muscles.

"Looks like you could use some help," said a masculine voice. I looked up to see a lanky youngster wearing an FFA cap.

"You think you could help us change a tire?" asked Louella.

I braced with my hands, eased forward to my knees and, without leaning on the precariously perched car, raised myself to a standing position. The movement lacked grace. I wanted to say I thought *we* were managing by ourselves, but I wasn't looking forward to wrestling the spare onto the wheel. My raw, grimy hands hurt.

Another boy sitting in the truck saw me stand. He grinned, then averted his eyes. And as I faced the future farmer, he suppressed a smirk.

"Your wig is crooked," whispered Louella.

"You two ladies lost?"

"Just out for a drive in the country," said Louella.

I threw my strawberry-blond curls into the car and pushed at the fly-away mop atop my head. "We were looking for the daughter of some people who used to live near here, but we can't seem to find their place. Did you know the Darnolds?"

"I hate to tell you this, lady, but the older Darnolds is dead. That boy there in the truck is their son, Vernon Darnold."

I recovered my composure as quickly as possible. "Yes, we'd heard about their accident."

At the mention of his name Vernon dismounted from the pickup and stood beside his friend. "You knew my folks?" he asked, leaping to a conclusion I hadn't intended. He was of slight build, and his deep brown eyes tilted pleasantly above prominent cheekbones. But a square jaw and thin lips gave his face a pronounced Caucasian aspect.

"Not really. My husband was a family friend."

"I'm Louella Finney, and this is Maggie Gilpin."

Vernon raised his eyebrows and he sounded excited. "Gilpin? You didn't know Dexter Gilpin, did you?"

"She's his widow," Louella told him.

He smiled broadly, then scuffed a toe. He seemed unused to offering condolences. "I sure hated to hear he died, ma'am. Man, I just couldn't believe it when I found out. For an old person he seemed to be in great shape. We was passing through Tulsa on a band trip when we stopped at the D. Q. for lunch. Someone had left a paper on one of the tables, and I just happened to see Dexter's, uh... Mr. Gilpin's picture."

"You sound like you knew him fairly well," said Louella.

"Oh, sure. He knew our folks when they were all in Korea. After my folks died he used to come by to help my sister with our taxes and stuff. She thought the world and all of him. You ladies have just got to stop and say hello to her."

In less than ten minutes the boys had finished changing the tire. After Vernon and his friend had secured the spare and lifted the flat into the trunk, Vernon insisted we follow them to the Darnold farm.

I protested, "We won't intrude. We'll come back when she's expecting us."

"Jody won't mind. She'll want to see you. Except for the neighbors we don't usually see people who knew our folks." He turned to the other boy. "We've got enough time to show them where I live before the others get here. You mind going back with me?"

"We were just out for a drive," I said. "The flat is going to make us very late getting home."

"You're this close. It won't take a minute to drive in and say, hello."

I was searching for a tactful response when Louella said, "Oh, Maggie, we might as well just drop by to say hello. We don't have to stay."

The boys headed for their truck as if they'd heard a starter's pistol, and I had to scramble to keep up with Louella.

"My clothes look as if I pulled them from the hamper," I said, as we followed the pickup.

Louella kept the Continental well back as gravel sprayed from their tires, then mixed in a plume of dust.

"I look a mess."

"Put your wig back on, dear."

But there seemed no point in wearing a wig now that Vernon knew I was Dexter's widow. I settled for removing the rubber bands and running a brush through my wild locks. I took a packet of sealed, treated cloths from my purse and wiped my hands. It made little difference.

"There's lotion in my purse," Louella said.

I decided the lotion felt good, but I needed industrial strength hand cleanser.

"What you need to do," said Louella, "once you've cleaned your hands real well, is take some petroleum jelly and just slather it on. Then put a pair of rubber gloves on top of that, and sleep that way every night for about a week. I have to do that sometimes when I mess up my hands from gardening."

I didn't say so, but to me the cure sounded worse than the disease.

Louella drove carelessly over the bumps and ruts, risking a broken tie rod or punctured fuel tank. As we bounced along she fished into her purse with one hand and removed a lipstick. While driving she applied makeup, alternately looking at the road and the mirror. I wondered how she kept from smearing "Shimmering Ruby Passion" outside her lined lips.

There seemed to be no way of avoiding my first meeting with Dexter's daughter, and it occurred to me we would have little privacy. Apparently Vernon did not know of Dexter's relationship to Jo Ann, and it wasn't my place to tell him.

"We'll have to be careful what we say in front of Vernon," I told Louella.

Instead of meeting Jo Ann while Louella accompanied me, I wished I could merely say to my friend, *Thanks for helping me look for Dexter's daughter for the past two weeks, and now that I've found her, would you mind if I took your car for a private visit and you just wait for me here by the side of the road?* I wondered if Louella had considered the awkwardness of the situation.

If only we hadn't run into Vernon, it would have been a simple matter to drive anonymously by the Gilpin farm, then head back to Redbud. We'd raise a little dust, maybe draw a few stares from farm windows, but I'd still be able to investigate Jo Ann's background further before our meeting. This was certainly not the intimate, controlled introduction I'd planned for myself and Dexter's daughter. A delicate situation which would require all the tact and diplomacy I could manage seemed headed for a Keystone Kops fiasco.

Twenty-Two

"I think," I started to say, "you should let me—"

"Oh, look," said Louella. "The mailbox says 'Darnold.' It's so faded, no wonder we missed it." She followed the pickup into the long, graveled drive.

"If you like, Louella, you may wait in the car. I mean, I'll understand if you don't want to get involved in something this... this shabby."

"And miss the excitement? Don't be silly, Maggie. I can't wait to see what Jo Ann looks like."

I had suspected Louella wanted to be a part of the reunion, but I never intended to include her. Now I had lost my last opportunity for privacy.

The house sat on a gentle rise. A large, unpainted barn lay far behind the house. Hollies broke the expanse of deciduous shrubs next to white clapboard walls of a two-story residence. A crude carport, several vehicles wide, stood nearby. We pulled to a stop behind a time-worn tractor, next to the pickup.

Vernon leaned across his friend and yelled, "We're supposed to meet some other guys down by the creek and we don't want to be late. I'll just run inside and tell Jody you're here."

Vernon ran to the house and took the back porch steps two at a time. The door slammed behind him. I imagined him telling his sister, "You remember that nice old gentleman who was stationed with Dad in Korea—the one who used to help you with the books? His name was Dexter Gilpin, remember? Well, I ran into his widow and her friend and I talked them into meeting you. They're out in the drive right now."

Her reaction would be one of shock. She would question him and learn the details of our chance meeting. Then tentatively, shyly, expectantly, she would make her way toward us where Vernon would, in his awkward manner, introduce us.

But the boy stayed inside only a few seconds before re-emerging through the back door, slamming it, then racing back to the truck.

"If I don't get home before you leave, it was nice meeting you," he yelled.

"Nice meeting you," I called as the truck spun its wheels and backed quickly onto the road.

The boys had hardly left the drive when a black Labrador bounded from the house, the fur of his ruff erect and his teeth bared. He barked furiously.

"Son of a bitch," yelled Louella. "Maggie, don't open the door!"

But, even as she spoke, I gently nudged the dog back with the car door. "Maverick," I said, almost hoping I hadn't guessed correctly, "is that you, boy?"

Perplexity flashed across the Lab's dark eyes, and he stood uncertainly a few seconds more. Then he tucked his tail between his legs, flattened his ears in embarrassment, and whined his apologies.

I stepped from the car and tried to protect myself from the joy of our reunion. "Mav, you old fake," I said. "Oh, you sweet boy, I'm glad to see you."

"You know that dog?" asked Louella.

"Since he was a pup. He used to belong to Don and Lori," I said, trying not to be toppled into the driveway. Chet's pediatrician had convinced them the baby was allergic to dogs, and Lori had reluctantly agreed to part with the animal. Dexter had volunteered to find a home for Maverick with "a business acquaintance who lives in the country." Lori had been depressed for weeks, but Dexter had assured her Maverick was happy in a wonderful new home.

Was there no end to my husband's treachery? Maverick had been my idea. After obtaining Don's permission, I'd shopped for a puppy with a perfect pedigree and brought him home to keep until we could give him to Lori for Christmas. In the intervening days I had cradled his soft body, answered his frightened whimpers, trained him to puddle on newspaper, comforted him on his first trip to the vet, and then Dexter and I had driven to Tulsa and given the Lab to our daughter's family. Now he ate crumbs from *her* table, slept at the foot of *her* bed.

While I petted Maverick his present owner arrived from the house, a leash in her hand. Her long hair was smoothed back from her face and caught at the neck by a barrette. As she bent to snap a lead on Maverick, her ponytail fell across a shoulder, and I caught the fragrance of scented shampoo mingled with perfume which might have been *L'air du Tempes*. She wore jeans no larger than size five and had topped them with a silk navy shirt and a jean jacket. If her smile had matched the radiance of her eyes, flawless skin, and delicate bone structure, she would have been beautiful. Absent any mirth or hint of civility, I could tell only that her features were classic and harmoniously proportioned.

Without glancing at us she gave the animal's chain collar a quick jerk. He yelped as she pulled him from me. "Sit," she told him. He obeyed quickly, raising brown eyes to me for sympathy.

I mentally cringed at the rough treatment, swallowing objections with the bile that rose from my stomach.

Jo Ann turned and met my gaze. Her expression was not inscrutable. I could read malice in it.

I cleared my throat. "I'm Maggie Gil—"

"I know who you are, Mrs. Gilpin." She stood with arms akimbo, still holding the leash. "And I see you've brought reinforcements with you."

Louella had come around the car and stood beside me. "I'm Louella Finney. I've been looking forward to meeting you, Jo... Miss Darnold." Louella's offered hand made no contact, and she withdrew it.

Jo Ann gave Louella only a cursory glance, then turned to me. "You were talking to my brother."

"He changed a flat tire for us. He—"

"What did you tell him?"

"Nothing. I thought you and I should talk before we tell anyone else about your relationship to Dexter."

She relaxed her squared shoulders, but only slightly. "I never dreamed you would come to see me here," she hissed. "I thought you might write or contact me through your lawyer, but I am amazed you have the gall to invite yourself to my home."

I felt my face grow hot. I should have realized our lawyer had been among those keeping Dexter's secret. For now I pushed that thought aside and tried to explain. "I apologize for dropping in on you unannounced. Please believe me—I had no intention of coming here today, but your brother insisted."

Louella tried to explain. "When he and his friend changed our flat, I told him our names, so he put two and two together about Maggie being Dexter's wife. Vernon seemed to think we were friends of your parents, although I assure you we didn't tell him that."

My heart pounded. I realized how much I had counted on liking Jo Ann and on her liking me. She was sister to Gil and Lori. She was my step-daughter. She was a part of Dexter. Iron-willed determination could not keep tears of disillusionment from the corners of my eyes.

"What are you two doing in Miracle Creek? Were you spying on me?"

Louella looked at me sheepishly and shrugged. With great effort I coaxed my face into what I hoped would appear to be a friendly and confident smile. "There has been so much secrecy, but I think the time has come for complete candor. After I learned Dexter is your father, I wanted to know something about you."

"I'm all for candor." She spat the words. "In all candor you have no rights where my family and I are concerned. And in all candor your curiosity about Dexter's Korean bastard strikes me as sleazy and cheap."

I gasped. Even baby jackals have a winsome, cuddly quality, and the vulnerable school child I'd seen in a photograph had apparently matured into a virago.

I took a deep breath. "You're wrong, Jo Ann. Dexter was my husband, and we loved each other very much. He thought you and I could be friends, and that's the reason I wanted to meet you. And to see if you had any plans to meet Lori and

Gil." She started to interrupt. "Please, let me finish. It took weeks to accept the fact you were an important part of his life, but once I came to terms with Dexter's… with his affair with your mother, I thought you might be someone worth knowing. His other children are."

Having said my speech, I turned and bolted toward the car.

Jo Ann stood, holding Maverick's lead, as Louella slid behind the wheel of the Continental. As the car rolled slowly backward I saw Jo Ann reach to pet the dog. She kept her back straight as she sat on her heels, her angry gaze fixed on us. When we were nearly to the road, Maverick lifted his head in a mournful cry. Jo Ann wrapped her slender arms around him and stroked his neck. I thought her eyes glistened, and for a moment she seemed about to call us back. Then I decided no such impulse had entered her mind.

I did not fully give into wracking sobs before she stood and turned toward her house. We swung onto Mulberry Road.

By the time I'd finished crying, Louella had found the highway, and we were headed toward Redbud. We drove in silence for a while, then she asked, "You hungry yet?"

"Starved."

"Yeah. A good crying jag always makes me hungry too." She located a truck stop. We sat in a corner booth and ordered coffee and burgers while Patsy Cline sang, "I Go to Pieces."

In a booth on the other side of the room sat a shriveled gnome dressed in jeans, cowboy shirt and roughouts. "His hat brim's wide enough to shade Texas," whispered Louella. "Have you ever listened to guys like him on the C.B.? Who'd ever believe quiet little squirts like him know so many words for human reproductive parts and functions."

I thought she sounded wistful. "I've had enough problems today," I told her. "If you make a move on anybody, I'll bean you with an ashtray and drive home by myself."

"But in person I'll bet he blushes when he talks about jack-asses, or canine bitches, or door knockers, or hot buns, and I'm sure he calls female felines mama kitties because he wouldn't want to waste a good word like pussy."

"Louella—"

"I bet he knows twelve words for female breasts, and not one of them is breast."

"Louella—"

"Bet I can get him to ask for my phone number."

"Don't you dare!"

"Just kidding. But at least you don't look like you're about to cry now. It's been gloom and doom since we left the Darnold farm."

The waitress brought our meal—steaming hot burgers shiny with grease and reeking of onions, and a tray filled with squirt bottles of mustard, catsup, and mayo to bury them in. "Hope you ladies enjoy your dinner," she said.

"I'm supposed to be watching my cholesterol count," said Louella as she devoured a bite of the sandwich. "But lordy, this is good."

The coffee tasted bitter—probably the last in the pot. I added water to it and thought about how the day had gone. "I'm sorry," I said. "I didn't mean to get you involved."

She rested her burger on the plate and looked at me. "Maggie, you haven't deserved any of this."

"How can you be so sure? Maybe if I hadn't been so textbook proper and perfect, Dexter would have told me about his affair, and we could have worked this out long ago."

"Why is it women always take the blame for things? You're not the one who screwed around, so why are you feeling guilty now?"

"Because I've made such a mess of meeting Jo Ann. And I was—disappointed. She wasn't what I expected at all."

"Disappointed? Disappointed?" She sounded incredulous. "I'd have been mad as hell," she said between sips of hot coffee. "What gave that little flower child license to talk to you the way she did? A skunk in a phone booth would have been a lot more cordial."

I thought Louella talked too loudly. But when I glanced at the nearest booth, no one seemed to have taken notice of her. Maybe they were all intent on Merle Haggard singing "Okie from Muskogee." The waitress refilled our cups.

Louella stirred two packets of sugar into her coffee. "What are you going to do now, Maggie?"

"Go home and take a hot bath. Gil and Peggy will be at my house next week for Thanksgiving. I'll need to plan my menu and make a grocery list. Tomorrow I'll go to church. On Monday and Tuesday, I'll clean my house. I'll bake the turkey and pump—"

"I was talking about Jo Ann."

"I'm going to do my best to forget her."

"Knowing you, it can't be done."

"What can't be done?"

"Forgetting Jo—oh, that's cute. What if someone tells your kids about her?"

I stared at Louella in horror. "You wouldn't!"

"I didn't mean me." She bit her lip. "Maggie, who else knows about Dexter being Jo Ann's father?"

She had a point. Lester Quinn and his office staff knew, and Jo Ann's allusion to our lawyer made me think he knew too. I had told J. Ronal Patrick. Jo Ann or her parents could have told people. Any of Dexter's buddies who served in Korea with him knew. Maybe Dexter had confided in Orin or some of our other friends.

I shook my head. "I suppose everyone in Redbud knows all about it. They're probably snickering at me for being such a stupid, trusting hausfrau."

"No they're not. I saw Flory and Amelia at least once a month all the time I lived in Tulsa. They never said a word, so you can bet there's been no gossip. But just because it isn't in the open yet doesn't mean Gil and Lori should be kept in the dark."

"Their half-sister is so... hateful."

"Hm. She didn't exactly throw her arms around us. But mad as I am about the way she talked to you, Maggie, I guess I do understand her reaction. We did kind of sneak up on her."

"I know, Louella. My plan was—after you and I learned what we could about her—to write to her and explain things— how Dexter wanted me to get in touch with her. Then we landed in her front yard like an invading army."

"Too late to change that."

"Exactly. And I guess I would have understood a little hostility, but she didn't even listen when you told her about the flat tire and about Vernon insisting we follow him home."

"You're going to contact her again." Louella spoke as if it were a foregone conclusion.

"When hogs fly."

"As soon as you've had time to think about it, you'll want to try again. Maybe you should hire a lawyer to act as a go-between—to set up a meeting."

"I bet Dexter's Tulsa lawyer knew all about it from the beginning. I wouldn't let him represent me on a traffic ticket now."

We finished the burgers and returned to the car. For half an hour we traveled through the darkening countryside in silence. I could think of nothing but the animosity in Jo Ann's words, the fire in her eyes when she'd accused me of prurient curiosity about Dexter's "Korean bastard."

Finally I broke the silence. "Louella, if she hadn't upset me to the point where I couldn't think, I'd have remembered to tell her how ridiculous she looked at the funeral."

"It would have been a hell of an ice breaker."

"You should have seen her. She must have worn her brother's clothes, but she looked bizarre. Just ask anyone who was there."

"Maggie, Redbud would still be talking if she hadn't disguised herself. Imagine—a young, attractive woman shows up at Dexter's funeral, distraught, sobbing. People would have concluded Dexter and she were having an affair. I think she did your family a favor by coming as a man, even if she wasn't very good at it."

"But to have dressed so outrageously... Lori told me she saw half the people at Dexter's funeral whispering."

"Look on the bright side. It wasn't Dexter's lover."

"If there's a bright side to all this, I haven't found it." I heard the quaver in my voice again. "Did you see how she treated Maverick? Lori would be devastated if she knew someone treated her dog like that."

"He looked well fed and happy."

"Please stop trying to make me feel better. I'm sure Maverick is miserable with her."

"Have it your way. She's probably fattening him up so she can serve doggie stew."

"That's disgusting."

"I hear Koreans eat dogs."

"Louella, please!" Thinking about Maverick brought tears to my eyes. I reached into the glove box and delved among the maps and documents for another tissue. I withdrew an empty box.

"There's a little packet way in the back there," said Louella.

While rummaging in the compartment I again touched a small metal object. It had not penetrated my consciousness before, but now, like a reader of Braille, I noted its shape and raised design.

As we sped down the highway I invented logical excuses for finding a spoon in the car: Louella found it on the ground at a picnic site; she bought it to add to her set of silverware; it was not a spoon at all, but an esoteric tool integral to the care of the Lincoln. While she concentrated on passing a semi on the two-lane highway, I folded several tissues around the object, and shoved it into my purse.

I intended to examine the mystery object as soon as I was alone. If I was mistaken in my suspicions, I would return it to Louella's glove compartment. If the glove compartment were locked, I would place it on the floor where it would appear to have fallen innocently. I reasoned no one would be hurt, and my mind would be relieved of all doubt.

And if I did recognize it? The idea of Louella stealing one of Elsie's sterling coffee spoons was too painful to contemplate. I disliked the cynical turn my thoughts had taken. Louella had never given me reason to distrust her.

But that wasn't quite so. My cloisonné brooch was still missing, and as I rode in the silent car, I mentally catalogued Louella's acquisitions in the months of our friendship. I thought of the scarf she had supposedly purchased the day she left the restaurant and told me to meet her in the mall parking lot. In recent weeks she had acquired two new eelskin purses, a half-dozen pairs of earrings, a new Seiko watch, an Ann Tyler novel, and several Vogue patterns I had seen her admire on our shopping trips. Had her purchases at the register matched her acquisitions? Most disquieting to me was the possibility I had been used as a foil for her mischief.

Elsie's attitude toward Louella began to make sense. And those Scriptures Elsie had given Louella to read at Circle—I hadn't memorized them, but the gist of one was fixed firmly in my memory: The thief must stop stealing and begin using her hands for honest work.

We approached Redbud, slowing to thirty-five miles per hour when we reached Main Street. "Maggie," said Louella, her forehead wrinkled in concern, "No one can tell you how to feel or what to do. But I know you well enough to know you won't be happy until you've done everything you can to follow Dexter's wishes."

"Is that what you'd do?"

In the light from my porch I saw her smile. "I'm not a great intellect, Maggie, but I have learned something in therapy. You can't be happy and angry at the same time, so I've learned how to forgive... or at least, I'm learning."

Dear God, I thought, *please don't let her be a thief. I didn't see how I could accommodate anymore disillusionment.*

When we parted, Louella said, "I'll see you next week."

"At choir practice, if not before," I said. We wished each other a happy holiday before she drove off.

As soon as I unwrapped the spoon, I had no doubt it belonged to Elsie.

It was not possible to confide in those with whom I most wanted to share this information—Dexter was dead and Louella was guilty. Elsie and Orin were spending Thanksgiving week with Candace and her family.

I could call Lori, but my children wouldn't give it the weight I felt it deserved.

Only one friend would be available to comfort me. I thought he might understand how sad and angry I was over Louella's treachery.

Twenty-Three

Ronal seemed surprised to see me in his office—I had already worked my scheduled two days at the nursing home that week.

"You look busy," I said.

"Not that busy. Come on in." He held a chair for me.

"Sorry, but I didn't come here to discuss literature."

"I don't think we have a prescribed list of topics, Mrs. Gilpin." His eyes were merry and his face crinkled with pleasure. I found his good humor irritating. "Let's throw caution to the wind," he said. "What's on your mind?"

I sighed, wondering where to begin. "I don't know why I tell you the things I do."

"I'm a trained listener."

"Is that what I'm doing? Spilling my guts to a trained analyst? Getting free advice? Let's hope you're better at effecting cures than Louella's shrink is."

"Maybe my listening skills help make me a better friend."

"At least if I paid you, you'd be bound by some sort of professional confidentiality."

A hurt expression replaced the cheerful look on his face. I always seemed to be unnecessarily rude to Ron, my "friendly" jibes carrying an edge. "I'm sorry. I know I can trust you."

"Nothing you say to me will ever leave this room without your permission, Maggie. I give that guarantee to my clients up front."

"I'm sorry," I said again, but he wasn't going to let me off with a simple apology.

"My friends seem to know it without asking."

I could feel my neck and face grow warm with embarrassment.

He walked to the door and closed it, then returned to his desk.

I said, "I used to be better at trusting people."

Like an August afternoon cloud burst, his anger vanished and he smiled. "Forget it, Maggie. What's wrong?"

He sat in his leather, overstuffed chair while I told him about meeting Jo Ann, and about Louella, and about finding Elsie's spoon in Louella's car. When I'd finished, he looked across his desk with a thoughtful expression, not saying a word.

Finally, I said, "Well?"

"I'm trying to take it all in. You've had quite a week."

"If you make fun of me—"

"I sure as hell am not amused by your pain."

"Well, that's something," I said.

The shiny glass reflected his hand tapping a pencil. "Why did you want to meet Jo Ann?"

I shrugged. "Curiosity." I stared at the garden beyond his window. All leaves were gone from the althea bush, and its bare limbs looked as dead as our town on a Sunday afternoon. "No, it's more than curiosity," I admitted. "She's half-sister to my children, and they may someday want to meet her. I thought... if I could find out more about her... I thought I might be able to help them understand."

He looked at me, those intense eyes peering deep. "And. ..."

"And she's Dexter's daughter. His flesh and blood. Maybe I'm perverted, but I had to see her for myself."

"Another link to him?"

"Yes."

He nodded. "And Louella?"

"I don't think I can ever trust her again."

"Because?"

"Because I know she stole my brooch."

"Assuming you're correct, why do you think she did it?"

"You're the one with the doctorate in psychology. I thought you might have some ideas."

"Why don't you ask her about it?"

"Oh, I will. But I hoped you would know how I should go about it."

"That depends on how much you value her as a person and a friend."

Psycho-babble, I thought, *and not very helpful. I didn't try to hide my disappointment.* "I could get more answers and advice from Elsie Wickfielder. She'd at least have a few platitudes or something she'd heard on a talk show."

He lowered his voice, but his words were sudden and angry about the edges. "What do you want from me, Maggie?"

His question jarred me. "I don't know."

We each stood, and he came close. The small space between us was electric, and my gaze never left his face. I thought how comforting it would be to lose myself in his arms, to let his embrace shut the world from my consciousness, but I stayed rooted in place.

He sighed and looked beyond me to the bookcase along the wall. "Hang in there, Maggie."

I followed his gaze to a picture of Helen seated on a sofa, surrounded by four of the Patrick grandchildren. My shoulder just brushed his arm as I pivoted and pushed the door open.

I remembered how he could watch me through his window to the parking lot, and my steps became heavy and self-conscious. I was home before I noticed the tail of my jacket, caught and trailing in the car door.

"What do you want from me, Maggie?"

The words echoed in my thoughts, and my mind could not deny the answer. I wanted J. Ronal Patrick to kiss me passionately, deeply, and for a long time. This wanting had nothing to do with vengeance for Dexter's betrayal. It was a physical yearning born of friendship and proximity. I wanted to succumb to flesh-melting embraces and the intimate, satisfying pleasures of sex, to welcome Ron's hands caressing my breasts, his whispers soft against my ear, to nest against his body in sleep.

There was no point in lying to myself. I was consumed by dizzying lust for a married man. Perhaps I had even fallen in love with him. The self-revelation amazed but did not shame me. After all, I reasoned, Maggie Gilpin still controlled her life. How could my secret wants hurt anyone?

Louella was wrong about my contacting Jo Ann again. I had given it a shot, now it was up to Jo Ann. Once I'd unburdened myself to Ron, I barely thought of her. Thinking about him was another matter. Like a tune that persists in the mind, ideas went round, repeating and building energy until I could barely contain them. "Hang in there, Maggie," may not have sounded like a summons to J. Ronal Patrick's bed, but I knew, *knew* his interest in me exceeded friendship. For now, I felt desirable and worthwhile, and I wanted to savor the pleasure of my feelings. Reproach was something at the very edge of my soul, and I was able to ignore it.

I sang as I cleaned house in preparation for the holiday visit of Gil's family. Their arrival brought me abruptly to solid ground. With great effort, I pushed away all thoughts of Ron. I was a miser hiding treasure against the time it could be retrieved and enjoyed.

Skip chose Thanksgiving Day to take his first steps. He was holding onto a coffee table when he let go and toddled over to Peggy, laughing as he lurched into her arms.

Gil opened an album and found a picture of his father taken when Dexter, Senior was two years old. In the sepia-toned portrait, a little boy wearing a cowboy hat and chaps sat astride a Shetland pony. And he looked like the child in my living room.

Peggy wrinkled her nose in mock disgust and said, "Maggie, we don't count for much against the Gilpin DNA."

"Gilpin DNA," I repeated, my thoughts diverted from the comfort of my family. *The Gilpin charm had somehow eluded Jo Ann,* I thought. Over the sweetness of Gil's family, Dexter's betrayal loomed more monstrous than ever.

"Yes," said Peggy. "He's even got his grandpa's flat feet."

Skip laughed as his mother tickled his toes, then Peggy handed the squirming child to me. A flash of light from Gil's Polaroid caught us in a candid embrace on the sofa.

"I'll put this one on the mantle for now, Mom," he said.

Still holding the baby I stood to see the picture better. Dim images defined themselves, became a woman and her grandchild. The scene had played before. I stared at it in fascination. The blurry face was no longer Helen Patrick's, but my own. I lifted Skip, turned him toward me and kissed his round tummy until he squealed with laughter.

I was still thinking about the picture when Helen Patrick phoned the next afternoon.

"Ronnie and I are having a small get-together, not tomorrow, but the next Saturday, in our home. We'd love to have you come."

I stuttered, and my voice sounded whiny and uncertain. "I... uh, what time, Mrs. Patrick?"

"Please call me Helen. I feel as if I already know you. We'll dine at seven, but please come earlier for cocktails. Sixish, I think. I'm looking forward to finally meeting you."

Oh, so formal. Cocktails and dinner. I wondered what one should wear to dinner at the home of her fantasy lover and his wife. I almost called Louella to get her advice, then remembered I wouldn't be relying on her fashion sense ever again.

An image of Scarlett O'Hara in adulterous red popped into my mind.

Twenty-Four

A day after the Wickfielder's return, Elsie sat in my kitchen drinking coffee and eating a slice of pumpkin pie.

"What did you put in here?" she asked, "Thyme?" She sniffed the pie as if Betty Crocker's reputation depended on Elsie's judgment. "Would you like my pumpkin pie recipe? It's the only one Orin will eat."

"Put some more whipped cream on it. I don't think I used anything more exotic than nutmeg."

I sat opposite her, the top button of my jeans loose under a big shirt to accommodate evidence I'd celebrated a Bacchanalian feast. The problem with my pumpkin pie and the rest of my holiday cooking was not the way it tasted.

Elsie looked trim as ever in red pants and matching tee which she'd painted in tones of mustard and turquoise. I stared briefly at what may have been a football with wings, took a deep breath, reached into my purse, and offered her the spoon.

Her eyes brightened. She took the delicately sculpted implement, turned it over and examined it the way a new mother counts her baby's toes and fingers. She sucked her lower lip, then peered at me through the upper lenses of her bifocals.

"Where did she hide it, Maggie?"

"Where did who hide it?"

"You know whom. Mrs.-Doctor Louella Finney, that's whom." She spat Louella's name as if it tasted sour.

"In the glove compartment of her car. When did you figure out it was Louella?"

Elsie stuck the spoon into her purse and folded her arms. Very smug. "Once a shoplifter, always a shoplifter."

"You knew she shoplifted?"

She didn't seem to notice how outraged I felt because of her keeping me in the dark. "The first time I knew anything about it, we were in the fifth grade. I saw her when she got busted at T. G. & Y. She had two vials of Blue Waltz perfume, a tube of pink Tangee lipstick, and some socks for her Sparkle Plenty doll. Chief Johnston and the store manager caught her on the sidewalk with the goods, but of course the Watsons had it hushed up."

I couldn't decide which I found most improbable— Louella's choice of toiletries or an image of her with a doll.

"Good grief, Elsie, that happened years ago."

"And you'd think she would have learned. But I've heard rumors her late doctor-husband bailed her out more than once."

"A woman like Louella? She could afford almost anything she wanted. Why steal?"

Elsie seized the opportunity to instruct me. "Jenny or Montel, I don't remember which one, had an expert on once. She said kleptomania was sort of a cry for attention, or the way some people reacted when their nerves were shot, or some such nonsense. And I seem to recall it might have had something to do with sex too. None of those educated liberals know how to call a thief a thief. Everyone in prison comes from what they call a dysfunctional family, and it's all their mother's fault."

"You're telling me Louella has a psychological problem?"

"You could call it that. I call it by its real name. She's a thief."

"Dammit, Elise, you should have told me."

Elsie shook her head in disgust. "Chicken spit, Maggie. As thick as the two of you were, you would have thought I was just jealous. I was waiting until I had some proof. I bet if we searched her house and her car, we'd find your brooch and your thimble too."

"Not my thimble. I found it in the bottom of my sewing tote." I took a deep swallow of coffee. "So, Louella stole my brooch."

"Does the sun rise in the east?"

I knew where the sun rose, but it was painful to admit Louella had stolen from me.

"Maggie, we ought to call the law."

I heard no hint of irony in her voice. "Now wait a minute. You wouldn't even accuse Louella to *me* without proof. She's a friend, Elsie. Maybe there's another explanation. We could be wrong." I thought again of the night Dexter had given me the brooch, and felt an empty place made worse by the possibility of losing Louella's friendship.

"We'd look like fools if we're wrong. Louella wouldn't speak to us ever again, and I wouldn't blame her."

"I'm not wrong, Maggie."

Schlegg waltzed into the kitchen, demanding to be stroked. He settled on my lap. "She has been a good friend, Elsie. And you used to like her too. If she is taking things, maybe she could be helped by counseling."

"She's on her third or fourth therapist now. None of them have helped so far as I can see."

So much, I thought, *for my promise of confidentiality about Louella's visits to a psychologist.*

"If you knew… if you knew she took things, how come you didn't warn me?"

"I thought she'd outgrown that kleptomania business, but Orin's aunt has a brother-in-law whose nephew is on the force in Tulsa, and he arrested Louella a week or two before she moved back to Redbud."

The corner of Elsie's mouth leaked a bit of pumpkin, and I had to resist the urge to look away. She must have seen my expression, because she dabbed at the corner of her lips with a napkin before continuing.

"All the rest I heard from Flory. Albert told her, and I guess he heard about it from his cousin who used to have his offices next door to Dr. Finney."

"Unimpeachable sources."

"You're the one who found my spoon."

I dumped Schlegg gently onto the floor and poured refills of coffee. "Are any of the other girls missing anything?"

"Let me see. There's Flory and Mattie and Sharla. Some of the others were missing stuff, but they found it. Flory can't find the key to her mantle clock, but then Flory can't find her car keys half the time."

"And Mattie and Sharla?"

Elsie sucked her lower lip, savoring the moment, enjoying the opportunity to educate me. "Mattie's missing a bottle of perfume Andy gave her a few years ago. *Poison*, or something."

I tried to outwait her, but plainly, I wasn't going to hear more without asking.

"And Sharla?"

"Sharla's looking for a milk glass salt cellar. It belonged to her great-aunt. She thought one of the kids might have carried it to the sandbox, but it's not there."

It could be anywhere, I thought.

"Louella took it. Trust me."

"Anyone else?"

"Not that I've heard so far."

I had the feeling she had canvassed the other members of Second Thursday Circle. She set her cup on the table and looked at me the way Mickey Rooney looked when he reported his idea for a musical review in the old barn.

"Say, Maggie, didn't Louella give you a key to her house?"

Elsie had been with me when Louella had entrusted me to water her African violets for two weeks while she was out of town. I bet it had taken supernatural will power not to mention that key earlier.

"I gave it back as soon as she returned from her vacation."

Elsie's face sagged with disappointment. "Oh. I just thought if you still had it, we might get someone to lure her away. Then we could take a look around to see what we could find."

"You would actually do that?"

"Maggie, she's a thief."

I shook my head. Had I been living in a dream world? In years past I hardly knew what treachery meant, now I felt as if I were drowning in it.

I said, "Even if I still had the key, I wouldn't want to sneak around. If I were going to accuse Louella, I'd give her the opportunity to defend herself. I'd talk to her face to face."

"Today?"

I heard my dryer buzz. "Excuse me. I need to fold my clothes so they won't wrinkle."

Elsie nearly overturned a kitchen chair as she hurried to my laundry room. She returned from the dryer and laid an armful of clothes on the table. In moments she had my linens folded in haphazard stacks.

I looked at the mess she'd made and said, "Thanks."

"Get your purse, Maggie. Hurry up."

"What are you talking about, Elsie?"

"I'm going to confront Louella, and you better go with me so I don't do something we'll both regret." She pulled me through my back door and urged me into her car. Then we sped across town to the Watson mansion.

Elsie wheeled her Buick onto the graveled drive and parked near Louella's front door.

On the way over I had tried to formulate what I would say to Louella. *My hand slipped innocently into your glove box, and I felt this suspicious object. I decided to take it, in case it was a spoon you had stolen from Elsie. And sure enough it was. Since we're such close friends I thought you might be able to explain yourself to me, and I'll try to explain to you why I burgled your glove compartment.*

I didn't like the way Elsie had painted me into a corner, yet I did have an overwhelming curiosity to get to the bottom of things.

I trailed Elsie up the porch steps. "I don't think this is a good idea. Since we're already here let's just invite Louella to dinner this evening. We can all three drive to the mall and take in a movie. My treat. Then maybe we can somehow work this thing into the conversation."

I might as well not have spoken.

"I can't wait to see her face when we tell her we know what she's been doing," said Elsie. She cranked the bell by the leaded glass door. We waited a few minutes, and she cranked the bell again. "She's here," said Elsie. "I saw her Lincoln in the carport."

"Maybe she can't hear us," I suggested.

"Maggie, that bell sounds like a fog horn in a stock pond." She tried the bell one more time. Then we walked down the steps and around the house to the back door. "The back door's open," she said, pushing into the kitchen.

"I don't think we should go in uninvited."

"What if she's been attacked and she's tied up and she's listening to the doorbell and waiting for us to rescue her? She might even have fallen and be unconscious. You'd feel terrible if she died, wouldn't you?" Elsie walked around the kitchen, picking up objects and examining them.

"What do you think you're doing?"

"Looking for clues, Maggie. Come on."

As we approached the stairs I heard an unfamiliar noise, like the sound of a soft waterfall.

"She's got her whirlpool tub going," Elsie explained. "Come on."

"But if she's in her bathtub—"

"She might have drowned. Come on."

Elsie tiptoed up the stairs, and I followed. "Louella," I called.

Elsie turned and gave me a withering stare. "Sh!"

"Well, we don't want to sneak up on her."

"If she's having a heart attack and you yell, you could flat kill her."

"Balderdash." I called Louella's name again, but the only response was the sound of roiling water.

I had been upstairs in the Watson House only once, when Louella's grandmother had allowed it to be part of a historical tour. As we topped the stairs and made our way into a spacious bedroom, Elsie walked slowly and on tiptoe. Our eyes were drawn to the bay windows, draped in satin and topped with wide cornices. Elsie tripped over the stand of a stationary bicycle and careened into a camel back trunk at the foot of a four poster. She looked shocked, put her fingers to her lips, and said, "Sh!"

A door stood part way open into a tiled bathroom. I couldn't see the tub, but the noises from the pump and the agitated water were loud. Elsie stooped to finger the satin spread. Her head brushed the bed canopy as she raised up. She crossed the room to begin examining objects on a mirrored vanity table, and I came to stand behind her. My cloisonné brooch rested on velvet in an open jewelry box. She lifted it from the velvet, turned and took my hand, then closed my fingers around the cool metal.

Beyond the bathroom door, almost lost in the noise of the whirling water, I heard Louella vocalizing as she exercised her soprano voice to strains of the "Hallelujah Chorus."

Twenty-Five

Shimmering mauve pillows on Louella's bed had at first seemed lovely, fashionable. Liver, I now thought, fighting queasiness. They reminded me of raw liver. The Victorian decor seemed cloyingly sentimental and false.

A woman I liked and admired had stolen from me, had betrayed my trust, had thought so little of our friendship, she had robbed me of a precious treasure. Until I held the proof in my hand, I had dealt with the growing conviction of Louella's treachery only on an intellectual level. Now that I'd been played for a fool, I trembled from head to toe.

"Damn it, Elsie! I thought she was my friend." I fought back tears of anger.

"Get control of yourself, Maggie."

"I didn't truly think she... how can a woman be my friend and still steal from me? I'm so angry, Elsie. Before, I was disappointed. Now, I'm mad as hell."

"We could take your brooch and anything else she might have stolen, and just leave."

"Is that what you want to do?"

"We could take some of her stuff—to pay her back, but I wouldn't want to be a part of that." She sucked her lip thoughtfully. "No. We've caught her red-handed. I think we should confront her with the evidence. Maybe we can shock her into getting reformed." She handed me a tissue from a box on the dresser.

The "Hallelujah Chorus" ended and Louella crooned, "Rudolph the Red-Nosed Reindeer." I wondered how she could have failed to hear us, but I was past caring.

"I still can't believe this." I held my brooch to the light of a Tiffany lamp and found no damage. Fire from the sapphire gleamed against the cobalt blue of the heart. *Almost as blue as your eyes*, Dexter had said.

Thinking of Dexter, and now Louella, I said, "I'm going to have a slogan tattooed onto my forehead: Maggie Gilpin is gullible. Feel free to cheat and lie to her."

"Orin has a joke about that—"

"Great. Now Orin has jokes about how gullible I am."

"It's a joke about a ranch with a long name. They don't have any cows, because the cows die every time they get branded. See, the brand takes off too much of their hide. I don't think your forehead could take all those words."

I doubted the comedian, Bill Dana, could have recognized the story.

Above the noise of the whirlpool, Louella sang, "You'll go down in his-to-ry," then, "Do you hear what I hear?"

"I think I've fallen down a rabbit hole," I said.

"What?"

"I'm having trouble believing this isn't a nightmare."

"You ought to be happy now that you've got your cloisonné pin back," said Elsie, folding her arms. "I still think it would have went good with my Halloween costume."

I squared my shoulders, took a deep breath, marched to the bathroom door, and flung it against the wall stop.

Time seemed to stretch, as perception of a car crash expands the time of breaking glass and flying metal. Louella wore ear phones, their cables linked to a battery operated cassette player on top of a marble vanity. Bubble bath foamed and tumbled as jets spewed from the sides of the tub. A lathery blanket undulated above everything between Louella's jaw and her ankles; she lay with her head resting on an air filled cushion; she had propped her feet on a towel placed on the wide ledge of the tub. In the instant before she saw us, serene satisfaction molded her features. Then, startled, she stopped singing and jerked the ear phones, pulling the entire apparatus to the floor. As she screamed she sat up in the tub, her feet drawing the towel into the bubbles. The sudden displacement splashed and slopped water onto the carpet. Recognition, relief, then surprise washed over her face in quick succession.

"What—what are you two doing in my bathroom?"

Foam slid from her shoulders, revealing her ample cleavage.

"Don't you dare get up naked," Elsie called above the tub's motor.

I flipped a switch, and the only noise left was a tinny sound from the cassette player.

"Maggie, Elsie, what's going on?" Without the noise of the whirlpool, her voice sounded loud. "Is my house on fire? Has something happened to my daughter?"

I put my hand close to her face and opened my fingers to reveal the brooch.

Louella blinked her eyes. At first there seemed to be no recognition. Then she looked at me and leaned back against the tub, her face blanching as white as the old fashioned, porcelain faucet handles.

"Where did you—"

Elsie pointed a finger at Louella. "You know where we found it. How much of that other stuff in your jewelry box is hot? I have a mind to call the sheriff and have him put you in jail."

Louella cowered and slid lower in the tub. I knelt and retrieved the tape player from the floor and turned it off.

"I can explain, Maggie."

I didn't say a word.

"I brought back everything else—Flory's silk scarf—even Amelia's pearl necklace and Lisa's turquoise ring. I don't think Lisa ever missed her ring."

"What about my spoon? I suppose you were going to present it to me in Sunday School," said Elsie.

Louella shook her head, and strands fell from the knot of henna-rinsed hair and collided with the foam at her neck.

"I can't find your spoon, Elsie. I know I put it in my car. I intended to slip it through the mail slot at Orin's plumbing shop, but when I looked for it, it was gone." She looked from me to Elsie, who did not reveal the spoon was safe in her purse. "I tried to order you a new spoon in Tulsa yesterday. It's out of stock, and they have to do a pattern search. But I will replace it. I always return what I take."

Louella didn't seem contrite, she was merely embarrassed.

I was no longer shaking and I made my words come out low and hard. "You weren't hungry. You have money in the bank. And I trusted you, Louella. I trusted you as much as I've ever trusted anyone outside my family. Stealing from strangers is despicable, but what kind of woman steals from her friends?"

Her voice had an edge too, and her gaze was direct. "We have been good friends, haven't we, Maggie? We've shared so many secrets."

Her implied threat fed my anger. "Nothing you could do now would hurt more than the knowledge you sneaked into my home and stole from me. Even after you knew how much that pin meant, you didn't return it."

"Now that you've broken into my house and barged into my bathroom, at least do me the courtesy of hearing me out, Maggie." Her brown eyes were devoid of makeup. All the tiny lines surgery couldn't quite erase stamped her with age, but defiance animated her face. "I would have returned your precious brooch. I tried to several times, but you made it very difficult. I couldn't just waltz into your house and put it back while I was visiting you, because then you'd have known who took it. I was going to return it the next time you had Circle."

I sighed. "And that would have made everything just hunky dory."

"Maggie, you know what's wrong with you? You think you're so damn perfect. Well, I like you…" Her voice grew quavery. "But you're not perfect. And you don't need to look down your nose at me because of my little problem."

"Little problem," I gasped, about the same time as Elsie said, "I don't call your stealing things a little problem."

"I knew she wouldn't understand," Louella said, dismissing Elsie with a toss of her head, "but I thought you could appreciate how much pressure I've been under since Bill died. Without sex and a loving partner to relieve the tension—"

"I don't want to hear this," said Elsie. "There's six dozen widows in town, and half of them are probably horny. You're the only one who steals, Mrs.-Doctor Finney. Your uppity Tulsa friends can call you a kleptomaniac if they like, but in Redbud, Oklahoma, you're nothing but a common thief."

"It's a psychological condition. I can't always help myself. Maggie...."

I thought I heard a hint of apology and regret in her voice, but my reservoir of forgiveness had expired. I shook my head slowly, then turned and headed out the door. "Wait," called Louella. "Please, Maggie, don't go."

I kept walking.

I heard Elsie again tell Louella to keep her naked body submerged. Then she joined me on the stairs. "One of us ought to have played the good cop."

"What?"

"Oh, don't act like you never saw *Law and Order* or *Barney Miller* reruns. You know, Maggie. Good cop, bad cop."

"Are you serious?"

"Well, I felt kind of sorry for her. It must be awful to lose friends like us, both in the same day."

"Elsie, I'm not playing at anything, but you do what you like. Go back and be 'the good cop.' I'm not sure I ever want to see Louella Watson Finney again."

I knew Elsie enjoyed the drama of the occasion, but I wanted to go home. I would replace my pin in its shadow box, find Schlegg so I could cuddle some one or some thing whose love I could count on, and have a good cry. We had driven Elsie's car, so I sat on the landing and waited while she returned to act out her scene with Louella.

Then I heard Elsie shout, "Ye gods and little fishes, Maggie, come quick!"

Louella hadn't done much more than splatter a few drops of blood into her sculpted marble sink. In the early days of his practice, Bill Finney had employed her as his office nurse. I was sure she could have slit her wrists efficiently if she'd wanted to. As it was, she had shown great skill with a scalpel, cutting deep into the flesh, but apparently not stabbing any major vessels. She lost more tears than blood, but I winced at how painful it must have been to have forced the sharp edge so deep into her wrist. She stood there in a velour beach towel, wrapped sarong style, and held her hand over the sink so that she wouldn't stain her carpet. I thought it considerate of her not to embarrass Elsie with nudity.

Elsie yelled, "Call Albert Santos."

"No!" Louella was emphatic. "He will tell everyone in town."

"If you actually bleed to death, or if you become rigid with lockjaw," I asked, "what do you want us to tell the reporter from *The Redbud Examiner?*"

Louella narrowed her reddened eyes. Then sadness replaced the choleric expression, and she shook her head and sighed. "I won't bleed to death. I might need a tetanus shot and a couple of stitches."

Elsie said, "I'll go call Doc Combs. Maybe he hasn't gone to lunch yet."

"No. Not Dr. Combs. I—would you drive me to County Memorial, Maggie?"

"Elsie's car is here. She can drop me at my house before she takes you."

"Maggie, good grief. What if she starts bleeding while I'm driving? You've got to come with us."

Again I met Louella's gaze. She had the grace to blush. "It's okay, Elsie. Maggie doesn't have to go if she doesn't want to."

"If you don't go with us, I'm not driving. We'll just call Albert."

"Okay, okay. I'll ride along. Louella, do you think, in your perilous condition, you would like some help getting dressed?"

"No. I'll wear a front closing bra," she said softly.

"Oh my," said Elsie. "I can see where you'd have trouble reaching around to your back."

"Where are your bandages?" I asked.

I thought it would make us all more comfortable not to have a clear view of Louella's wrist. Elsie helped me cover the wound which most definitely would need stitches.

"Do you think it's safe to leave her by herself while she dresses?" Elsie whispered, as if Louella weren't present.

"Why don't you stay with her, Elsie? Then you won't worry," I said.

But Elsie stood outside the door and kept up a stream of chatter while Louella put on her clothes.

Louella staggered a bit on the way to the car, and she accepted Elsie's offered assistance without a murmur.

"For Pete's sake," I said. "You haven't lost that much blood."

"Sit in the back with her, Maggie. Just in case."

Elsie drove ten miles above the speed limit, and we rode in near silence. Unsympathetic as I was I couldn't help noticing Louella did indeed seem to be in distress. A bluish tinge outlined her mouth, while the rest of her face was extraordinarily pale.

"I can't seem to get my breath," she said.

By the time we pulled into the emergency drive, I was concerned. I went inside for a wheelchair, and a nurse accompanied me to the car.

"I'm having a heart attack," Louella told her.

"You can't be having a heart attack," Elsie said. "You only jabbed yourself in the wrist."

"Let's just take her inside, and I'll get the doctor," said the nurse, as she eased Louella into the chair.

Twenty-Six

Before they whisked her away Louella gasped, "Call my daughter." There wasn't time for any of us to say more. Hospital personnel helped her onto a gurney, and she disappeared behind large swinging doors.

I remembered Elsie's admonition of a few hours ago, "You'd feel terrible if she died, wouldn't you?" A chill swept over me, shaking my shoulders and raising goose bumps.

There had been an accident on the freeway, and the relatives and friends of the victims filled the waiting room. Elsie and I stood in the hall.

"There's a lounge on the third floor, down the hall from the Cardiac Care Unit," said the nurse. "You'd probably be more comfortable up there, and there's a phone in the hall you can use. I'll have one of the doctors speak to you after they've done the work-up." She handed us a bag containing Louella's purse and clothes, and told us how to get to the elevator.

We found Louella's address book in her purse. I'd never met her daughter and I was too nervous to recall the name.

"That's probably it on the first page," said Elsie. "See? Right there where it says 'Notify in Case of Emergency.'" I then recognized the name Rebecca Atchley.

We located a pay phone outside the waiting room, and Elsie elbowed me aside. "Give me some quarters, Maggie," she said, already dialing the Tulsa exchange. I fished in my purse for change, then stepped into the waiting room and sat down.

Through the glass wall that separated us, I watched Elsie hang up and dial a second number. I wondered if her voice conveyed as much information as her dramatic gestures. She talked several minutes, pausing occasionally to deposit more of my quarters. When she'd finished she breezed into the waiting room.

"Louella's daughter isn't home. I had to call that other number. It turned out to be her son-in-law's office. Corey will bring her here as soon as he finds her, and Brother Pierce's wife said she would try to locate him."

I leaned my head against the plump upholstered back of the sofa. The decor of the waiting room was obscenely rosy, as if a Southwest motif of desert sunsets and fabrics of turquoise and shrimp could vaporize nail biting worry and the bitter realities of bereavement. Dozens of magazines, neatly spaced on tables of glass and pale wood, told how to bake the best chocolate cookies, what the royals really wore to bed, and all the dirt about the talk show wars. The titles were no different from those I'd barely glimpsed in the room downstairs on the night of Dexter's death.

Elsie sat in a chair at right angles to the sofa. "Maggie, do you think we're responsible for... for...."

"Elsie, I...."

We were alone, except for a man at the far end of the room. He shifted in his chair and turned the pages of a newspaper.

"We didn't mean to."

"No."

"Did she say anything to you while I parked the car?"

"Like what?"

"You know. Like, did she forgive us for scaring her into a heart attack, or anything like that?"

"I imagine slicing into her wrist had more to do with giving her a heart attack," I said. But I couldn't convince myself that was true.

"Do you think she'll live? Because, if she dies, I'll never forgive myself." Elsie started to cry.

A woman wearing a hospital tag strode down the hall toward us, and came into the waiting room. "Did you ladies just bring Mrs. Finney in downstairs?" Her tag said "Kerry Cathers, Admitting."

"Yes," I said. "How is she?"

"They're still evaluating her. I'll need to get some more

information from you." She sat in one of the desert streaked chairs, and laid her clipboard on the pale wood coffee table. "What can you tell me about the wound to Mrs. Finney's wrist?"

"I suppose you're talking about her accident. I wasn't with her when it happened," I said.

"If you ask me, she's lucky she didn't hit a vein," said Elsie.

"Then you think it was self-inflicted?"

"If you've talked to Mrs. Finney, I'm sure you know we weren't with her when the accident occurred," I said.

"Did Mrs. Finney tell you it was an accident?"

"What she said was, 'I'm going to need some stitches and a tetanus shot.'"

"Ladies, we have a responsibility to the patient to keep her from harm. If Mrs. Finney tried to commit suicide, now would be a good time to get her the help she needs."

"Louella wouldn't want to be committed to some crazy ward," said Elsie.

I looked pointedly at Elsie, then spoke to the admitting clerk. "Ms. Cathers, if Louella Finney had wanted to kill herself, she had the expertise to do it. And she could have accomplished it more neatly and with less pain than jabbing herself with a sharp instrument. In my own mind I'm sure she didn't try to kill herself. I believe when she's better Mrs. Finney will confirm that."

Elsie and I had most of the other answers Ms. Cathers needed for the admission forms. When she had finished writing she stood to leave, then turned to face me. "That must have been one tough turkey," she said.

"I beg your pardon?"

"The turkey Mrs. Finney said she was boning. I figure he was still alive when she went after him. Otherwise, you'd think she would have quit after the first wound. Imagine, accidentally plunging that sharp little knife so deep. Twice."

After the nurse left, Elsie began to pray softly for Louella. In a few moments she said, "You shouldn't be ashamed to pray out loud, Maggie."

"You're doing fine for both of us, Elsie."

She glanced at the man reading his newspaper, and whispered, "Should I ask him to join us?"

The man stood and walked to the elevator.

I rose from the sofa and walked toward the soft drink machines in the hall outside. "I need to stretch my legs."

I caught a glimpse of Elsie through the glass walls of the waiting room. She stayed sitting in the chair and buried her face in her hands.

I'd have given anything to have the day back. I couldn't blame Elsie—it had taken little persuasion to lead me into Louella's bedroom and to the jewelry box where we'd found my brooch. I wondered what Ron would think about me now —that I was impetuous and judgmental? Instead of confronting Louella I wished I'd taken the brooch and returned home. Elsie and I probably had caused Louella's heart attack. Not that she didn't deserve my anger, but I didn't think she should die for her theft.

I stood alone in the hall and prayed silently for forgiveness —for treating Louella so harshly, for judging Dexter, for my adulterous flights of fancy. "As we forgive our debtors," went the prayer. Did the Lord count all the times I'd been on the receiving end, all the times I'd been wronged? My list of debtors was growing rapidly, with Dexter at the top, followed by Jo Ann and Louella. "Seventy times seven," said a voice in my head.

"Is that always the answer, Lord?"

"Always."

"Please let Louella live," I prayed.

De ja vu. I had prayed so hard that my husband would survive his heart attack. Nearly a year had passed since I'd ridden in the ambulance as it brought Dexter to County Memorial. I'd held his hand all the way, talked to him, urged him to breathe, while a medic performed his ministrations. That event was so vivid I could recall every word.

"You've got to revive him," I had told the doctor. My voice had sounded like a claxon, echoing down the hospital corridors. "He's barely past sixty, and he's never been sick a day in his life."

"Mrs. Gilpin, we tried. I'm sorry, but your husband was

dead when they carried him in," the doctor told me softly. "He probably died before you even had a chance to call for an ambulance."

"You quit too soon. You need to open his chest and massage his heart, shock him with those electric paddles, give him a shot of adrenaline, do something!"

"Dear lady, what your husband needed...." he shook his head. "What he needed was beyond the ability of any human doctor. I'm sorry."

"I should have taken him on to Tulsa," I wept, "where they have real doctors."

The huge man's shoulders sagged. "You're upset. And I'm tired... so tired and worn out I'm having trouble remaining civil. So if you'll excuse me, I'll send someone from staff to help you make a decision about the body."

When the doctor recalled the event, I hoped he realized I had spoken from grief. I wanted to apologize, to thank him for trying to help my husband, but I never saw him again.

I was jarred into the present by a man in scrubs, a stethoscope hanging from his neck, coming toward me.

"Hello," he said. "I'm Dr. Wood. Are you a relative of Mrs. Finney's?"

Through the window I saw Elsie leave the sofa in the waiting room and hurry to join the conversation.

"I'm one of Louella's friends too, Doctor. How's she doing?"

He nodded at Elsie, then his eyes met mine, and his brow furrowed. "We're making her comfortable. Haven't we met before?"

"Yes, I'm Maggie Gilpin. I volunteer at the nursing home in Redbud, and I've seen you making rounds there. Is Louella going to be okay?"

"I volunteer at the nursing home too, Dr. Wood. My mother-in-law is a patient there. Divinity Wickfielder—she's the bald-headed lady in Room two-oh-four."

I said, "Please tell us about Louella."

"We have only a preliminary diagnosis. The EKG shows a second degree bundle branch block."

"I'm sorry. I don't understand. Will she be okay?"

"We won't have results from the CPK profile for a while, but the EKG indicates she's throwing occasional PVC's. Of course, we won't be able to tell much until we complete more of her tests, but, for the present, she seems to be stable. There was no ventricular fibrillation."

"In English?" I requested.

He folded his arms. "Mrs. Finney appears to have suffered a mild heart attack, but I don't think you have to worry unduly at this point. However, we're going to need some time to evaluate her condition."

"How long will that take?" asked Elsie.

"Hmm, I'd estimate a week, give or take a few days."

"Is she conscious?" I asked.

"We sedated her a little but we didn't knock her out. Even though I'm optimistic about the outcome, I think it would be a good idea to notify her family."

"Her daughter will be here soon," I said.

"When can we see her?" asked Elsie.

"Well, I'm going to break a few rules here. The patient has assured me it's in her best interests to see you both. I promised Mrs. Finney I'd allow each of you a half-minute with her. Reassure her, and whatever you do, don't upset her."

Elsie saw Louella first. "I told her we'd pray for her. She can't talk plain, but she sort of nodded her head at me."

Resentment swelled in me when I saw Louella. She was too sick for me to scold, too perilously close to death to rally, too sedated to listen to the saga of my non-romance with J. Ronal Patrick. The only option I had was to try to ease her mind, but I wondered what I could possibly say as she lay there, tubes protruding and monitors recording her every breath.

"You remember my date with Mickey Holden?"

She stared at me blankly, then broke into a faint smile.

"His wife left him again. When he called me for a date, I gave him your name."

Louella's reply was unintelligible.

"I didn't quite get that, Louella."

"I shed, I liszhinhope."

"Oh, you live in hope. So do I, friend. So do I." And then, the nurse hurried me into the hall.

Twenty-Seven

When the doctors determined Louella was in no immediate danger, the Atchleys insisted on treating us to dinner at a restaurant near the hospital. It was the first time I had met any of Louella's family, though Elsie remembered Rebecca from her childhood visits to Redbud. Louella's daughter had intense blue eyes and fine bones. I imagined how vivacious she must be when she wasn't worried.

She plunged her fork into a cube of cheese and left it resting in her chef's salad while she spoke. "I'm so grateful that you two were at Mother's house when she had her heart attack."

I contemplated my soup, swirling the confetti with a spoon.

Elsie gushed, "Oh, we didn't know she was having a heart attack until we got to the emergency room. We were taking her to the hospital to get her wrist sewed up."

"Her wrist? Nobody said anything to us about her wrist."

I thought the Atchleys had all the problems they could handle for one evening, so I kicked Elsie under the table. She ignored me.

"Louella slit her wrist—almost to the bone. My stomach turned flip flops when I saw all that blood. There was—"

"We're not exactly sure how she hurt her wrist," I said, kicking Elsie again. "We didn't see the accident."

"That's right," said Elsie, her voice higher, her words faster. "We don't have any idea how it happened. I mean, it was an unusual accident, wasn't it, Maggie?"

"You don't need to explain," said Rebecca. She sighed and looked at Corey. "With Mother, the unusual is normal."

Elsie smiled and nodded, as if encouraging Rebecca to continue.

"Mom likes to be the center of attention," said Corey.

I was surprised that I could so easily tell Rebecca had kicked Corey. The leg movement rocked her backward a fraction of an inch, and Corey reacted with a barely perceptible start.

"I mean," he said, "there's never a dull moment when my mother-in-law is around."

"That's one of the reasons you love her so much," said Rebecca. "Daddy's favorite name for her was 'Miss Excitement.' He said she could make an adventure out of tying her shoes."

The remainder of the evening passed in a blur of banalities. It was late before we returned with the Atchleys to the hospital, then headed home. It seemed as if we'd been away from Redbud several days.

"Rebecca and her husband are real nice," said Elsie as she maneuvered her Buick through city traffic and onto the highway.

"You know what, Elsie? I'd be willing to bet Rebecca and Corey know all about Louella's kleptomania."

"Margaret Gilpin, I'm surprised at you," Elsie scolded as we turned onto the Redbud cut-off. "The woman is practically at death's door, even though she probably will get over it. I don't think now's the time to bring up Louella's peculiarities."

"I'm not sure I consider stealing valuables from friends to be mere peculiarities," I said.

In truth, my emotions were at war. I wanted to be loyal to Louella, to continue to enjoy her effervescent personality. I longed to confide in her about my attraction to Ron—she would probably tell me I deserved a little happiness after so many months of widowhood. But her betrayal dismayed me. How could I resume a friendship with someone who had stolen from me? And it wasn't only the brooch Louella had taken. For months I had been unable to see other members of Second Thursday Circle without silently questioning their honesty.

"As tight as you've been with Louella Finney, you sure are being hard-nosed about things," said Elsie. She drove faster now that we were away from the city.

"You were the one ready to call the police to have her arrested," I pointed out. "I'm just wondering what sort of friendship she and I will be able to have now."

Elsie shrugged. "You certainly can't arrest her tonight, not with her locked in a desperate life and death struggle to survive. Besides, she literally melted my heart when she asked us to help her."

I didn't let Elsie's imagery deter me. "Am I to understand you think I should forget she stole my brooch?"

"It's called turning the other cheek. Besides, you got it back. Now if she comes over and steals something else, then maybe we should have her arrested." Elsie sucked her lips and wrinkled her forehead. The habit always seemed to be followed by a sermonette. "My philosophy is, sometimes you have to overlook your friends' faults. The good Lord knows I'm openminded. Otherwise, whom would any of us have to pal around with?"

I asked, "Do you think the other women of Second Thursday Circle are going to forgive and forget?"

We were whizzing along at seventy-five when a motorist in the opposite lane flashed his headlights at us.

Elsie eased off the accelerator before addressing my question. "Most of the Second Thursdays don't see how a doctor's wife could actually be a thief. Not having grown up in Redbud, you wouldn't know this, but the Watsons have generally had good reputations. And since the stuff Louella takes turns up sooner or later, they don't think any permanent harm has been done. Of course I knew all along whom the perpetrator was, but the girls wouldn't believe me until Flory found out about Louella from her nephew. I can't wait to see the look on Lisa's face—she says she's from Missouri. I hope you'll back me up, now that we've got proof."

"It sounds as though there have been several discussions about Louella's kleptomania. Am I the last to know?"

Elsie had the grace to look a bit sheepish before answering, "Well, some of the others thought you might be the one taking things."

"Me?" I was dumbfounded. "But my brooch was taken!"

She tried to laugh. It was a false, anemic sound. "Some of the girls thought that was a cover-up. I told them you wouldn't steal a glass of water if you was crossing the desert with a leaky canteen, but they thought losing Dexter might have made you go off your rocker."

I gasped in disbelief. "But surely they know me well enough to know I've never stolen anything in my life."

"It's just that the rest of us either grew up in Redbud, or else we had family here. And we didn't really know you until you married Dexter."

"I married and moved here more than thirty years ago, Elsie. And besides, you told me that Chief Johnston had caught Louella shoplifting one time."

"When she was just a kid. And her family was in such an uproar about it, some of the girls were sure she'd learned her lesson back then."

I rode the rest of the way in silence, bristling at the knowledge some of the Second Thursdays had harbored suspicions about me. My mind raced to other hurts. I wondered how Redbud would react when it learned about Jo Ann. I knew the revelation of my husband's illegitimate daughter would flash with the speed of wildfire through the town.

But perhaps I was like the proverbial wronged wife—the last to know—and had been the subject of pity for years. Maybe the town had already identified Jo Ann as the unseemly mourner at Dexter's funeral and enjoyed gossiping about the spectacle.

As we pulled into my driveway, Elsie said, "Who did *you* think stole your brooch, Maggie?"

I could feel my face grow hot with embarrassment, remembering how I'd voiced my suspicion to Louella. "I suppose," she said, "you thought I took it because you wouldn't loan it to me."

"Elsie, I—"

"The point is, Maggie, you don't have the right to get mad

at the girls for wondering about you." She reached for my hand. "I love you like a sister, but you're an awful hard woman at times. If I was you I'd climb down off that high horse. What's done is done. There's a psychiatrist who wrote a book about people like you—people who carry grudges."

I choked back tears of anger. "Tell me, Elsie, did the psychiatrist say how one is supposed to react to humiliation and betrayal?"

She dropped her voice to a confidential whisper. "There was this one woman who hadn't spoke to her mother for twelve years. That psychiatrist showed them how picky they was being, and their reunion was just beautiful. I cried."

I stepped from the car hurriedly, slammed the door, and walked around to the driver's side. Elsie rolled down her window, and I raised my voice above the other pearls of wisdom she tried to impart. "Just tell my dear friends—friends whose children I've chauffeured, friends whose businesses I've patronized, friends who've asked for advice in constructing job resumés—just tell all the ladies who consider being born in Redbud some sort of divine gift, I think they're all a bunch of supercilious, small-town hypocrites!"

As I strode to my back door I mumbled a parting shot. "And stop using 'whom' until you know how."

My phone was ringing as I unlocked the kitchen door. As soon as I picked it up, Lori said, "Good grief, Mother, where on earth have you been all day? I've been trying to reach you since noon."

"I'm sorry, Lori. Elsie and I took Louella to the hospital. She had a heart attack. They think it's a mild one, and that she'll recover."

"Oh, I'm sorry. About the heart attack, I mean. But I'm glad she's going to recover."

"Thank you, dear."

"Mother, you could have called someone to let them know where you were." The edge in Lori's voice alerted me. This was not a social call. "I really needed to talk to you," she said.

I thought, oh no, and sat down, anticipating bad news. "What's wrong, dear? Are the children okay?"

"Calm down and don't get excited. Nothing's wrong. I just needed to see if you could come to Tulsa on the twenty-first to baby-sit the kids. I'm supposed to go with Don to his office party, and we thought since we're going to be out so late, Chet and Sara would rather be with you than with our regular sitter."

"The twenty-first? Oh, sweetheart, I'd love to, but that's the night of our Christmas cantata."

"Your what?"

"The Christmas cantata at church. Remember? I invited you. I asked you several weeks ago, and you said you'd write it on your calendar."

"Oh, that. Well, I can't really do anything about the date of the office party, and his boss has already mentioned to Don how he looks forward to my pineapple kolaches. Are you sure you have to go to the cantata?"

"I beg your pardon?"

"Don't get all defensive, Mom. I was just asking if it was something you'd mind skipping."

"Yes, Lori."

"Yes? You mean you'd mind, or do you mean you would skip it."

"Our choir has been practicing for weeks. I know the others are depending on me to be there. I'm sorry."

"Mom, it's not as if you're Barbra Streisand. I'm sure there are plenty of altos in your choir."

I took a deep breath. "Is that all?"

"What?"

"Is that all you called about, dear?"

"I was really counting on you, you know."

"No, dear, I didn't know a thing about it until you called to-night. And much as I love Chet and Sara Jane, you'll need to get someone else to baby-sit on the twenty-first."

While I was on the phone with Lori, Schlegg had bounded into the kitchen, *ptrdurping* all the way. My cupboards were bare of canned cat food.

"This dry stuff is supposed to be really good for you," I told Schlegg as I filled his bowl. "It has all the nutrients you need for a healthy coat and a sound digestive tract."

My cat walked stiffly to his dish, smelled the mice-shaped bits, waved his tail, then stalked to the back door.

"Go find a home with one of the town natives," I told him, as I boosted him from my kitchen.

Twenty-Eight

The way my life was going, I thought I should consider analysis on live TV by a panel of talk show experts. True, Gil and Peggy were still speaking to me. But, considering my recent track record, I opted to keep my distance and not risk the ruination of those relationships.

The next morning I indulged in self-pity and strong coffee, then reported for the early shift at the nursing home. Seeing Ron guaranteed a lift of my spirits, and I promised myself I would maintain a platonic attitude.

A silver plastic tree filled a corner of the cafeteria. Someone had decorated it with red metallic balls and tossed a few handfuls of icicles on the branches. Gifts for each resident, compliments of the Second Thursdays, piled against the base of the tree. Wrapping paper hid cologne, stationery, and large print editions of the *New Testament*. I noted the bulletin board announcing caroling programs—the Congregationalists and Methodists on Tuesday, the Catholics and Lutherans on Friday. Rabbi Lehman from Tulsa was scheduled for a visit on Wednesday.

Along the corridor leading to Ron's office, a life-sized smiling Santa sat in his toy-filled sleigh, flying his team of reindeer through the ether of antiseptics, soap, stale cooking oil, and urine.

Ron's office door was closed. "He's taking Mrs. Crew to Tulsa for her MRI," said the receptionist.

He hadn't told me of his plans—there was no real reason he should have, but I felt hurt.

Hiding my disappointment I headed for Bella Shariff's

room. A visit with her was like warm sunshine after a blizzard, and I needed the soothing serenity of her friendship. But she was not in her bed—it had been stripped to its plastic mattress cover.

"She just slipped away after supper last night," her roommate, Mrs. Hansen, told me.

When I could speak I said, "I'm sorry. I'll miss her." I brushed at a tear.

Death is not an unusual event in a nursing home. Many of the residents are marking time, waiting for the close of this life, but the vibrant Bella had been a special person. Until that moment, I hadn't realized how much I had counted on her affection and wisdom. "She was a lovely lady...."

Mrs. Hansen's rasping voice grew quavery. "I've seen it before, you know."

I nodded.

With a clicking sound she blinked papery lids over her pale eyes. "Lots of times. The minute she quit snoring, I knew she was gone."

I put my arm around her. I preferred dying in peaceful slumber at an advanced age to any other death I could imagine. Bella had lived a productive life for most of her ninety years. She had told me that, because of her faith, she didn't fear death.

Mrs. Hansen reached for my hands. Hers were cold and mapped with islands the color of grocery bags. She stared at my face, as if searching for understanding. "She and her husband was both Lesbians."

"Oh?"

"Yep. They come over right after the war from Bay Root. She told me all them Lesbians snored. Ever one in her family was noisier than buzz saws." She let go my hands and stopped talking to sip orange juice. She drank the juice, then swirled catsup into the reconstituted scrambled eggs. "If I have to have a roommate again, I hope staff will put someone in here who doesn't snore. Will you tell them at the desk to put somebody in here who sleeps quiet? I ain't prejudiced, but I don't want no more A-rabs."

Knowing that Happy Heart Care Center strove for amicable relationships, I asked, "Did you have another person in mind to be your new roommate?"

Mrs. Hansen covered her mouth with her hands and giggled. "I wouldn't mind if they moved Chief Johnston in."

After my shift at the nursing home, I phoned the hospital. The nurse reported that, although Louella would continue to be in the Coronary Care Unit for a while, the doctors were cautiously optimistic about her progress. "I'll tell her you called," said the nurse. "May I please have your name?"

"Just tell her one of the members from her church called," I said and hung up.

As I lay in bed that night, I took stock of my life. On the plus side, my spice jars were alphabetized in their rack. I'd filled twelve albums with photos, all neatly labeled and put in chronological order. Nothing remained in my house which could be mended or ironed.

On the debit side, I'd alienated half my children. My husband was dead. I slept alone. My persistent sexual fantasies involved a married man. A young woman I had met only once hated me. Two of my closest friends were disloyal. And feline affection was mine only as long as the tuna held out.

I imagined an epitaph for my tombstone: *Here lies Maggie. She died with a clean lint trap.* No one would step forward with more flattering praise.

When I drifted to sleep I found myself atop a giant horse. I was afraid to dismount because of the distance to the ground.

Elsie took the reins and yelled up to me. "Get off your high horse, Maggie. Slide down. We'll catch you."

Without knowing how I had managed, I stood in my back-yard.

A young woman handed me a hammer and a bucket of nails. "Your fences need mending," she said. I didn't recognize the woman, but then she became Dexter's daughter, Jo Ann.

"This fence is made of brick," I protested.

Now the woman was not Jo Ann, but Lori. "Take the hammer and tear down the wall," she said.

Mrs. Hansen materialized. "Do it without snoring," she said.

As a vision my dream was flawed. Jacob hadn't contended with anything so silly when he saw the ladder reaching into Heaven. Nor did the Bible report any extraneous clutter in the warning to Joseph to flee into Egypt. As the machinations of a troubled mind, it was realistic and uncomfortable. Simply interpreted it meant I would be miserable until I'd set things right.

I woke too early to call Lori. When I next noticed the time, it was eight o'clock. What I had to say couldn't wait until evening, so I spoke to the answering machine. "Lori, I still can't baby-sit on the twenty-first, but I hope you'll give me a rain check. I'm sorry I was abrupt last night. I love you, baby."

Then I ordered flowers to be sent to Louella at the hospital. "What shall I put on the card?" the woman asked.

I searched for honest but gentle words to express my feelings. You couldn't fit volumes onto a florist's card. I wasn't sure we were ever going to be comfortable again in our friendship, but I wanted to make a start. "Just say, "Hurry and get well. Life is dull without you. Love, Maggie."

Next, I called Elsie. "I'm sorry I was rude last night, Elsie."

"I forgive you," she told me, "but you might want to get your estrogen supplement increased."

I clenched my fists and bit my tongue.

Into the silence Elsie gushed, "Rebecca's going to take Louella to her house as soon as the doctor releases her."

"I'm sure that's best."

"If she's well enough, she's going to come to the cantata."

"Too bad she can't sing with us."

"What are you going to do about Louella, Maggie?"

"Do? Rebecca gave me the key to the Watson place. I told her I'd water Louella's house plants."

"That's not what I meant."

Forgiveness doesn't have a simple on-off switch, I thought. My emotions were roiling. "Elsie, can I get back to you on that?"

Twenty-Nine

It was six-fifteen on Saturday when I arrived in the Patricks' neighborhood for the party Helen and Ronal were giving. My mouth felt dry as cotton and my heart beat rapidly as I approached their house. Before leaving the car I checked my purse for Tums, knowing they wouldn't do much to ease the fire in my stomach. I checked my makeup for the umpteenth time, unwrapped a breath mint and bit into it.

The Patricks did not live in Redbud, but in a community a few miles closer to Tulsa. Cars were parked along the curb and in their drive, so I had to walk a good distance in new, toe-pinching pumps. By myself. Unescorted. Alone. No arm to take as I stepped up the curb onto the root-buckled sidewalk.

A mental image of Rhett leaving Scarlett at the Wilkes' front door popped into my mind.

The number of cars indicated the party was larger than I'd imagined, possibly more formal than I'd supposed. Had I dressed appropriately? Even if Louella and I had been on the best of terms, she was too ill to give me advice. After trying every ensemble in my closet, I'd driven to Tulsa and spent enough on clothing, nails, and hair to feed a third world country. I hoped turquoise shantung would be appropriate—not too young-looking or too dressy. The front buttoned low, revealing a sheer inset of tulle that barely concealed décolletage. A side slit in the skirt stopped an inch above my left knee. Ron usually saw me in the shapeless, pink uniform of the nursing home, and I wanted to dazzle him tonight. I hoped any comparison between Helen and me would be in my favor. I reached for the doorbell.

Perhaps my attire was too flagrantly sexy. I hugged the velvet cape tight as I considered turning back to the car. I could call from home and plead sudden illness.

"Hello," said the man holding the door. "Come on in. I'm Helen's brother Daniel." We shook hands, mine were cold and trembly, and I told him my name. "Oh, so you're Maggie Gilpin. I've been wanting to meet you." Before I could react to that remark, he took my cape, then led me through a small crowd to the wet bar, stopping along the way for introductions.

The Patrick's neighbors, a few relatives, and some of Redbud's most prominent citizens stood or sat in clusters in the large, cheery room. I surmised the Mitchells, the Santoses, and the Wickfielders had been invited because of their positions on the board at Happy Heart.

A perfume of greenery and candle wax reminded me of childhood Christmases. Near a large, flocked tree, Elsie stood with Albert and some of the Patrick relatives.

"Well, didn't you put on the dog," she said to me. "If I didn't know better, I'd say there was a new man in your life." The pin and tiara she wore matched her earrings, but each piece of jewelry flashed in different neon rhythms.

"I live in hope," I said, tossing off Louella's one-liner with as much assurance as I could muster.

Albert leered. "That outfit looks a whole lot better on you than men's trousers."

"Best leave Helen's brother Daniel alone," said Elsie in a loud whisper. "He's a priest."

I felt a blush crawl from my neck to my face, and I reached nervously to finger my pearl necklace. "Elsie, I—"

Father Daniel bestowed a good natured smile on our little group. "My cover's blown." He turned to me. "No doubt it was just in time to keep you from flinging yourself at my manly charms."

"Not a moment too soon," I agreed.

And then Ron was by my side, his arm casually around my shoulder. "Hello," he said, meeting my gaze. "I'm glad you could make it, Maggie. I see you've met my favorite brother-in-law."

He walked on, taking drink orders, making small talk, acting the convivial host. I heard him tell Shirley, "Helen will be back down in a few moments. She's still looking for that art catalog to show you."

I had not sipped my first drink when she glided down the greenery draped staircase into the room, regally in command of our attention. Sienna-colored eyes contrasted with pale skin and chestnut hair. The photograph in Ron's office had led my expectations astray—the woman was a knockout.

She quickly surveyed the crowd, then crossed to where I stood. She took my free hand in hers, her long fingers wrapping mine in warmth. "Maggie Gilpin? Of course. Ron's told me so much about you."

"And I've heard so much about you," I lied.

Soft folds of her bronze-colored jumpsuit draped a well toned body. Gold chains looped her slender neck. Fine lines near her mouth and eyes were the only signs of age.

"Shirley," she said, moving on, "I'm afraid I've misplaced that catalog, but I'll drop it by your house."

I saw Ron watching me and realized I must have looked as crestfallen as I felt. I managed to smile weakly as he crossed the room to my side. "Elsie tells me your friend Louella seems to be recovering," he said.

"So far, so good."

"You two must have had quite a time of it, stemming the flow of blood, lugging her to the car, saving her life and all."

"Elsie does have a way with words," I said. "Has she told everyone?"

He laughed and touched my arm. "Well, Elsie may be dramatic, but I think it's no exaggeration Louella was lucky to have you." He gave my hand a brief squeeze. Intimate, secret. His voice lowered. "I'm glad you came."

"I stopped by your office to—my confrontation with Louella may have been the last straw for her heart, you know. I... I needed to... to talk to a friend."

"I wish I could have been there for you, Maggie."

His soft voice had such a loving quality, I could almost believe we were alone in his office. I tried to smile. "Your wife is beautiful."

He withdrew his hand. "Helen has always taken good care

of herself." The phrase sounded automatic, as if he had memorized the words.

Elsie elbowed her way between us. "Did I hear my name a minute ago? My ears are literally burning."

"You told Ron about Louella. We were talking about that."

"Oh. I'm just so grateful we could save her." She looked at me in horror and raised her voice several decibels. "Maggie, is that another screwdriver? You know you can't drink." She looked at Ron. "Maggie just gets sicker than a dog chasing hornets."

I glared at Elsie and kept a tight hold on my drink. "I'm fine, Elsie. Really."

"I've heard that before. Just remember, I tried to warn you."

A dinner bell spared me. At Ron's request Father Daniel blessed the food. I followed the other guests to an enclosed porch which accommodated a buffet and three large tables. After filling a plate I found my place card next to Orin and across from Elsie. Father Daniel sat to my left at the head of the table.

Shades on a long wall were up so we could look onto the patio. White lights twinkled in holly bushes, and a spotlight illuminated a plywood crèche.

"Orin, I wish you'd look at that patio," said Elsie. "You could wire ours next year."

Helen sat at a round table, her profile just beyond Elsie. Albert Santos whispered something, and she laughed a rich musical laugh. I thought Albert was smitten with her. She turned toward us and winked, as if to say, isn't this fun? Isn't it wonderful to be so admired? Her brother nodded and smiled. I envied her confident manner, and it was disconcerting to think I could probably like her very much.

I looked at my plate and pondered the intricate maneuvers and coordination required to satisfactorily move food to my mouth and worried someone would see me dribble sauce down my chin and onto the white lace tablecloth, or that I would propel a glass of wine onto Father Daniel.

Orin surveyed his place setting with a frown and didn't take a bite until he'd checked to see which fork other diners were using. I wanted to hug him. "This sure is fancy," he muttered.

Draping a napkin across my exposed left knee, I turned to Father Daniel. "I hope Mrs. Patrick will share her recipe for duck a l'orange. This is delicious."

"I'm sure she will. Helen is a generous lady."

"I won a ribbon at the State Fair one year with my chicken casserole," said Elsie. "Remember that, Orin? I make it with crushed potato chips and canned mushroom soup." She giggled. "But the secret ingredients are what won it for me."

She laid her fork on her plate, folded her hands in her lap, and looked directly at the priest.

Finally, he said, "If you'd send me the recipe, Mrs. Wickfielder, I'd love to sample it."

"A jar of pimentos, a dash of lime juice, and a package of onion soup mix. That's what makes it so good—the secret ingredients. Orin loves it, don't you, Orin."

Father Daniel turned to me. "I understand you share Ron's interest in English literature."

"We've had some lively discussions."

"He greatly admires you, Mrs. Gilpin."

I swallowed quickly and looked at him. His expression was humorless. "He told you he admired me?"

"Not in so many words. But it's obvious he appreciates your work at the nursing home and has come to depend on your friendship."

"You two must have had quite a talk."

He drank some water. "Ron says you have a fine sense of moral duty."

Did I merely imagine his tone had become reproachful?

"That's a fine quality in any woman, particularly one struggling with the burdens of widowhood."

Elsie, who had been scribbling on the back of a check deposit slip, thrust it into Father Daniel's hand. "Just give this to your housekeeper," she said. "It's real easy to make."

"I don't have a housekeeper, Mrs. Wickfielder."

"But I thought… I mean Father Dowling… you Catholics… oh, well. I guess one of the nuns could do it for you."

"Probably not in this world. Actually, I cook for myself. But I'll give the recipe a try when I get back to Boston. Thank you." He smoothly shifted his attention to one of the Patricks' neighbors seated by Orin. I scanned guests at the farthest table until I saw Ron. When our eyes met, he looked away.

Thirty

The rest of the evening at the Patricks' passed as comfortably as the night Dexter and I found ourselves ensconced in a pew at the wrong wedding. Guests gathered around a concert grand. Its shiny surface reflected a collection of framed family pictures while Helen flawlessly played several carols for a jolly singalong.

When the first couples gathered at the door to say their good-byes, I retrieved my cape. I suppose I made the proper farewells, but I don't remember.

On the drive home I thought about the evening. Did Helen's brother know of the attraction between Ron and me, or was I reading too much into his remarks about my "fine sense of moral duty?" Was Helen suspicious? And what sort of woman was she? Her accomplishments and talent were apparent, but I told myself I could detect a certain coldness of character—a selfish drive for perfection that overlooked the needs of all about her.

The phone rang as I opened the back door. Warmth shot through me when I heard his voice. "We... I wanted to make sure you got safely home, Maggie."

My knees melted. I collapsed onto a kitchen chair and Schlegg jumped into my lap. "It was good of you to call, Ron."

His voice dropped to a whisper. "I'll be away until the first of the year—a training session in Boston."

"I know," I said. "I... be careful, Ron."

"I've missed you. Take care of yourself, Maggie."

"Ron—"

Then his voice changed, as if someone had walked into the

room. "I'm glad the roads were clear and you got home all right, Orin. Good-bye."

He'd called me Orin, no mistake—I heard him clearly. Had Helen walked into the room? Was Father Daniel eavesdropping? Ron wouldn't hide my identity unless....

I knew with more certainty than ever he contemplated the same direction for our friendship as I did. I held the phone a few moments, even after hearing the dial tone. There was so much more I'd wanted to hear him say. And I wouldn't even see him until after the holidays. My hands were trembling as I replaced the receiver. *Louella,* I thought, *if you don't hurry and get well enough for me to talk about this, I'm going to lose my mind.* I dumped Schlegg and went to look for my tranquilizers.

Louella stayed in the hospital a week. Then, temporarily, she moved into the Atchleys' home in Tulsa. A few days later, she called to invite me to visit her there. "We need to talk," she said.

"Are you up to it? I mean, are you sure it's okay for your heart?"

"Bring your walking shoes, Maggie. I have to walk every-day now and I could use the company."

The next morning after strolling once around the park, we settled into Rebecca Atchley's kitchen. She and her husband had taken their children to a day-care center before going to their respective jobs. I sat while Louella made us a pot of coffee.

"I... do you think you could do some Christmas shopping for me, Maggie?"

"What?"

"It's awkward to shop for Becca while I'm living in her house. There are only three items, and I wrote everything down for you."

"There's not much time left before Christmas, Louella. But I'll do what I can."

She poured two cups of coffee, then sat across the table from me. "That's not the reason I asked you to drive all the way to Tulsa."

"No, I suppose not," I said.

"Oh, Maggie. I don't know where to begin." Her voice trembled and I noticed her hand shook when she lifted her coffee cup.

"I don't think you should get upset," I said. "Maybe we should wait until you're well before we talk about—about your problem."

"Oh, good grief," she bristled. "You don't have to worry about me stabbing my wrist again. And besides, I didn't seriously try to kill myself."

"I know, but I'm thinking of your heart. Please don't get worked up."

"I'm fine. I'm glad it's all out in the open—about my taking your brooch and all."

Her words unleashed anger, but I tried to be careful with my response. "If you're well enough—if you really want to talk about my brooch, I have to tell you—nothing has hurt me so much since I found out about Dexter's affair."

"I know and I'm sorry."

I jabbed my fork into a chocolate doughnut.

"I said I was sorry, Maggie."

As if she'd accidentally broken a coffee cup or stepped on my toe. She put her hand on my arm. I looked at her, fighting to keep my voice level. "I think I deserve more than that."

She shook her head sadly. "I can't give you a good explanation."

"I can't say I'm really surprised. Elsie says you've been shoplifting since you were in grade school."

"What?" She looked incredulous. "Maggie, that's a crock! She's probably talking about the time I took some things from the dime store. I was only ten years old."

"And someone told her you'd been arrested in Tulsa for shoplifting."

"That dirty gossip. I would like to know... who...." Our eyes met and she slumped in her chair, a look of defeat on her face. "I hardly ever took things while Bill was alive, then when he died... oh, Maggie," she sobbed, then buried her face in her arms. "I miss him so much."

I stood and patted her back. "Don't cry," I said, knowing I'd pressed her too far. I hurried to get her a glass of water. "Maybe we should talk about something else. It can't be good for you to get this upset."

"I'm so sorry. I never meant to hurt you. I don't know why I took the brooch, but you've just got to forgive me."

"Of course," I said, trying not to sound as alarmed as I felt. "As far as I'm concerned, it never happened. Please calm down."

"Sometimes I get out of control. But I do enjoy the excitement."

"Excitement?"

She raised her head. There was a faint smile on her lips. "The thrill of putting something over and not getting caught, the satisfaction of getting even." Her tear-glistened eyes shone with fervor. "My endorphins go wild."

She must have seen my shocked expression. "And sometimes, like with your brooch, I never even realize I've taken something until I find it in my purse or on my dresser." She stared at me, as if waiting for some sign of comprehension.

I didn't understand but I nodded anyway.

"I'm going to live one day at a time. When I get the urge to steal, I'll take up bungee jumping, or maybe I'll call Elsie and let her get me a date."

"Bungee jumping is safer," I said.

"But not half as much fun."

"Probably not."

She took another sip of water and regarded me thoughtfully. "Don't you ever get desperate to snuggle up to Prince Charming?"

"Snuggling just wouldn't do it for me."

Louella raised her eyebrows in mock disapproval. "Why, Maggie Gilpin."

"Do you remember J. Ronal Patrick?"

Her brown eyes widened as I told her about him.

"What are you going to do?"

"God help me. I know it's wrong, but when he gets home from Boston, I'm going to invite him into my bed."

"Oh, Maggie," she said shaking her head. "You mean... you're going to do 'the wild thing'?"

I laughed. "You make it sound so trivial."

"Not trivial, Maggie. But...."

"I thought you would understand."

"You thought more than that. You thought I would approve."

"Damn it, Louella, don't lecture me."

She frowned. "Lectures aren't my style, dear. I don't have to tell you how wrong it is. You already know. I won't love you any less, but I'll worry about you."

"I bet that's how you talk to your daughter."

She shrugged. "Sometimes it even works."

I gave her a hug and left for home. When I arrived in my kitchen, I found a hungry cat and a message from Don on my answering machine. My son-in-law greeted me, "Hi, Effie," letting me know he wasn't too upset to use his favorite pet name for me. "Don't sweat the baby-sitting on the twenty-first. It ain't that important. By the way, where have you been, you old sea hag?" A reassuring chuckle followed his question, then a dial tone.

I opened a can of tuna and dumped it into Furr Schleggener's dish. He ate, drawing his lips back from sharp teeth, not contaminating his face with food. Then I set the table with bone china and sterling silver—for one—popped the cork on a bottle of peach wine Dex and I had bought while on vacation in Arkansas a few years ago, and zapped a frozen meal in the microwave. After dinner Schlegg allowed me to carry him into the living room. As I tried to read he lay in my lap, swishing his tail onto the pages of a novel I'd borrowed from Louella.

I read somewhere most people who live alone talk to themselves. Schlegg saves me from that.

"Schlegg, old boy, time flies when you're having fun, waiting for your lover to return from Boston, and all, but I must be off to choir practice."

He responded with one of his *ptrdurping* noises.

I didn't want to go to choir practice, but there was no escaping the obligation. After Christmas I planned to look for a large church in Tulsa where any sermon on adultery wouldn't make me feel as if the preacher had tailored it to my sin.

Maybe I would take a vacation from church, rid my heart of its confusion, then return to some other house of worship.

Meanwhile I honored my obligation to the church where Gilpins had worshipped for nine decades. Hopes were high for the Christmas cantata. As it drew nearer, Brother Lee held extra rehearsals. Shirley said it would be too stressful for the children to rehearse with us every time, but when we finally combined the choirs for our dress run-through, the little ones performed beautifully. The boys swaggered in their shepherd and wise men costumes, and the girls looked properly pious as angels. Phoebe Kearny played softly, and the children's voices rang sweet and clear above her notes.

Mary, the innkeeper, Herod, the shepherds and angels—all knew their few lines. Lindsay McCoy substituted for her son as Joseph, reading, "Since King David was my ancestor, Mary and I traveled to Bethlehem to be taxed. It was a long, hard trip, and when we got to Bethlehem, there was no place for us to stay in the inn."

Sharla, Lindsay and Shirley kept control of the children, whose behavior was exemplary. After their part of the program, the children sat quietly on stage as the church choir sang behind them.

Louella wouldn't be able to sing with us, though she'd promised to be in the audience for the performance. The cantata ended with a thunderous, abridged version of "The Hallelujah Chorus."

Brother Lee smiled as he brought his baton down on the last note. "Children, adult choir members, you were wonderful. I'm proud of you."

"Is Lindsay going to read the part of Joseph tomorrow night?" asked Albert Santos, provoking hearty laughter.

"How is Little Carter?" asked Amelia.

"Oh, his chicken pox is completely scabbed over," Shirley told us. "I wanted him here tonight, but his dad couldn't see fit to bring him home until noon tomorrow."

While Shirley's daughter Lindsay flushed beet red, Flory clucked her tongue. "It must have tore up Big Carter to have to deprive himself of a trip to the race track at Remington Park just so he could have Little Carter for a few days."

After the singing ended Elsie stared pensively at her music, oblivious to conversations around her. Now her voice rose above the hum, demanding to be heard. "Brother Lee, do you think the piano is too loud during my oratorio?"

Brother Lee rocked on his heels while pondering Elsie's concern, one finger pointing thoughtfully toward his chin.

"I'm playing mezzo piano now," said Phoebe.

"Elsie, I thought it sounded just right," said Brother Lee.

Elsie sucked her lip, frowning. "I suppose I could sing a little louder. I trained for the stage where you really have to belt it out."

Nervous laughter rippled through the choir loft.

"Let's leave it the way it is, Elsie. Folks, go on home, get a good rest, and be here ready to get into your robes at six o'clock tomorrow evening." Then he dismissed us with prayer.

Since early October we'd practiced long and conscientiously. Like all performers who know they've been well-rehearsed and are confident of their parts, we were eager for opening night so we could show off. But not all my joyous feelings were a result of the season—Christmas would follow the cantata, New Year would follow Christmas, and then Ron would be home from Boston.

On the way to my car with Elsie, we noticed Shirley limping. "What happened?" asked Elsie. "Did you get kicked by a horse, or what?"

"Mother has a rash on her leg," said Lindsay. "I tried all last week to get her to go to the doctor. She's hurting bad enough now, I think she'll let me take her tomorrow."

Shirley winced. "It hurts like the devil."

"Let me see that," said Elsie. Shirley lifted a pant leg. As Elsie peered, the light of the parking lot lamp revealed a raw pattern on Shirley's flesh. "You been in the woods?"

"It's nearly Christmas, and it's too cold to be in the woods."

"Well, it looks to me like you picked up some poison ivy somewhere. Cook some oatmeal, cool it just to warm, and make a poultice. It'll be well in three days."

"No," said Shirley. "I've had poison ivy. It itches enough to drive you insane, but it doesn't hurt like this."

"You just watch," Elsie told me after we'd settled into my car. "If that isn't poison ivy, I'll go naked to General Assembly."

Thirty-One

Polished loafers and Mary Janes peeked from beneath flowing robes as the children lined up in the ante room. Little Carter McCoy still had a few pink spots among his freckles, but Lindsay assured us he was not contagious and that the doctor had said her son was well enough to participate in the program. "Mother's the one suffering now," said Lindsay. "She has shingles on her left leg, and the doctor doped her up on pain medication. She's going to sit out front tonight with Daddy."

"Well, of course," said Elsie, "shingles looks exactly like poison ivy."

"I won't hold you to your promise," I told her.

She sniffed. "I'll bring my medical remedy book and show you the pictures."

Lindsay and Sharla managed the children. I wondered if the absence of Shirley's discipline bode well for the evening, but the two younger women kept order in the ranks, straightening glittering halos, flowing robes, and bejeweled crowns while the adult choir filed into the sanctuary.

My place next to Amelia was on the edge of a semi-circle facing Lisa Beach who stood across from us on the other side of the chancel.

In the glow of the candlelight, I stole glances into the auditorium and found Gil and Peggy. To my astonishment and pleasure, Don, Lori, Chet and Sara Jane sat next to them. Through moist eyes I could make out Sara's tiny hand—two middle fingers bent, thumb, forefinger and pinkie extended—waving to me. I wanted to signal, "I love you too," but I merely smiled, hoping she would see my acknowledgement. The presence of Lori and her family warmed me. Sometimes, I thought, one has to be assertive with grown children. That doesn't mean they'll love you less. I'd have to learn to take over that role now that Dexter was gone.

While I waited for the costumed children to enter, I caught sight of Louella. A tall gentleman held her arm as an usher escorted them to the alcove where late arrivals were seated.

Brother Pierce welcomed our visitors and took his place in the choir, organ music melded with piano, and the youngsters stepped purposefully to the raised platform at the front of the church. The angels stood in the center of the stage, behind Joseph and Mary, with shepherds and wise men flanking them. Because I stood so far to one side of the choir, I could see the wide-eyed wonder on each scrubbed face.

One tot, awed by the importance of the occasion, sobbed. Amid sympathetic laughter Sharla stepped into the chancel, gathered the little boy in her arms and carried him to his parents. Then she took her place next to Lindsay in the front pew, facing the children. The pianist began the first carol. The children sang, tentatively at first, then with charming abandon.

Mary, one of the angels, the narrator, and a shepherd delivered their speeches without incident. While Phoebe played in the background Little Carter McCoy stepped to the microphone. Blue velvet folds of his robe accented his carrot-colored hair. Innocence framed freckled wholesomeness, and he smiled sweetly. He took the microphone from the narrator, blew into it, drew back in exaggerated surprise as the discordant sputter shot through the sound system. Like a vaudeville veteran he waited for the small ripple of laughter to sweep through the congregation, then he launched into his part.

"King David is my ancestor, and Mary and I had to go over to Bethlehem to catch up with the I.R.S. on our taxes. It was a long, hard trip, especially since she was about nine months pregnant, and when we got to Bethlehem, there was no place for us to stay in the inn because they was booked solid."

Mary and the innkeeper stared at Joseph in puzzlement, and several choir members froze. The words, "pregnant" and "I.R.S." definitely had not been in the script. Shirley, seated behind Lindsay and Sharla, glared at Little Carter, while

Brother Lee sat with a fixed smile that denied his having noticed any departure from the speech as written.

Lindsay stood. We all knew Little Carter had intentionally reworked his part, and I wondered if his mother would pull him from the stage. But Phoebe began to play, and Lindsay directed the boys and girls in another song. The children delivered their remaining lines and music as rehearsed. When they had finished their part of the program and settled into chairs on the stage, relief was palpable.

Brother Lee strode to the podium, commanded every eye, nodded to Phoebe, then directed us in harmonious melody. I sang, blending my voice until it became part of a worshipful entity of praise and wonder.

Near the end of the cantata Elsie began her solo. I followed closely, determined to come in at the proper moment for the altos and tenors. Restless movement among the children caught my eye and broke my concentration. Then I noticed inappropriate smiles and smothered giggles among the congregation. I looked over the audience and found Gil. He shook his head in disbelief. Don buried his face in a handkerchief.

Elsie, near the beginning of her solo, was doing a fine job. The drama of Jesus' birth seemed to fill her whole being with passion. Her eyes were closed, her hands folded together in the center of her chest. Some of the notes were quite high, causing her voice to stretch beyond its finest range, but I could detect no cause for amusement.

Then I saw Little Carter. His hands were folded together in the center of his chest, his eyes were closed, and he mouthed the words to Elsie's solo. Every time she hit a high note, Little Carter rose from his chair to stand on tiptoe, his mouth grimacing, his eyes squinting grotesquely. At one point he put his hands over his ears as if in pain. His behavior was rude and jarring; but to my disgust, I had to suppress a giggle of my own.

Sharla sat in the front pew with her mouth open, as if watching a horrible accident she had no power to stop. Lindsay stared at Elsie's face, apparently trying to blot her son from her consciousness by fixing her attention on the soloist.

As if on signal two people from opposite sides of the church stepped into the aisle and started for the front. Though she was closest, Shirley's sore leg and medicated state slowed her down, so Orin leapt onto the stage just as Elsie reached the most passionate section of the music. Wordlessly, he lifted Little Carter high over his stunned contemporaries and carried the child from the church as Shirley shuffled after them. Little Carter did not go quietly. His screams, "Help, help! Put me down!" and, "Daddy, I want my daddy!" finally penetrated Elsie's awareness. She and Phoebe stopped.

Brother Lee's face blanched pale gray. He trembled with righteous anger. I don't know what he would have done if Phoebe hadn't replayed the introduction for Elsie's solo. Her voice now thoroughly limbered, Elsie apparently saw the situation as a not-to-be-missed opportunity. She launched into song. Brother Lee calmed enough to direct us in our background hums, and by the fourth stanza the full choir followed his baton.

Before the song ended I heard one person clapping. Like a snowball beginning an avalanche the congregation's applause rose in volume. I saw Orin standing alone at the back of the church, a smile on his face, enjoying Elsie's moment of triumph.

Thirty-Two

Orin's tirades are impressive because they occur so infrequently and are such a contrast to his usual laid back attitude. He marched around their living room claiming allowances were made for Little Carter just because he was Richard Mitchell's grandson. Orin said if Richard's brother hadn't been the banker, Little Carter would have been barred from joining the Cub Scouts, overlooked when time came to cast the school play, would have been benched the whole Little League season. And when he was older he would not have been allowed to caddie at the Redbud Country Club. Orin seemed to believe if a child from the bottom of the social ladder had behaved so scandalously, his family would have been forced to move.

"Maggie, you know I'm telling the truth," he said. "Things was different in the old days, back when law officers was more interested in doing the right thing than in pussyfooting around some juva-nile delinquent's civil rights."

Elsie said, "Shirley made him apologize to me, but his voice was so hateful you'd have thought he was challenging me to a duel. I was glad Orin was there to back me up." She looked at Orin adoringly, then returned her attention to me. "'Spare the rod and spoil the child' is what Orin says. He doesn't go for coddling juveniles. He says that's the way you raise a full-fledged criminal."

"If I was sheriff," said Orin, "you can bet I'd haul his— I'd take that little stinker to jail. At least give him a good scare."

Elsie turned to me, wanting, it seemed, for me to lead a lynch party.

I cleared my throat. "Well, you each handled yourselves

very well at the cantata. I thought it was nice of the congregation to give you a standing ovation, Elsie."

"Standing ovations are always rewarding to me," she said.

She had me taste one of her pumpkin pies so I could see how much better it was than mine.

I was too content to let Elsie Wickfielder annoy me. I had spent a lovely Christmas with my children, during which Lori apologized for taking me for granted. Our first Christmas without Dexter had been filled with poignancy, but there were happy moments too.

And Ron was due back the first Monday of the new year from his seminar in Boston. The thought energized me with girlish fervor as I contemplated hideouts and romantic scenarios for our trysts. I shared some of those thoughts with Louella. Though she didn't try to talk me out of my plans, I knew she disapproved.

The Saturday before Ron's scheduled return I gathered some food and cleaning supplies and headed for the camping trailer at Lake Redbud. I had considered selling the camp until Lori had made it plain how much her family loved the place. Now I was happy I hadn't put it on the market.

I rarely went there. Even after Dexter had dug a well and septic tank, its primitive comforts didn't appeal to me as they did to my children and grandchildren.

But it would make a perfect lovers' hideaway for Ron and me. The small building rested atop wheels far back on a lot surrounded by acres of thick woods. Almost no one ventured near the place from September to May.

I drove past town to the narrow lane. Tree limbs scratched the car doors as I drove down the rutted road. Between the highway and our camp I saw no one. A brisk wind blew from the small lake, shaking the bare cottonwoods and dancing the tire swing eerily. I parked, flipped the breaker switch, and hurried inside the trailer. My hands were chilled to stiffness, but I managed to light the kerosene wall heater.

The kitchen was furnished with Mother's embroidered cup towels and mismatched cutlery. Old quilts, too tattered for our bedrooms in town, covered the beds.

In a few hours the clean smell of soap filled the trailer. I crammed champagne, cheeses, and chicken pâté into the tiny refrigerator. I washed a colander of fresh fruit in the tiny sink. I imagined hearing tires crunching across the leafy clearing, imagined welcoming Ron to the cozy warmth of feather-stuffed pillows and rustic bedclothes, imagined our passionate tangled embraces. I thought about how it would feel to lie in his arms, skin touching skin, his hands and mouth searching me to release all the unbearably exquisite pleasures ready to burst and consume me.

I surveyed the scene one last time. I considered bringing my stereo and a stack of Sinatra tapes, but the sound would overwhelm the small space. No, it was perfect the way it was. I closed and locked the door, sealing my expectations inside.

When I arrived at Happy Heart early on the first Monday of the year, Ron had already parked his car and gone inside. I had to stop myself from rushing as I approached his office, but I couldn't suppress a smile.

I halted abruptly at the door, my smile frozen, my throat constricting.

"Oh, Mrs. Gilpin," said Helen. "Ron and I were just having coffee. Can I pour you a cup?"

Somehow I found my voice. "No, thank you. I already drank two cups this morning."

She buzzed around in her new volunteer's uniform, straightening Ron's desk. He had the grace to look slightly uncomfortable.

"Please sit down any way," she said, pointing to the chair across from the desk and pulling one close to Ron for herself. "We didn't get to talk much the night of the party."

I looked at Ron, but his blank expression gave me no help. "Did you enjoy your trip?" I asked.

Helen turned to him, smiling, as if I had stumbled onto their secret. "Ronnie and I had a wonderful time." She straightened his tie and patted his hand.

He looked as if he enjoyed the attention, as if he'd forgotten I was there.

Helen continued, "None of the boys have room for us, what

with their growing families. So after the conference we stayed on at the hotel." The look she gave me could only be characterized as "meaningful."

It seemed to be my turn again, but I could think of little to say. "The conference?"

"I was so proud of him. His speech had those stuffed shirts on the edge of their seats."

There was another long silence. I think Ron cleared his throat. Then Helen suddenly beamed a dazzling smile at me, a little too dazzling to be genuine.

"Ronnie's asked me to head up the volunteer program here, Mrs. Gilpin, so I expect we'll be seeing a lot of each other."

"I see," I said as Ron turned his gaze to the bookcase. I swallowed hard and too noisily. "Actually, although I've enjoyed my days here more than I can say, I just stopped by this morning to resign." I willed my voice to sound normal, my eyes to stay dry, but I nearly lost the battle. "I'm rather involved with some personal interests now. I hope you don't mind, but this is the last shift I can work."

"Oh, goodness, don't worry," said Helen. In contrast to the words, her voice held no warmth. "I can take your place today. I've arranged my schedule so I can give Ronnie all the help he needs, and I may as well begin now."

"Oh, well then...." I stood and backed toward the door, lingering, waiting for one word of protest from Ron, a flicker of regret in his eyes, a subtle, conspiratorial nod.

"Thanks for all your help," he said as I stepped to the door. What struck me most was that, until that moment, he hadn't spoken to me at all.

In less than a year I'd had a date with one married man and made a foolish, unsuccessful play for another. It seemed to me I'd made a mess of my life. "Dexter would have been so shocked," I wailed.

"Hell," said Louella. "The Wickfielders and all of Redbud would be shocked. Dexter would be apoplectic."

After I called her she had arrived with flowers and homemade fudge. "If my pecan fudge isn't better than sex, it's a

close second," she promised, pushing it toward me while I
blubbered the humiliating details of my last trip to Ron's
office.

"He acted as though I'd never been anything more than—
more than a woman who carried bedpans down the hall."

She patted my hand. "Maybe, in his mind, that's all you
were, dear."

"Then why did he call me 'Orin' before he hung up the
phone the night of the party? You don't believe I imagined it
all, do you?"

"What I really think is you're lucky you didn't have a
chance to throw yourself at that skirt-chasing wimp. You're too
good for him, Maggie."

"But he's not a skirt-chaser, and I did throw myself at him."

"Still," she mused, "you notice how quickly his wife picked
up on things. I just bet it wouldn't have been the first time he'd
strayed.

"And you," she said, her voice turning quavery, "have no
idea how bad it feels to...."

"To do the wild thing with someone besides your husband?"

"To wake up one morning, face the mirror, and feel so
cheap."

The next day she insisted I dress and accompany her shopping. "You need someone with you on your first trip out. This
time I'll keep *you* from pilfering."

And though I'd declared to Elsie I'd never shop with
Louella again, I went.

When Louella dropped me off, she said, "I don't want you
to wonder about it. I paid for everything I took today."

And I believed her. She'd stolen from me and deceived me,
but I believed her because I had to. I had to have one friend to
whom I could reveal the true Maggie Gilpin, someone who
wouldn't judge or scold. Louella understood how I could be so
hungry for a man's arms that I would yearn for someone else's
husband, and she liked me anyway.

Now all I had to do was learn to like myself again.

Thirty-Three

On the night of the cantata Louella had introduced me to her "date." "A first cousin is not a date, Maggie. Besides I'm six years older than Jim and I could never date someone whom I remember wearing diapers."

He had a craggy face and handsome middle-aged features. Laughter lurked behind eyes the color of wood smoke. His belly looked flat in a black worsted suit, and I thought he'd be at home on the links or fly casting.

"She's worse than my sisters," he'd said, "and they're both merciless." He'd taken my hand firmly. "Enjoyed the music, Mrs. Gilpin."

Louella had explained that she and her doctor decided she was well enough to move home. She'd invited Jim to visit her for the holidays. "He lost his wife two years ago, and came here to get away from all the women who are chasing him. He didn't want to meet you until I told him you're only interested in married men."

My face had grown hot, and Jim had blushed. "Lulu, you're going to have to come out of your shell," he'd told her.

Now as she sat in my living room tickling Schlegg, Louella asked me, "Remember my cousin Jim Dugger—my 'date' for the cantata? He's rented a cabin and a boat on Lake Tenkiller, and he's invited you and me to spend a few days with him there."

I bit my lip and frowned. "Louella, I never expected you'd try to play matchmaker, but if you did I thought you'd be more subtle."

She shook her head. "Would I be so predictable? Honestly,

Jim thinks you're attractive, but he's really on the defensive—
all those women who've been chasing him since his wife died.
He'd like to pay me back for keeping him through the holidays,
and he just thought the three of us could act like kids at camp.
You know—hike, fish, toast marshmallows in the fireplace.
What could be wrong with having a good time?"

"Nothing, so long as everyone knows I'm not ready for a
relationship. You do understand that, don't you?"

"Bring along your embroidery hoop and stitch it on a
sampler— 'Maggie Gilpin isn't ready.'"

We left on a Wednesday afternoon in Jim's van. He laughed
when he saw all the boxes of food Louella and I brought. "I
only have the place through Saturday," he said, loading
Louella's crate of wine. "You don't plan to stay snockered the
whole time, do you, Lulu?"

On the drive they decided to detour to the dam. I remembered visiting the site with Dexter. It had seemed the perfect place
to tell my husband I was pregnant with our second child.

Louella called to me, "Aren't you going to get out?" So I
walked with them to view the water as it tumbled relentlessly
down concrete slopes.

I shuddered in the stiff breeze. We stood, silent, and after a
few moments Jim turned and smiled. "Ready?" Back in the van
he said, "You forget how powerful it is until you get that close.
Quite a feat of engineering."

"It always scares me," said Louella.

"It looks lovely by starlight," I said, thinking of the only
other time I'd seen it. Louella poked me in the ribs, and I
wished I'd kept my thoughts to myself.

Cozy didn't quite describe the limitations of the cabin, and
delightful was too pale a word for its rugged charm. Jim slept
on a sofa bed in the living room, Louella and I slept on a
double bed in the only bedroom. All three mornings I woke to
cold floors and a wait for the bathroom. There was no TV, but
the fireplace cast lovely shadows on log walls. We saw deer
through the kitchen window. While hiking up a steep hill, we
gathered pine cones and paused to listen as quail whistled in
the morning sun. We ate on paper plates, and Louella and I
took turns cleaning the kitchen and washing the few dishes. In

the evenings we played Rummy, worked jigsaw puzzles, and talked.

Jim volunteered to pop the evening's supply of popcorn. He moved the pan noisily in the fireplace as he recited:

Red men found it shooting to the sky
Growing beneath a roasting sun.
And it blossomed in their cookfires
When the warrior's day was done.
They gave it to the white man
Back when they all were friendly.
His woman cooked it in a frying pan
And now we think it's real trendy.

He looked up sheepishly. "I wrote it myself."

"Well," I said, smiling brightly and hoping I sounded enthusiastic, "you certainly have an ear for rhyming words, don't you."

"What do you think of it?"

I squirmed beneath his hopeful gaze, but Louella leapt into the breach. "Don't give up your day job, Jimbo."

"I bet your grandchildren love it," I said.

He poured the popped corn into three bowls and gave me one. "My wife appreciated poetry. She used to clip poems out of the newspaper and tape them to the refrigerator." He handed me salt and melted butter, then sat next to me on the sofa. "She sent the one about popcorn to the newspaper without ever telling me." He cleared his throat and fixed his gaze on the fire. "When they published it she never said a word—just taped it up there with all the rest of those poems she kept."

On Friday afternoon while the sun was high and the winds calm, Jim said, "Come on, you land lubbers. Cap'n Jim will take you for a sail."

"Yeah," Louella shouted. "Before I catch cabin fever."

At his direction Louella and I hauled sails, pulled ropes, and tried not to resemble Lucy and Ethel. His hearty laugh told us how often we failed, but we managed not to capsize or fall overboard.

That evening after supper we carried our wine glasses to the boat dock. In a curve of land that brought the trees to the water's edge, raccoons foraged. They dipped their tiny paws into the lake and rippled the moon's reflection. We watched in silence for several minutes before I heard Jim's low chuckle. "I think Louella slipped off to give us time to be alone."

"And after she swore she wasn't playing Cupid." I laughed to cover my irritation. "Will the real Dolly Gallagher Levi please stand up."

"Who?"

"Oh, that was the name of the matchmaker in *Hello, Dolly.*"

"Sorry. I don't know too much about movies." He kicked a stray pebble into the water. "Want to take a walk?"

I helped him stow the deck chairs, then followed him on a rocky path that hugged the shore. He turned his flashlight toward a trail into the woods.

"If we're lucky, maybe we'll see more raccoons or some deer."

"And if we're lucky, maybe we won't."

He laughed, took my hand, and pulled me along. "Watch your step on those rocks."

"Jim, we're not going to get lost, are we?"

"If you look over your right shoulder, you can see the lights of the cabin."

"Oh."

"I've had a swell time with you here this week, Maggie."

"Me too, Jim. And I know Louella's had fun."

He edged closer—too close, and I tried to turn toward the cabin. "I, uh, of course Louella always has a good—"

Then he pulled me close and kissed my lips gently, tentatively. His face felt cold and bristly and smelled faintly of Old Spice.

I drew back, wishing Louella had stayed on the dock with us, wondering if Jim sensed my embarrassment.

He looked away as if he knew the kiss had been a mistake. He cleared his throat. "I wish you could see this place in the spring."

I kept my voice light. "I'm sure it's lovely."

"It was Linda's favorite time of year."

"Linda? Oh. Your wife."

"I—"

"You must miss her."

"I never knew anything could hurt so much. I guess it's the same for you?"

"Yes," I said, realizing how often I found myself grieving for Dexter. We stood a moment longer, the silence between us growing.

Finally he turned toward the cabin. "I guess Lulu could use some help with the dishes."

"It's not her favorite pastime," I agreed.

He was a decent man and I liked him. I wanted to say: Look, you're a great guy. You don't repulse me. It's that you're moving too fast, and I just want to be friends.

I thought I might invite him and Louella for Sunday dinner. If he didn't feel humiliated by my lack of response to his romantic overtures, perhaps we could forge a genuine friendship. Yes, I liked him, but there was no chemistry. He was a solid, steady man. Salt of the earth type.

He probably thought Sylvia Plath was a Congresswoman from Texas and Chaucer a dinnerware pattern. And he wasn't George Dexter Gilpin. He wasn't even J. Ronal Patrick.

Thirty-Four

Elsie's voice cut into my reverie. "Then you don't mind?"

"Mind what?"

"Just what I've been telling you for the past fifteen minutes, Maggie. You haven't heard a word, have you?"

"Of course I heard you. You said Orin has decided to run for sheriff."

"I knew you wouldn't mind." She wore a satisfied smile. "He'll be here around two this afternoon."

As it turned out, some significant points of Elsie's conversation had escaped me. Apparently I had agreed to assist with Orin's campaign by posting signs, handing out flyers, and helping him with his public speaking.

"After all," said Elsie, "you've got all that time on your hands since you quit Happy Heart. And even you don't have enough money to go shopping in Tulsa every day."

Orin's gestures were as fluid as brick, and his delivery as entertaining as a dripping faucet. "At this point in time law enforcement is in a loogerbus predicament."

"Stop," said Elsie. "That's lugubrious."

"Hell, Elsie, I can't say loo—looboogerbus. I don't even know what it means."

"Can't he say law enforcement is in a sorry state, and he wants to improve it, Elsie?"

She fixed me with a withering stare. "Lugubrious is a good word. I looked it up in my thesaurus. English teachers aren't the only people who know how to use a thesaurus."

"I'm dog tired," said Orin. "And I've got to be up with the chickens in the morning. We're putting in a new septic tank out to the Reynolds' farm."

"What will become of your plumbing business if you're elected sheriff?"

"I hadn't got that far in my thinking, Maggie. I'm gonna float a trial balloon to see if anybody salutes it."

Elsie nodded encouragement. "We need to root out corruption in law enforcement."

"I gather you're not happy with Sheriff Williamson."

"He's a bleeding-heart liberal," said Elsie.

"Really?"

"I guess you didn't hear," said Orin. "He fired Shorty Cook just cause a bunch of do-gooders caught Shorty shooting hawks off telephone poles."

"Wasn't Shorty breaking the law?"

"Hawks are thick as flies around here. And besides that, Williamson wants more tax money to build a new jail."

"I heard the old one was getting pretty crowded."

"I don't believe in coddling prisoners."

"The paper said the sheriff wants to be able to separate the occasional hardened offender he arrests from the kids he's hauled in for mischief."

Orin, his patience obviously wearing thin, shook his head. "If Dex was around he could set you straight. All Williamson wants is to get his hands on some of that tax money hisself."

"Well, I don't know how much help I can be to your campaign, Orin. But I don't recommend you try to deliver a memorized speech."

"I was up all night writing that speech," said Elsie.

"And it makes some good points. But it doesn't quite sound like Orin."

"All we want from you is help with Orin's gestures."

"Fair enough," I said. I knew that when the time came, Orin would throw out Elsie's speech and address his constituents in his own charming, aw shucks style. The scary part was he might win.

On Dexter's birthday I drove to the cemetery, parked my car, and walked the last several yards along the cobbled path. As I approached his grave I saw her kneeling before the stone marker. Her attention seemed absorbed by the wreath of poinsettias and holly she placed there. She must have heard my steps on the path, but she kept her gaze toward Dexter's head-stone.

"It was good of you to remember Dexter's birthday," I said. "Thank you."

Jo Ann stood and faced me. "I don't need your thanks for visiting my father's grave."

"No, I suppose not." As she watched I stooped to place my own floral arrangement on the mounded earth, then stepped back to assess the effect. "You came to the funeral, didn't you?"

"Yes." She raised her chin defiantly.

"I dressed in my brother's clothes. I didn't want people to think... whatever you choose to believe about me, I didn't want to embarrass your family."

I wondered what the good townsfolk would have said if she'd worn the purple wool suit I saw her in now, and what they'd have thought if she'd ridden in the family car. It must have hurt her to have been excluded from every facet of the service. "It isn't right he didn't tell me about you as soon as he returned from Korea."

"Right? There was never anything 'right' about the way he treated my mother." She held her arms stiff at her side as the sexton's truck crunched by on the graveled lane, then she turned to leave.

"Wait, please," I said. A cool breeze blew from the north and she paused, shivering. "Would you like to sit in my car with me for a few moments?"

"No. My brother and grandmother expect me home soon."

"I won't keep you long. We're both adults, and I'd like to believe we can have a civil conversation about Dex... about your father."

She hesitated as if considering my invitation. She was so small and delicate, she somehow reminded me of a fragile woodland creature trapped by the gaze of a predator. I wanted to reassure her.

"Just for a few moments, please."

At last she nodded and followed me down the path to my car. I opened the door for her and settled myself behind the wheel. After all these weeks we were alone and face to face. I still wasn't sure what I should say.

"Jo Ann, your father was very idealistic. He wanted us to be friends."

She turned, her brown eyes glistening with fury. "You kept him from us." I started to protest, but she held up her hand. "I don't mean you knew. But it's a fact. Without you and your children, he would have married my mother." She sounded close to tears. "Mama felt so betrayed."

I gasped, "*She* felt betrayed! Jo Ann, he was *my* husband. I could write volumes on how it feels to be betrayed."

She clenched her fists and closed her eyes, as if trying to quell her anger. "Oh damn, damn, damn." Sobs shook her and I handed her a tissue.

Long moments later she seemed to have spent herself.

"I hadn't given much thought to your side of things," I said. "But...."

I searched for words to phrase my thoughts. Jo Ann and her mother seemed to have lived well in this country. I wondered if her anger had more to do with the grief of losing her parents and Dexter. I said, "I suppose we can agree there has been hurt enough to go around."

"Yes." She settled against the headrest. For a few moments we sat without speaking. Then she turned toward me. "Vernon told me he insisted you and your friend come to the house the day you had the flat tire. I regret being rude, but that doesn't mean we're going to be friends."

"Of course not. Dexter's expectations were unrealistic."

Her face was swollen and her words had a nasal quality. "Yes. Very unrealistic." She drummed her long nails on the padded door handle. "What do Gil and Lori think of me?"

"Gil and Lori?" I couldn't keep concern from my voice. "Nothing, really. We don't talk about it."

Her gaze swept my face. "You haven't told them."

"You must understand—they think Dexter hung the moon. His death nearly destroyed them." I gulped. "They couldn't handle hearing about his affair yet."

"I want to meet them."

"Of course, Jo Ann. I'll let you know when they're ready."

"Mrs. Gilpin, if I wait until you think they're ready, I'll never meet them. I want to see them now."

Anger sent new surges of adrenaline through me. "I've never heard of anything so self-centered and inconsiderate. You've got to give me time."

She shook her head. "Just listen to yourself. Lori and Gil aren't babies. Even if they don't know exactly what's gone on, I'd be surprised if they hadn't heard some gossip. Wouldn't you rather the full story come from you?"

"If they'd heard anything, I'd have heard it too."

"It's only a matter of time until someone talks. The insurance agent knows, his secretary knows, so does the lawyer in Tulsa. And I've told my brother."

"God help us," I said. "It will destroy them."

"Not likely. You need to give us all more credit than that."

I thought, perhaps she's right. If my children were to know of their father's infidelity, I wanted to be the one to tell them. I shivered and pulled my coat tight. "All right. Can you come next Saturday? I'll invite them all for lunch."

We planned her arrival for two o'clock. I watched from my kitchen window as Peggy, Lori and I cleaned up after the meal. As soon as I saw her in the drive, I hurried outside. "They don't know yet," I whispered.

I ignored the looks on Lori's and Peggy's faces as I led Jo Ann through the kitchen. I told them to follow.

"Mother?" said Lori, but I kept moving through the dining room toward the living room.

Chet and Sara Jane had gone to play with Little Carter at the Mitchells' house, and Don and Gil were doing a half-hearted job of corralling Skippy while they watched a hockey game on TV. I ignored their groans as I hit the "Off" button.

"Jo Ann Darnold, I'd like you to meet my daughter, Lori,

her husband, Don Shepherd; and my son, Gil Gilpin, and his wife, Peggy."

"How do you do," Jo Ann said stiffly. Standing near my family she looked even smaller, more vulnerable.

Lori and Don exchanged puzzled looks with Gil while Peggy settled on the floor to help Skippy build a tower of blocks.

"Well," I said. "Everyone, please sit down. There's something Miss Darnold and I need to tell you." The silence hung over us. "Miss Darnold... Jo Ann... she..." I turned to smile at her, "I wanted you to get to know her."

"Oh, oh." Lori collapsed onto one end of the sofa next to Don. Her eyes widened as if she'd received a kangaroo punch. "You're Weird Wilmer."

The way Lori said it made hair stand up on the back of my neck. I laughed nervously. "Weird Wilmer is what we called Wilmer Darling—before we knew it was you, Jo Ann. You did sign the guest book that way at the funeral, didn't you?"

She sat next to me, facing the others. I wondered if they could see how her hands trembled. "Oh, that. When I was a toddler my step-dad and I played a game where I was Wilma Flintstone and he was Fred. He often called me Wilma Darling, so when I signed the guest book, I made it into Wilmer Darling."

Gil sat forward. His lips made a tight line across his face. When he spoke his voice was a shade too loud. "I don't understand. A joke at my dad's funeral? I don't understand, Miss Darnold. I mean, what sort of person gets into a baggy suit and tries to make a joke out of a funeral? Seems to me it's a hell of a way to behave."

Jo Ann held up her hand as if to ward off his words, "I didn't—"

"If you came here to apologize," said Lori, "forget it. You ruined things, and there's no way to fix that now. Everyone wondered about you. Why did you do it? For God's sake, why?"

Jo Ann turned to me. Except for a tiny quiver on her lips, her face was a mask of composure. "I think your mother will explain to you," she said.

Panic rose in my chest, and my voice sounded shrill. "I have a tape your father made for me before he died. I think you should listen to it."

Don stood. "I think we should go before the roads get too slippery," he said.

Lori pulled him down beside her. "We have to wait for the kids to get back from the Mitchells'. Besides I'm not leaving now until I hear Daddy's tape." She stared at Jo Ann. "If it really is his tape."

Don looked uncomfortable, and Peggy kept her eyes on Skippy. But Gil and Lori were like hungry wolves at a deer carcass.

"It's not supposed to ice until late this evening," I said. "And the kids were going to watch a movie at Lindsay's. I'm sure they can't be through yet." As Don hesitated, I crossed to the audio equipment and punched the button to play the tape.

As his words filled the room I looked away from the pain I saw in my children's faces and fled to the kitchen. I sat at the table, sobbing and praying.

Hearing Dexter's voice I imagined their reactions when he said, "You're a strong woman, Maggie darling, and somehow I think you'll handle this tape better if… if I'm dead before you play it." He began his confession. I pictured all eyes turning to Jo Ann when he said, "It happened in Korea, Maggie. You were so far away. And I was so lonely."

Jo Ann was hearing the tape for the first time too—hearing how he'd loved me more than her mother, how he'd gone to Jo Ann when he'd learned of the auto accident. "She was a senior in high school, just a few months older than our Lori. And I knew I had to help her, Maggie. I hadn't been a real daddy to her, but after her mother and step-father were killed, I tried. I helped settle the estate and flew her grandma over to help raise her little brother. I made sure she enrolled at the university and got on with her education—I used to meet her at O.U. when Lester and I went to the games. At first she didn't trust me— she was so bitter about the way I'd treated Lee An. But she never closed the door on me, and little by little I tried to make her understand how it was back then in Korea… why I couldn't marry her mother. One of the happiest days of my life was when she said she loved me...."

My kitchen felt cold and my eyes ached.

"I know you can't be like a mother to her, Maggie, but I hope someday you'll meet her and that you two can be friends."

At last I felt soft hands on my shoulders. "Are you okay, Lori?"

But it was Jo Ann. "They want you in the living room," she said.

"What do you think? How did they take it?"

Her laugh was brief. "I think Dexter would have called them bumfoozled, but I don't think they still want to attack me."

"This is going to take time," I said. "Time for healing."

"Well, you know how we Orientals are."

"I'm afraid I don't understand your meaning."

"Surely everyone knows we are as patient as we are inscrutable."

I thought about reminding her of her "inscrutable tears," but didn't want to offend her. She had her coat on and carried her purse. "You don't have to leave now."

"I think it's best if I do, Mrs. Gilpin"

"Do you think you could call me 'Maggie?'"

"Maggie, yes." She smiled. "He really did want us to be friends, didn't he?"

"We can try," I said.

"One more thing about us Orientals. We pay great respect to the wishes of our parents."

"Frankly, all this talk about Oriental mysticism kind of gets in my way. It's the American part of you that belonged to Dexter."

She shrugged. "I try to use whatever works. See you later."

As she closed the door to my carport, I walked into the living room. I thought of Dexter's words, "If you do tell them, please tell them I loved their mother."

"He really did love each of us," I said.

"I know," said Lori. "He was just insignificantly unfaithful and he probably didn't have more than one bastard child, so it doesn't count."

"He was young and lonely. We have to forgive him, dear."

"Forgive him?" she said, whirling to face me. "Mother, how can you speak of forgiveness after what he did to you? To all of us?"

"See a lawyer," said Don. "If Jo Ann can prove paternity, she could really take you to the cleaners."

"Shit," said Lori.

"I'm sure your dad covered all the legalities. I'm not worried about that."

Gil caught Skippy before he could pull more books from the shelves. "I suppose it's all over town by now."

"I really don't know or care. But I wanted you to hear it from me first."

"I—I just can't imagine Dad looking at another woman. He was so straight-arrow."

Lori glared at her brother. "He was a damned hypocrite."

Gil and Peggy gathered their things into the car. "Are you going to be okay?" Gil asked.

"Never better, dear."

Peggy cried as she settled Skippy into his car seat, then hugged me good-bye.

"Son of a bitch," said Gil before he closed his car door and roared off with his family.

"I could have gone the rest of my life without knowing he… without hearing about his affair," said Lori.

"And I would have let you, sweetheart. But I'm sure the stories would have reached you very soon. I wanted to be the one to tell you."

Don reached to give her a comforting pat, but she shrugged angrily and slid into their car.

Would they ever be able to work through their hurt? To understand Dexter never meant to betray us? Merciful Lord, I prayed, please don't let them find out about their mother's despicable behavior.

Thirty-Five

Dexter's progeny would have to find a way through their own problems. Bitterness clung to them, but there were hopeful signs. When Jo Ann introduced Gil to her fiancé, she introduced him as one of her brothers; and she gave Chet a birthday present, signing it "Aunt Jo Ann."

I dwelt on my own hurt and dashed hopes.

And then one day as I searched the trunk for some pictures I wanted to give the kids, I came across a letter Dexter had written me just before his return from Korea. It had been months since I'd seen it, and I read it now with new meaning.

"My heart has never left you, Maggie. God knows I don't deserve you, but at any cost I would banish the world to be in your arms."

Nothing, not even another woman and her baby, had truly stolen his heart from me. Through his affair with Lee An, through the infrequent quarrels and multitude of accomplishments that marked our years together, through pain and happiness, to his death, he had loved me. I couldn't allow his betrayal to blot that fact from my mind.

Our lovemaking had confirmed all that was good between us. Why had I pursued a sham relationship of secret trysts with a man who would never be mine? Why would I damage someone else's marriage?

"Oh, God, forgive me," I pleaded. My sins had been ongoing, worse than Dexter's. Had Providence intervened to stop me from having sex with Ron? My soul was still damaged. My needs were deep, my adultery genuine.

No excuses were possible but when I saw Louella, who has

learned a few things in her therapy sessions, I asked her for help in understanding why I'd behaved the way I did.

"Why couldn't I have left Ron's and my friendship where it was? Two people who enjoyed each other's company. Now I've destroyed that too."

"You were ripe for the picking, Maggie. Most widows are."

"But I never was the sort of woman to go looking for an affair."

"Not until you heard Dexter's confession. It crushed you."

"I felt like a failure as a woman, that's for sure."

"Dr. Mulvaney thinks women of our generation fall into a trap. We want a man to validate our worth, to give us confidence in ourselves. But you've got to see that you're a person in your own right, not just Dexter's widow."

I squared my shoulders. "'I am woman, hear me roar.'"

She sniffed. "We cultured types disapprove of roaring. It's so very crass and unfeminine."

I took a sip of hot coffee. Was I really as vulnerable as she painted me? Was I shifting the blame, not taking responsibility for my actions? Was she excusing me with psycho-babble?

"Louella," I said, looking into her dark, laughing eyes, "what if I acted the way I did because I was... you know... what if I was just—"

"Horny?"

"I was going to say 'selfish and thoughtless.'"

"I don't know about selfish and thoughtless, but horny will make you forget everything you ever promised your mother."

Some time in February, I'd received the notice for my high school reunion. I reserved a room in an Oklahoma City hotel at the site of the get-together. I remembered thinking it would be a fun trip to make with Louella. But when the event drew close she told me she promised to baby-sit for the Atchleys while they cruised in the Caribbean. Even if I'd wanted to take Elsie, she couldn't leave Orin until after the run-off election.

I needed to get away from Redbud, away from thoughts of my children and their distress. I'd attended my last reunion ten years ago, cozy and relaxed at Dexter's side—Dexter who sparked all social occasions with affable charm. Now seemed a perfect time to prove Louella's theory about becoming my own person. Surely among my former classmates I would be more than George Dexter Gilpin's widow.

Dressed in the silk turquoise outfit I'd purchased for the Patricks' Christmas party, I walked into the hotel banquet hall. An older couple sat behind the registration table.

"Who are you?" asked the woman. "Guest or alumnus... oh, for heavens sakes, it's Maggie Martin. I'd know you anywhere."

Her name tag read "Lynne Smith Cummings," saving me from having to guess. Lynne, the titian-haired cheerleader, had turned into Granny Cummings, a comfortably round matron of flaming orange locks.

I registered and pasted a small square bearing the likeness of a young and naïve Margaret Lorraine Martin on my chest.

People met, smiled tentatively, lowered their heads to read name tags, then whooped with recognition. I'd bet hundreds of pairs of bifocals hid in purses and vest pockets that night as we desperately tried to match the photos on the name tags to lined faces and graying hair.

But the novelty soon wore off as cliques formed and re-formed. Everyone I remembered seemed securely included in a group—closed circles of good humor focused on themselves. As the time of the banquet approached, my palms grew moist. I feared having to find an empty chair, having to approach strangers to ask if I could join them. Suppose someone said, "Oh, sorry, but this is reserved for one of our friends." I felt like the new kid in junior high, struggling with acne and wearing clothes my mother had chosen for me.

So I was happier than I ever thought I'd be to see Karley Jacobson. "Sorry to hear about your husband's death," she said, placing an arm around my shoulder. Though our only connections had been Sunday School and a shared algebra class, I welcomed the invitation to join her and her friends.

"You remember Otis Whittington and his wife Judy, used to be Judy Bell, and Benton Landry and his wife Avis—she went to Central."

I didn't, but said I did, though I vaguely remembered

Benton had some affiliation with a girl on my debate team. Maybe Dolores Thomas had been Benton's cousin—I couldn't remember. I listened as the group chatted about memories that bound them together and tried not to feel as out of place as they would have been at Second Thursday Circle.

When my silence finally became too noticeable, I joined in. "Whatever happened to Dolores Thomas?" I asked Benton. Our table fell silent. He cleared his throat. "Far as I know she's still in South America with her second husband. At least, that's where she went when we split up."

"Oh, I'm sorry. I didn't know."

Avis wore a pained expression.

I decided I would stay a little longer, then excuse myself to make a phone call. They'd think I'd slipped away to visit another table, and I need never return. The hotel gift shop sold paperbacks, so I could buy one to read in my room. Or I could watch TV. I could try out the jacuzzi or re-do my nails. I could tear up my application for membership in N.O.W.

It was a moment before I realized Karley spoke to me and not to one of the others at the table. "He's divorced now." I looked at her without comprehension. "Michael James. He just walked through the door and he's headed our way."

I smiled, remembering the lanky kid with the burr haircut who'd been my partner in adolescent passion—kisses on hayrides, hand holding at the movies, tentative gropings I easily thwarted. Though I had worn his ring on a chain around my neck our junior and senior years, attraction hadn't survived separate colleges. It surprised me that I could recognize him now. His hair line had receded and he wore a mustache. His shoulders were broader than I remembered, but he had the same rolling walk and cat-like grace. I wished for a picture to back my claims about "the one that got away." Louella was certainly going to hear about him.

He stopped near the door to shake hands, and a man tried to steer him to a table on the other side of the room. I couldn't hear what Mike said, but he smiled and shook his head. Then he scanned the room, obviously looking for someone. He frowned, then headed for the bar.

"I think he was looking for you," Karley whispered.

"You haven't changed a bit. I bet you still pray for Bruce and Demi to get back together."

"I gave up on them but I'm working on Tom and Nicole." She finished the last of her beer. "Don't tell me you're not interested in him."

I laughed. "Well, I did some hard breathing when he walked in, but I bet he dates women half his age." I lowered my voice. "But it's okay. My life is full. I'll survive very well if I never have another date."

She unpacked a bottle of bourbon. "Anybody ready for another drink?"

"Karley, you drink now? Remember the night that visiting evangelist wanted us to pledge never... never to—"

"'Never to engage in the use or sale of alcoholic beverages.' Sure, I remember, but that was almost forty years ago. And I'll tell you something else—except for murder, I've probably broken every one of the commandments too." She punched the man she'd introduced as her husband. "And if Fred don't straighten up, I may break that one too." She winked at the others as she rose to leave.

"Be back with drinks for Maggie and me."

"But I—"

"If you don't drink it, I will," she said over her shoulder. She snaked her way between tables toward the bar to where Mike stood chatting with two men. She touched his shoulder and they talked briefly. Then she pointed in my direction.

Oh, no, I thought in embarrassment. What is she telling him? Then he headed my way, smiling warmly.

"Maggie Martin—I mean Gilpin," he said, pulling me to my feet and kissing my cheek. "Gosh, you look good."

"You too, Mike. How've you been?"

"Fine. You here by yourself?"

My heart gave an involuntary skip, a delicious feeling that proves true love for a sixteen year old, but is probably life-threatening for someone my age. "Yes. By myself."

"Well, if there's room for me, I'd like to sit with you."

Karley pointed to the vacant chair. "We've been saving it just for you."

"Oh, please stay until whoever you're with shows up," I

said as we sat. He raised puzzled brows. "I saw you when you came in. Weren't you looking for someone?"

"A friendly face." He lowered his voice. "Someone who would rescue me from Barbara Wainscot and her husband. They're trying to fix me up with his sister, so I told them I was meeting a date here. Now you know how thrilled I am you showed up."

"Hm."

"I think Maggie would have been happier if you hadn't been so desperate," said Karley.

He ducked his head, a gesture I well remembered. "If I could have learned to be sensitive and say the right thing, I might still be in a condition of wedded bliss."

I joined the others in agreeable laughter, but I remembered how Mike used to make fun of himself to cover hurts—his dad's drinking, the loss of the student council election, the teasing he took when his mother gave him a bad haircut with her new clippers.

"And I always thought," I said, "that you, more than any man except the guy I married, could charm the birds from the trees."

"Hey, why the hell did we break up?"

There's nothing so glorious, I thought, *as feeling you look wonderful when you meet an old beau.* Maybe I would write a letter to the hotel to thank them for the dim overhead lighting.

"I heard you'd lost your husband," said Mike. "I'm sorry."

"We were married a long time, and I still miss him. Thanks."

After we ate, the class president read our "Last Will and Testament." It seems I had willed my ballet slippers to one of the junior varsity football players. I'd forgotten I ever owned a pair.

Mike winked and whispered, "You'd think a ballerina wouldn't have had so much trouble trying to do the bop."

We stood in silence as the emcee read a list of members known to have died. We joined hands and sang the school song. Then, as we sat to face the stage, spotlights danced to illuminate the evening's entertainment—a series of skits too predictable to be funny unless you knew the participants, and side-splitting fun if you did. At the finale we pushed back our chairs and gave the "actors" a standing ovation.

"I helped on the planning committee, so I saw your name on the reservation list," Mike told me as people on their way from the room strained to see whom they might have missed, might yet recognize. "I've gone out a few times since my divorce, but after being married so long it's really weird. You wouldn't believe how aggressive the women are. Not like our generation. I really was looking for you, Maggie."

I could feel myself blushing. "That's the nicest thing anybody's said to me in a long while."

"Do you think they still dance until the wee hours the way we used to at *The Pines*?"

"I heard they tore it down. Or maybe it burned."

"Good thing," he said, his eyes lively with humor. "You never could dance."

We had moved into the foyer where knots of people stood exchanging pictures, addresses, phone numbers, and meaningless promises to keep in touch. I moved toward the elevator. "Well, it was good to see you again."

"There's a Denny's around the corner. You suppose they'd split a chocolate sundae for us?"

I laughed at his reference to my once-upon-a-time addiction. "I had to give up sundaes about nineteen-seventy-one when I thought I might outweigh Dexter, but I'd drink a cup of coffee with you."

"Unleaded."

"Certainly. I give up the real stuff by five o'clock now."

Outside the hotel and onto the lamp-lighted sidewalk, he took my arm as we walked the short distance to Denny's. No one had opened the door for me in a long while. I caught myself just in time to let him do it.

We sat across from each other in a small booth and told life stories, though I wasn't yet ready to tell him about Dexter and Lee An.

"Your kids sound wonderful," he said.

"So do yours."

When I looked at my watch, it was four in the morning.

"I better walk you back," he said. "I'm supposed to call on one of our plants about four hours from now."

Our conversations had been so natural and comfortable—two old friends who cared for each other.

At my door he said, "I don't know quite how to ask you." He ducked his head, and for the first time since we'd left for Denny's, I sensed an awkwardness. "I... uh, I know you lost your husband a while back, and I don't want to sound crass. But I guess what I want to know is if you've thought about dating again."

Hysterical laughter threatened to bray from my throat, but I managed not to tell him about the naked asthmatic who'd fainted in my kitchen, the love nest I'd made in the camping trailer for an unfulfilled tryst with Ron, the awkward walk in the woods I'd shared with Jim. "I hope you're asking me to go out with you," I said.

"One of my branches is in Tulsa, not too far from Redbud. I get over there almost every week. I'd like to call you."

I fished a Denny's napkin from my purse and wrote my address and phone number on it. "If you lose this, it's in the book under Dexter Gilpin." I folded the napkin and put it in his shirt pocket.

"I won't lose it, Maggie."

I put the key into the lock and opened my door. "Good night," I said. Then I blew him a kiss and closed the door.

I kicked off my shoes, turned out the lamp, and walked onto the patio, six floors above the pool and with a view of the parking lot. Minutes later I saw Mike striding to his car.

I liked him very much. We had a history, we were friends, he was sweet and manly, and we'd be good together. I hoped he'd call soon.

I still couldn't say I had things down pat. I hoped I would never again be so shaken, so rudderless, but maybe there was hope for me. I'd matured, learned a few things about living, about being Maggie Gilpin.

Unbidden words came to my mind: No pain, no gain.

Grandmother Martin had visited my family once when I was four years old. I had wanted her to lift me, to raise me high as she had when I'd last seen her. She'd laughed. "Sorry, honey.

Grandma's old back can't do that now that you've got so big."
I pouted, and she said, "Oh, sweetheart, growth is such a
painful thing."

Through the years it seemed to be her favorite theme. To all
my problems—whether I complained about the difficulties of
classroom studies or the fickle attentions of some young man,
she comforted me with her wisdom. And when she'd aged to a
withered shell of her former self, she picked up the vernacular
of the day— "No pain, no gain, sweetheart."

Wounds, many of them self-inflicted, had festered in my
soul for more than a year. I hadn't been crushed, so maybe I'd
grown. And what I'd said to Karley was true—with or without
a man, my life would be productive and worthwhile. It had
taken me a long time to feel whole and complete.

There was no going back now.